FILE UNDER: JEOPARDY

Sarah Lacey

Hodder & Stoughton

Copyright © 1995 Sarah Lacey

The right of Sarah Lacey to be identified as the Author of
the Work has been asserted by her in accordance with the
Copyright, Designs and Patents Act 1988.

First published in Great Britain in 1995
by Hodder and Stoughton
A division of Hodder Headline PLC

10 9 8 7 6 5 4 3 2 1

A CIP catalogue record for this title is available from the British Library

ISBN 0-340-60786-6

Typeset by Avon Dataset Ltd, Bidford-on-Avon, B50 4JH

Printed and bound in Great Britain by
Mackays of Chatham PLC, Chatham, Kent

Hodder and Stoughton
A division of Hodder Headline PLC
338 Euston Road
London NW1 3BH

For the Jude the Obscure
in Ocala, U.S.A.

1

In the beginning was the word. Two of them to be precise. Hanging in the air between us along the lines of get lost – but a lot less polite. I might even have been offended if it wasn't for the fact that her eyes were sending out an altogether different message. They were eyes I remembered well. It wasn't that long ago since Bramfield Girls' College had tried to turn us both into ladies. A second after her last, loud *f* stopped vibrating, two of Bramfield's finest hauled her into the charge room and out of sight.

Which is a shining example of the way Providence manages to manœuvre me into being in the wrong place, at the wrong time, for my own good.

Maybe I should introduce myself.

My name is Leah Hunter, dark hair, dark eyes, twenty-six years old and single. The single part is from choice: I appreciate freedom and domesticity is low on my list of priorities. Which is not to say I don't also appreciate men, it's just that I prefer the kind who do their own chores. I was born and still live in Bramfield – a Yorkshire town where Sunday morning pavements bear witness to Saturday night blood sports – and by profession I'm a tax inspector, a small fact that can stop a conversation dead in its tracks. It's amazing how many people carry a guilty conscience.

That particular Thursday I'd been cooling my heels in the front office of Bramfield Police HQ, innocently chatting up the desk sergeant while I waited for DI David Nicholls to finish up some little thing or other and take me to dinner. At that point I swear the only thing on my mind was an urgent need to be fed, and it would have stayed that way if Jeannie Johnson hadn't got herself propelled in through the outer door, kicking and screaming like a banshee.

It took a second or two for me to recognise her – the bucking cursing female giving two uniforms a peck of grief was nothing like the quiet Jeannie Johnson I remembered from school, and when the inner doors closed behind her I brooded on the short sharp answer given to my 'Jeannie?', and its total conflict with the look in her eyes.

A couple of minutes later Nicholls strolled in with a happy grin on his face, Bunsen blue eyes untroubled until I began to bend his ear. Then he got a look of pained vexation and told me how people didn't get arrested unless they deserved it.

Such untruths are easily recognised. 'Oh yeah?' I said sweetly.

'Oh yeah,' he snapped.

'Well, if you're that sure it can't hurt for you to wander through into the charge room and check it out.'

'Leah . . .'

'Hey,' I said. 'Who's fault is it? If you were ever on time I wouldn't even know she was here.'

He glowered at such an incontrovertible truism and walked out. A couple of seconds later I went after him. The charge room doors have neat round spy windows. I took a peek through one. Jeannie was leaning up against the custody sergeant's desk sipping something hot from a canteen mug, and looking like she was good buddies with everyone in there – including Nicholls. Life is just full of surprises. Maybe I didn't need to worry too much about her after all.

I wandered back to the front office and did some more waiting. By and by Nicholls came back and told me a load of bullshit. When he paused for breath I grabbed my bag and walked out.

'Now what?' he said plaintively when we hit the pavement. 'Didn't I do what you asked?'

'I don't know,' I said. 'You tell me.'

'I already did.'

'That stuff about Jeannie being banged up in the cells until she quietens down and co-operates? Is that what you mean?'

'Look, I put in a good word. She'll probably get let off with a caution.'

'That so?'

'That's so. Leah . . . Dammit, woman! What more do you want?'

Nicholls is really good, I've got to admit that, he'd got the aggrieved note just about right, enough so that if I hadn't known him better I'd have believed every word.

'What is she?' I asked casually. 'Out of area? Fraud squad? Drugs? Regional?' He tucked his head down and swore. 'Spy holes are for spies,' I reminded him tartly. 'Next time you want to keep a secret, drop the blinds.'

'Thanks.'

'You're welcome. Going to tell me what's going on?'

'None of your business, Leah.'

'I'll remember that,' I told him. 'Next time you come up with any good questions of your own.' We walked the rest of the way to La Dolce Vita in silence, and when he drove me home I didn't ask him in for coffee. Such small slappings down are good for his soul.

Next day I hunted up Jeannie's old address and stopped by on my way home. Jeannie's mother was there, but not Jeannie. I scribbled down my own address and telephone number. 'If she calls,' I said. 'Ask her to get in touch, I'd really like to catch up on things.' On my way out the door I popped another question, casually, as if it wasn't the most important thing on my mind. 'What's she doing these days? Anything exciting?' Mrs Johnson pinked up with pride.

'She deals with antiques. Valuing, going around salerooms, and you know I'm so proud of her! I knew my Jeannie would make good use of her education, and she has. Her job takes her all over the world . . . Athens, Amsterdam, New York, Hong Kong . . . She seems very happy.'

'Sounds great,' I said.

She pulled herself back down to ground level and gave me a speculative look. 'And what kind of work are you doing now?' she asked kindly.

'Nothing anywhere near as exciting as jetting off to Paris or somewhere,' I said, abstractedly trying to square what I'd just been told with what I'd seen at the local cop shop, and finding an unjumpable chasm between the two. 'What kind of firm is Jeannie with?'

'Oh-um,' she sounded cautious. 'Well, right now she's doing valuation work for a London firm. But she's an independent expert, you know, which is how she gets to travel around so much.'

'That so? Maybe I know it. What's the name?'

She struggled for a couple of seconds. 'Ensis,' she said finally. 'It's something like Sotheby's.' She tipped her head and frowned a little. 'What made you think she was home?'

'Mistaken identity I guess. I thought I saw her in town, you know how it is, catch a brief glimpse and find it's a look-alike.' I wondered why that little lie should make her look so relieved. She nodded and smiled, promised to pass on my phone number, and closed the door. I saw the vague shape of her standing behind the net curtains as I drove away.

Ensis.

There *might* be a firm of art auctioneers with that name, but from what I'd seen yesterday Mrs Johnson's Ensis was more likely to be NCIS, a London firm Nicholls would be only too familiar with since they were in his own line of work. It would also fit in beautifully with the job Jeannie was supposed to do.

The initials stood for the National Criminal Intelligence Service, whose business it is to gather intelligence on criminal activities – particularly money laundering by organised crime, where, with all the new banking regulations, an offshore clean-up is the easiest option. The buying up of expensive art and antiques as a way of getting rid of dirty money is something the big men of crime have always been good at, especially on the American scene where revenue laws have long been tight enough to demand such inventiveness. The sad fact is that, on both sides of the Atlantic, art and antique dealers don't exactly fret themselves over where the money comes from to buy their baubles. Neither do they raise a fuss at being paid in large amounts of small denomination notes that would raise eyebrows if introduced into the banking system. In fact – since a recent change in UK law forced banks and building societies to notify NCIS of all suspiciously large amounts of money being deposited with them – the antique trade is going into boom time.

And with Customs barriers no longer in force, it's a relatively easy scam.

Art treasures and antiques bought in England can be shipped to the Continent and freely resold, a loophole that provides a neat and easy way for low-lifes to launder their dirty money – most of it from the drugs trade – into nice clean cash. All in all, I guess the criminal fraternity are really glad we joined the EEC.

Driving back to my attic home I gave some thought to that, and also to the notion that Jeannie might be tracking some such laundering activities in Bramfield. If she was, I'd bet my boots Nicholls knew all about it, just like he knew laundered money went hand in hand with undeclared profits, and to a snoopy tax inspector like myself undeclared profits are as honey to a bear.

It really bugs me sometimes the way he tries to hide things.

* * *

A couple of days later Jeannie came round to the flat. We shared a pot of coffee and did some reminiscing about times past, which was easy – the hard part was nudging the conversation into times present.

Jeannie neatly fended a question about her friendliness with Bramfield police, and wandered over to the window, looking out at the scrawny garden where nothing much grew except a few tubs of plants and three dustbins. 'I don't suppose there's much point in my saying forget you saw me the other night?' she said.

'No point at all,' I assured her cheerfully. 'An act like that deserves to be remembered.'

'Oscar material?'

'Definitely. But for whose benefit? Not mine, that's for sure. Which makes me wonder where the audience was. Outside looking in?'

'Suppose I say, no act – I drank too much and got picked up. Is that so unbelievable? Do I look like a goody-two-shoes?'

'Picked up for what?'

'Public affray.'

'Uh-huh. How come you sobered up so fast?' She didn't answer that. I said, 'Come on, Jeannie, this is me, I saw you sizing up the talent in the charge room.'

'Speaking of talent,' she said chattily, 'I hear you've got something going there. Nice guy.'

'Isn't he though.' A little silence grew and stretched itself tight. I said, 'How's the antique trade?'

'Holding its own.'

'That's good, except that NCIS doesn't deal in antiques.'

She sighed. 'Never tell your mother anything you wouldn't want the world to know.'

'Why did you then?'

'She overheard a telephone conversation, and it was the best story I could come up with at the time. Look . . .' She turned around. 'We never were a close family, remember? After university I sort of dropped out of touch for a while and never got around to telling her where I was or what I was doing. When I finally came home to make peace I told her I was in antiques and travelled a lot. It saved questions, and it was the kind of thing she wanted to hear – something she could stuff up her cronies at coffee mornings.'

'What was so hard in admitting you were a policewoman?'

She laughed. 'A policewoman? Me? God, no. Flatfooting around with a trusty truncheon? Give me a break.'

'But I thought NCIS . . . ?'

'You got the right firm, but NCIS isn't comprised solely of police officers. It takes all kinds of disciplines to make up a team. Customs and Excise, VAT officers,' – she squinted at me, her mouth curving up at one side – 'even the odd Inland Revenuer.' I took that new piece of information on board for future reference and waited for the next revelation. 'I'm Customs,' she said. 'So relax, your territory's safe.'

'Uh-huh. That's nice. So how about filling me in on crime in Bramfield. No airport. No sea-link. I'm really curious to know what kind of scam would make Customs busy themselves around here?'

She wandered back to the settee and sat down. Picked up her mug and looked at the dregs. Sighed a little and put it down. As a hostess I have faults. Guilt drove me hastily into the kitchen to start a fresh brew, totally forgetting I wasn't the only one in the world with a devious mind.

Coffee in one hand, spoon in the other, I heard the flat door make its familiar snicking sound and Jeannie's feet on the stairs. Going after her got me nowhere. Her blue Metro was already on the move when I got to the front door. She ducked her head to look out the window and mouthed, 'Sorry.'

I was sorry too, but I told myself there'd be other times.

The trouble is, seeing into the future has never been my strong point.

2

Being a Nosy Parker doesn't mean I have no respect for confidentiality; on the contrary, where my own job is concerned I'm as tight lipped as the next person. But that doesn't stop me trying to find out as much as I can about everybody else's line of work. Snoopyness goes with the territory – as does knowing when to quit.

I shoved Jeannie, NCIS and thoughts of money-laundering to the back of my mind, knowing the one sure thing about criminality is that by and by, like rotten fish, it floats to the surface. Time enough when that happened for Inland Revenue to catch up with the profits. Or so I thought.

Providence had other ideas.

A week after Jeannie drove away I had a telephone call from her mother. Mrs Johnson said in a fractured kind of way that she was worried about Jeannie and needed to talk. How would I feel about meeting with her at Benson's Café when I finished work? I said if it was that important I'd clear my desk early and be there a little before five. Silence drifted down the line. 'Unless you want to leave it until tomorrow?' I suggested.

Her '*No!*' came back really fast. So did another hesitation after it. Then she asked if I'd act surprised, like I hadn't expected to see her there.

'Why would I want to do that?' I asked cautiously.

'If anyone's watching, I don't want them to think we're meeting by arrangement,' she said.

'What kind of anyone are we talking about, Mrs Johnson?'

'I don't know that. *Who*, is one of the things I need to talk about.' A note of hysteria eased in. 'I think I'm being followed, Leah, in fact I'm sure of it.'

'Have you contacted the police?'

7

'*No!*'

'I think you ought to do that, Mrs Johnson. If you're being harassed, they're the people you should be talking to.'

Another silence. Then, 'When Jeannie came back from her visit with you, we had a long talk. She told me she was with Customs and Excise.'

'Is that why you're worried?'

'No. I'm worried that someone's watching me – and that Jeannie might be in trouble.'

'In which case the police would be the best people to help you.'

'I don't think so. Jeannie said . . . She said if I was worried I should talk to you.'

Thank you Jeannie.

'OK, I'll meet you in Benson's,' I said, 'and I'll act like you're my long lost aunt.'

'I have something for you. A packet. Jeannie left it with me and said if she didn't contact me for a week I should give it to you. She said you'd know what to do with it.'

We had another little silence, while I used up some thinking time. 'What kind of a packet?'

'A fat envelope.'

'You didn't take a peek?'

'It's addressed to you,' she said virtuously, and I thought how much I admire people who can contain their curiosity. She added, 'And it's well sealed with Sellotape.' I caught the note of frustration and grinned. We said goodbye and hung up.

Over a sandwich and Pils lunch with Nicholls, I casually dropped Jeannie's name into the conversation and asked how the NCIS fishing trip was getting along. He stopped chewing to stare at the sandwich like it had just bit him back, then said primly that he wasn't privy to NCIS activities.

'But you know who is,' I reminded gently. 'Which means you could ask.'

'Given a good enough reason.'

'Personal interest.'

'Don't have any.'

'I do.'

'Not good enough,' he said.

'You've heard something you don't want to talk about,' I accused.

This time he lowered his butty long enough to look at me. 'Like what?'

I shrugged. 'Take your pick. The bad guys found out what Jeannie was up to. She had a breakdown. Stole the crown jewels. Who cares what? Just find out if she's OK.'

'What's the real reason?'

'Her mother's worried.'

He went back to eating while he worked on whether or not I might be telling him the truth.

'She rang me this morning,' I told him acidly.

He sighed, wiped his mouth, put his elbows on the table and looked me in the eye. 'I'll ask around,' he said. 'But I'm not promising.'

'Do it fast and come round tonight to tell me about it,' I said. 'Maybe I'll make cocoa.' As a ploy that seldom fails. His eyes took on a hopeful sparkle. They also took on something else, something dopily proprietorial that I wasn't ready to see. Don't get me wrong – if Nicholls wasn't around I'd miss him like hell, but I'm still a long way from ready for the housewife bit. 'Remember the word maybe,' I told him crisply. 'If I don't get to hear something interesting I'll be too depressed to bother.' He took the message away with him. Nicholls always knows where his best interests lie.

I spent the afternoon checking out eccentrically inventive accounting figures and marvelling at the amount of creativity let loose among the general public. At four-thirty-two I signed myself out in the flexitime book and walked briskly to Benson's, neatly avoiding attempts to seat me near the kitchen with the rest of the *hoi polloi*, when what I wanted was a window table from where I could see the street. I swallowed down two cups of tea, ate a scone piled high with jam and cream, and began to wonder if I'd got the right day. At five-thirty, when the café closed, Jeannie's mother still hadn't shown, and that worried me enough to send me knocking on her door.

I was peering through the kitchen window, wondering why she didn't answer, when her neighbour popped out from her own back door and told me about the hit and run.

By the time I got back to my attic home Nicholls was already there – an easy thing to achieve when he hadn't needed to hang around a hospital for two hours waiting to hear if Mrs Johnson was going to make it. And I still didn't know. All I'd managed to prise out of the hospital staff was a maybe. By and by, when her son arrived from Windermere, frazzled by a long drive and worry, I gave him my phone number and left him to keep vigil on his own. Don't ask me why I felt guilty when I walked away, it's enough that I did, and it was a burden heavy enough to make me shirty with Nicholls when he peeled himself up from off the top stair and complained about his ass growing roots.

'So, who asked you to wait?' I said nastily. 'Go haunt your own place.'

'If I'd had a key I could have got the coffee going.'

'If you had a key you could have got a lot of things going,' I said darkly. 'Which is why you don't have one.' I let myself in and stalked to the kitchen. 'I hope you aren't looking to be fed, that wasn't part of the deal.'

He wandered to the sink, looked at the pile of pots, and started hunting in the cupboard for clean mugs. 'I can go to the take-away,' he offered helpfully.

I watched him take the lid off the biscuit tin and peer inside. 'Whatever.'

'You've eaten all the Ginger Nuts.'

'Tough.'

He folded his arms and looked at me. 'Going to tell me what's brought on the grump?'

Grump?

'Going to tell me you couldn't find out a damn thing about Jeannie?' I said crisply.

'I'm going to tell you you're not the only one wanting to know where she is and what she's doing.'

'NCIS? They've lost her?'

'They seem to have a problem making contact.' He began to forage in the fridge. 'And don't take that as an invitation to mess with their affairs, Leah, because it isn't one, it's an attempt to head you off. As far as Mrs Johnson is concerned, tell her Jeannie is fine. OK?'

'Hey, don't bother about it,' I said icily. 'Someone already took care of Mrs Johnson's curiosity.' The filter machine burbled and spat behind me. I turned around and looked at the dark brew. 'Which is why I'm so damn late, I've been waiting around at the hospital.'

Nicholls' voice got edgy. 'Let's hear it.'

'You mean you don't know already? I thought CID bright sparks knew everything.'

'Not this one. Tell me.'

'She was run down crossing the street outside her home. Quite a coincidence really, happening right after she'd asked me to meet her at Benson's. She'd got this silly idea someone was following her around, so when she didn't turn up I went looking for her. Her next-door neighbour passed on the news.'

This time he didn't say anything smart, just trotted into the hall and started using the phone. When I followed him to do a little eavesdropping, he put on a scowl and waved me away dismissively. Who did he think he was? I stayed put. He slammed the receiver and stalked away. As he went out the hall door I said, 'If you're going for a take-away make mine Italian.' He didn't answer, just clattered downstairs and closed the outside door with a little too much emphasis.

It was close to ten when he showed his face again, leaning on my bell-push, a pizza box balanced on one hand. We sat in the kitchen and ate the contents straight out of the box to save on washing up, but I guess my powers of persuasion were at an all time low. All I could get out of him about Jeannie was that NCIS wouldn't thank me for stirring up dust.

'Which at least proves there's dust to stir,' I said with pointed logic. 'Besides which, Jeannie has to be told about her mother.'

'When she surfaces again she will be.'

'Surfaces? Does that mean she's undercover? I thought NCIS operatives weren't supposed to take an active part in investigations? From what I've seen of their remit, they only gather information, after that it's up to the local police to investigate and make arrests.'

'Jeannie seems to have seen herself as a wild card,' Nicholls said heavily. 'This was her first attachment and she doesn't appear to have understood the rules. When they find her she'll be replaced.'

'That's nice,' I answered, with equal slowness and weight. 'Always provided she hasn't got herself killed by then, because some superior male hadn't communicated the limits of intelligence gathering.'

'She knew the rules,' he said, eyeing the last piece of pizza.

I shoved the box closer to him. 'Take it,' I invited, and then as it disappeared asked casually, 'By the way, where had she been hanging out when uniform picked her up?'

He gave me one of those eye-shifting, skittering looks like a saddle-shy horse.

'Why?'

'Why do you think?'

'Forget it, Leah.'

'Thanks.'

'You're welcome.'

I dumped the empty pizza box in the trash, then went into the sitting-room to catch the end of *Newsnight*. It didn't take Nicholls much more than a minute to come and sit on the settee and slide an arm along the back of it.

'How about cocoa?' he asked hopefully.

'Huh! You want cocoa, take the tin home with you.'

'But I thought . . .'

'You assumed,' I said. 'That's your trouble Nicholls. You assume too damn much.' He took his arm back, sulked for a couple of minutes, then stomped to the door.

'So do you,' he said gruffly, and walked out.

I turned off the lights and went to bed.

At six-thirty next morning I was out on the pavements, running at a nice, easy pace, a feathery breeze stroking my skin and the sky an even blue. On the back streets, with no traffic, no trannies, and birds singing fit to bust, it was easy to pretend the world was in good shape. Such illusions last only until the next news bulletin. At eight, showered and fed, I rang the hospital. 'Poorly but stable' didn't sound good, but it was better than the terse word 'critical' they'd handed me the day before. It also prompted me to give a little extra thought to Bramfield road accident statistics.

Did I have any real cause to think Molly Johnson's brush with death had been due to more than careless driving? Wasn't I jumping the gun a bit, seeing bogeymen when there weren't any around? It's a sad fact of life that worried people unintentionally walk out in front of cars every day, and not every driver is bright enough, or brave enough, to stop. It was an attractive notion, one of those really clever thoughts that fitted in with what I wanted to believe, and it made things look a lot less complicated.

Of course, there was still Mrs Johnson's notion that she was being followed to explain away, but that wasn't something either of needed us to worry about for a while.

I went off to work in a more cheerful mood, dropped by the hospital at lunchtime and found Jeannie's brother, Martin, also looking a lot happier than he had the night before. I handed some flowers I'd brought with me to a passing nurse. Martin said, 'Nice thought, thanks.'

'I guess she's improved,' I said, 'or you wouldn't be so relaxed.'

'She came round a couple of hours ago and spoke to me. According to the doctor she isn't out of the woods yet, but things are starting to look better.'

'I'm glad.'

'I was going to ring up later. Let you know.'

'Thanks.'

Mrs Johnson's eyes were closed tight, and she gave no sign that she could hear us. I said, 'Any news of Jeannie?' Martin shook his head, just a single sweep from right to left. I wondered if he knew how much he looked like Billy Crystal.

'I wish she'd get in touch.'

'Martin, did your mother have a handbag with her when they brought her in?'

'No, she didn't.' He stared at me reflectively. 'That was the first thing on her mind when she woke up, and now you're asking the same question. Why? What's so important about her handbag?'

'She was carrying a letter in it, from Jeannie to me. I don't know what the letter contained, but your mother thought it important enough to set up a meeting so she could hand it over.'

'And now it's missing.'

'Looks that way. If the police drop by maybe you could mention it to them. It's possible someone who gave help after the accident saw what happened to it.'

'Or stole it,' he said bitterly. 'That'd be more like it.'

I didn't contradict him. Such coincidences are seldom accidental, and I couldn't shake the thought that Jeannie's letter might have held importance to someone prepared to go to extremes to get hold of it. If they'd known it existed, and that Mrs Johnson had it with her.

Martin let some anger spill, grabbing his mother's hand and scowling across the bed. 'Stella had better have a damn good reason for this. You know what makes me sick? It's when all she needed to do was pick up a phone and say she was all right. What's difficult about that?'

I didn't enlighten him, it seemed best to let him unload while he had the chance, and right then I had no direct evidence that things were any different from the way he envisaged.

'Things come up,' I said. 'Maybe she didn't have the opportunity.'

'Maybe.' He stared back at the ICU bed. Mrs Johnson's eyes were still closed. 'You were at school with Jeannie, weren't you?'

'That's right.'

'Then you'll know she broke with the family for a while.'

'I think she regrets that.'

'It wasn't all her fault, Dad was giving Mum a hard time, and she more or less passed it on to Jeannie. When Dad finally walked out, Mum went to pieces and Jeannie took the brunt of it in her A-level year. I remember the struggle she had to get her grades.'

'Parental problems can be tough on the kids.'

'You can say that again. I expected the bad-feeling would heal over when she went to uni, but instead they fell apart. She came home just once at the end of her first term, done up in all that Goth stuff, and Mum hit the roof. That was it. I didn't see Jeannie again for six years, by which time I was married with two kids of my own.'

'You didn't go looking for her?'

He shook his head. 'I wrote half a dozen times, but when nothing came back I gave up. If it happened again I guess I'd do it differently.'

Mrs Johnson's eyes were still closed. I said, 'I'd better go now, I'll drop by tomorrow.'

He said, 'If Jeannie gets in touch with you . . . ?'

'I'll tell her what's been happening,' I promised. 'If she knew about it, she'd be here, you can bet on it.' He nodded and I moved away, wondering if just once I might get a little co-operation out of Nicholls without being told to mind my own business.

3

Nicholls was playing hard to get, acting like he was the injured party. I put the lid on a few grizzles of my own, and pointed out nicely that offering to cook dinner was by way of a peace offering, and not to be sniffed at.

'Cook what?' he asked critically. 'Curled ham omelette with pre-cracked eggs? Green cheese salad? Or maybe it's that last pack of lasagne – the one that needs an ice-pick.'

'Take or leave it,' I said. 'If you're not there at seven-thirty I'll invite Marcie round instead.' Marcie is my neighbour on the middle floor, a brilliant freelance illustrator who's also a single parent with a three-year-old son. We get on fine. I watched Nicholls take a walk around his damaged pride and try to figure out a way to climb down. 'I chipped out the lasagne this morning,' I said. 'It was real good exercise.' He scowled a little. I said, 'Seven-thirty,' and left him to it.

On the way home I dropped in at the supermarket and did some shopping, picking up the stuff I'd need for a good moussaka and splashing out on a bottle of retsina to go with it. By seven-thirty the cooking smelled pretty good, and if he hadn't made it with a minute to spare I'd have been hungry enough to start without him. It took roughly five minutes' eating and a couple of glasses of wine to remind him where his best interests lay, and after that he loosened up enough to tell me he'd dropped by the hospital.

'That's nice,' I said. 'Learn anything interesting?'

'What's all this about a handbag?'

'Looks like some opportunist must have picked it up.' I poured him a little more wine. 'Seems to be worrying Mrs Johnson though. Martin said it was the first thing she asked about.' He gave me a quick look and got

15

busy with his fork again. I said innocently, 'There was a letter in it, for me from Jeannie, but maybe it was just gossip and holiday snaps. Guess we'll never know now until she surfaces again.'

He set his fork down. 'Is that the truth? You don't know what was in the letter?'

'Scout's honour, Nicholls. Until yesterday I didn't know it existed. Weird how the minute Mrs Johnson walks out with it in her handbag she gets hit by a car. A suspiciously minded person counting up coincidences might think her phone had been bugged.' His forehead creased up. Such things are a dead giveaway. 'If you want to call the office,' I said graciously, 'feel free, I won't listen.' He took another swallow of retsina and went out into the hall, closing the door behind him.

Such trust is really touching.

Trying to square raw materials with end product can be very time consuming, and things got pretty busy again at work. The notion of having your cake and eating it seemed to have appealed to one of Bramfield's bakers, and it took a couple of hairy interviews to put him back on the straight and narrow. The size of fiscal penalties imposed for tax evasion concentrated his mind beautifully; enough so for him to come up with a new set of figures that didn't leave him eating, trashing, or giving to the poor close on half his weekly output.

I let two days go by without calling in at the hospital, and when next I saw Mrs Johnson she was out of ICU and in a four-bedded ward. Martin was absent. 'I sent him home,' Mrs Johnson said. 'He has a life and a business, there's no sense in him staying here when I'll be up and about in no time.' She eased her head on the pillows so she could see me better. 'Any news of Jeannie yet?'

I shook my head.

'The police wanted my house keys,' she said. 'Something about checking my telephone.'

'Did you let them?'

She shrugged. 'Told them they'd have to get a locksmith, the house keys were in the handbag along with Jeannie's letter.'

Nice one, I thought. No wonder Nicholls hadn't found a bug when whoever planted it had had free access to get it back.

'I guess they wanted to cover themselves,' I said.

'There'll be one or other of them back again soon, asking more questions. Sometimes, Leah, they make it sound like Jeannie is a criminal.'

'It's just the indelicate way they put things. Maybe charm school would help.' I examined her face and wondered which had caused her the most havoc, the accident or Jeannie's disappearance. Her eyes had sunk into brown-soaked hollows while her skin had taken on the colour of pale parchment, and I wished I could tell her something positive to combat the negativity of police questions. She moved her head again, the high plastic collar giving her discomfort.

'Suppose something terrible has happened?' she said. 'Suppose Jeannie really is in trouble? The police seem to think she's missing voluntarily, but suppose they're wrong?' She was looking at me with a kind of pleading, wanting me to say reassuring things that would take away the images in her mind. I wished I could do that, but the right words wouldn't come.

I said, 'Whatever Jeannie's doing, there's one thing you can be sure of, she won't let you down. I know how close Jeannie feels to you now, and how sorry she is that she stayed away so long. She was pleased to bits you were proud of her.'

'She told you that?'

'When she called by the flat.' Gran used to say white lies got you into heaven. I hoped she was right because I'd just told a whole bunch.

Wetness welled. Mrs Johnson groped for a handkerchief and stemmed the flow. Her lips moved. I only just caught the words. 'I wish I could believe that.'

'Is there any good reason why you shouldn't?' I asked.

She didn't answer that, instead she said, 'Leah, will you try to find her for me?'

I shook my head. 'I don't think I can do that. The police are looking for her and they have a lot more resources than me. Besides which,' I looked at her squarely, 'it could be that she doesn't want to be found, that it's important to her work for her to stay out of contact for a while. Maybe she's working undercover.'

'No. Jeannie's in trouble. I know she is. I feel it.' The wetness came back. I got the tissues from her locker top and put them on the bed.

I said, 'Do you know where Jeannie was living?'

'She found a flat on St Giles' Square. I had a key for it but . . .'

'That was in the handbag too?' She nodded. 'Maybe it'll turn up,' I said. 'The police seem to think an opportunist grabbed the bag after the accident.'

Something very like a smile moved her lips. 'Is that what they told you?' I nodded. 'It isn't the truth you know, my neighbour saw it through her front window. Some man got out of the car and stole my handbag. That's what really happened to it.'

Great, I thought. No wonder Nicholls had been looking so shifty. I said, 'The police know about that?'

'Oh yes,' she said. 'They know. Molly told them all about it.' I sighed, thinking that if I'd known the right questions, neighbour Molly would have told me too. But I hadn't asked the right questions. I hadn't asked any questions. Instead I'd climbed back into my car and driven to the hospital, which just shows how dumb I can be.

In London, St Giles' would be called a garden square, a patch of grass enclosed by Georgian houses that still manage to look, for the most part, tall and elegant, although some of them have been allowed to become sagging and sad. Most of those are owner-occupied by ageing citizens crippled by repair bills and community tax. Number twenty seven, where Jeannie had housed herself, was crisp with new paint and freshly pointed brickwork, its black front door gleaming with brass furnishings. Nice. I pressed the bell push by Jeannie's name, unsurprised when nothing happened. I was toying with the idea of pushing the other three in quick succession when the pizza delivery van drew up. I gave the driver an ingenuous smile and fished for my purse, 'Is that mine?'

He said, 'Marsden?'

'Got it in one. How much?' I paid the price, balanced the box and started fishing around my bag some more. Van and driver moved away, cornering briskly, unconcerned about right of title. I pressed the Marsden bell. A tinny voice asked what I wanted. 'Pizza,' I said cheerfully, and got buzzed up. Dutifully I made the delivery and got paid. Fraudulent entry gets easier by the day.

Jeannie's flat was on the first floor and it would have helped to have had the keys but there are other ways of gaining entry, like the neat set of picklocks supplied to me a while ago by an acquaintance named Sidney, whose business affairs it's best not to delve into. Lessons in lockpicking had been included in the price and had already served me well. It took around a minute to open Jeannie's door. I guess the landlord thought that providing a secure entrance system relieved him of spending overmuch on indiidual locks. It's lucky I'm on the side of the angels.

I admired Jeannie's nice hall carpet and thought I really ought to do something about my own, and then I went into the sitting-room and admired the un-neat way some person had been through her things. Cassette cases were open, contents in a pile. Record sleeves were adrift from records. I eyed the open drawers and cupboards and stepped over the settee cushions. Someone had done a messy if thorough job, and I didn't think it had been the police. For one thing Nicholls and his crew wouldn't have wanted anybody to know they'd been in there, and for another magistrates' warrants aren't all that easy to come by. I righted the settee, put the cushions back, and looked at the disarray. A specific search or a random fishing trip? Either way the place had been turned over so thoroughly there didn't seem much point in doing it all again.

Except for the sofa and two easy chairs, the furniture was black ash, and I guessed it would be pretty uniform to all the flats. A two-shelf trolley supported a television and VCR, and a wide bookcase with drawers and cupboards below stood against the long back wall. It's a pity everything it held had been transferred to the carpet. If the place wasn't such a mess it'd be really nice.

I went down the hall and into the bedroom. There's something to be said for having a meagre wardrobe. Jeannie had a lot of clothes and they were all on view, piled on the floor, thrown over a chair, everywhere they shouldn't be. I took a peek in the empty wardrobe, stepped over a pile of frivolous underwear that would have had Nicholls drooling were I in it, and fingered through the letters, photographs and miscellaneous papers scattered over the dressing-table. Jeannie's passport and savings book were among them. Her chequebook and driving licence were not. Wherever Jeannie had gone she hadn't expected to need either. Idly I opened her building society passbook and blinked at the balance.

I was still looking at the £25,000 deposited four weeks and three days ago when somebody put a key in the lock and I wasn't alone any more.

4

Hiding out in a room with no closets, a bare wardrobe and a divan low enough to give a skulking cat trouble gave me some worry. My heart picked up a little speed. A couple of voices, male by the sound of them, mumbled something too subdued for me to catch. Great! Whoever was out there had brought a friend along. I looked around for a handy weapon. Mother Hubbard would have felt right at home. Maybe I should try for a little nonchalance. Make out like I was the cleaning lady.

The mumble shifted into the sitting-room and I moved out into the hallway, adrenaline flowing, soft-footing it to the flat door and easing back the latch. Two more seconds and I would have made it.

A hand, lean and well sprinkled with hairs, came past my head and flattened against the wood. Reflexively I knuckled right hand into left and elbowed back, hard, striking home and hearing a grunt of pain. I grabbed for the latch. Nicholls' voice said peevishly, 'Leah, what the hell are you doing here?'

Shit!

I let go the latch and turned around. 'Nicholls,' I said. 'Your timing's lousy, a trick like that could give me heart failure.' From the look on his face anyone would think he didn't care. He stayed where he was in the sitting-room doorway, and scowled some more.

'Breaking and entering . . .'

I squinted over at DC Dixon, up against the wall and doing a little self-massage. 'Uh-uh,' I said. 'Forget it. I'm here by invitation – who asked you along?'

'How'd you get in?'

'Through the door, how else? I guess whoever wrecked the place left it open.' Sometimes lies slip off my tongue so easily it scares me. 'And how come you suddenly turn up with a key? Where'd you get it?'

'None of your damn business, Leah.'

I shrugged. 'If you found the handbag I bet Jeannie's letter wasn't in there. And how come you're working so late?'

The scowl looked pretty permanent. 'Going by the book, I should arrest you.'

'For what?'

'For what? Illegal entry, assaulting a police officer . . .'

'How was I supposed to know he was a police officer? He could have been the guy who trashed the place.'

' . . . interfering with evidence . . .'

'What evidence?'

'Touched anything?' he said.

I shrugged. 'You already have my prints.'

He nodded. 'Be interesting to see where we find them.'

'Jeannie's passport is one place,' I said. 'You'll find it in the bedroom, along with her bankbook. I guess she didn't plan on going very far, even without a passport she'd need to get at her money.'

'Maybe she had more than one account.'

'What's that supposed to mean?'

He reached past me and opened the door. 'It means go home,' he said flatly.

'You think she just grabbed a pair of clean underpants and left? Those are good clothes in there, Nicholls, why the hell would she dump them? And how come her vanity case is still here? To me that kind of thing suggests she didn't plan on being away too long – or that something happened that prevented her coming home.'

'Like what?'

I shrugged again. 'You tell me. Not an accident or you'd know about it, and my guess is, if you talked with her boss at Customs and Excise he'd tell you it isn't like her to just take off.'

'Maybe he would,' Nicholls said.

'You asked him already?'

He opened the door a bit wider and gave me a little shove. 'Go home, Leah.'

I turned around and walked away. Times are when strategic retreat is best, and I had other things to do, like go back and talk with Mrs Johnson's neighbour, so I could ask a few questions I'd forgotten to ask before.

One of the nice things about early July is the length of daylight; for one thing it lets people see who's knocking on their door at eight-thirty when they're not expecting callers. Mrs Johnson's neighbour took a good look at me through the net curtain. I smiled, waved, and hoped if she didn't remember me she wouldn't just write me off as an Avon lady and go back to the television. After about ten seconds she backed away from the window, and a couple of seconds after that opened the door.

'You're the young woman who came looking for Mrs Johnson,' she said.

'That's right. I've just come from the hospital. She's worried about a handbag she had with her when the accident happened.'

'I know that, I called in myself yesterday and talked with her. I suppose she told you what I said?'

'That you saw someone take it? Yes, she told me that, that's why I've come to talk to you.'

'Better come in then,' she said, stepping back and letting me into the hall. 'I was about to make a pot of tea, but I can do you an instant coffee if you'd like that better?'

'Tea would be nice,' I said, following her down the hall. When we got to the sitting-room she waved me through.

'Make yourself at home, I won't be long.' I smiled in response and hoped the soles of my shoes were clean as I trod across the pink Chinese carpet, sinking into a cream and pink tasselled armchair that threatened to swallow me up in its cushions. I wished I knew Molly's surname, but whatever it was she was very house-proud, dust wouldn't dare show its nose in a room like this, and the shine on the furniture made it look like it had been lacquered. Not a room I could ever feel comfortable in, no place for a slobby person to put their feet up and relax. Even the television was an elegant number in a hideaway cabinet. I hitched up a little in the chair, eyeing a Degas print of a ballet class, and knowing if I spilled tea I'd feel guilty till I died.

The television was still turned on, a food programme of sorts, some female I'd never seen before using pints of cream to make the kinds of cakes most people only have to look at to put on pounds. I could feel my stomach gear itself up, anticipating a treat it wasn't going to get. Maybe on the way home I'd pick up a pizza.

By and by Molly came back with a tray that she set on the shiny coffee table without so much as a worried look. I took my cup from her carefully. 'Nice room,' I said. She looked pleased.

'You like it? I don't know why, but it seems to make some people feel uneasy.' She smiled and bent her head a little as if we were part of a conspiracy. 'You know, when the children were young the place was always such a tip, toys and books and fingermarks. I promised myself, one day, Molly, one day.' She sighed, and looked around. 'There are times when I'd like the clutter back, but life won't stand for any stepping back.' I made some sympathetic noises. She took a gulp of tea and looked at me. 'You didn't come to hear all that, you came to talk about Stella and her handbag. What is it you want to know?'

'Would you tell me about the accident, everything you saw?'

'There isn't all that much to tell, it happened so fast. Stella and I live alone, you know? We both picked the wrong men to marry so it gave us something in common, and we've dropped into the habit of, when one of us goes out, letting the other one know.'

'When Mrs Johnson called round did she tell you where she was going?'

'She mentioned taking a letter to one of Jeannie's friends.' She looked at me. 'That was you I suppose?' I nodded. 'I don't know where that girl's got to,' she sighed.

'That's what I'm hoping to find out,' I said, and steered her back to the hit and run. 'There's a possibility Jeannie might have mentioned her intentions in that letter, which is why I need to know what happened to it.'

'One of the men took it. There were two of them in the car and it didn't seem to me they tried to avoid Stella at all.'

'Which direction were they going?'

'That way.' She faced the window and waved her hand from left to right. 'There wasn't anything else on the road, they could have gone around her if they'd wanted to.'

I nodded. 'I don't want to upset you by going over it, but can you tell me what happened next?'

'Well, the telephone is on the windowsill, so naturally I picked it up and dialled 999 before I went out to Stella. While I was doing that I saw a man get out of the passenger door and come back up the road. At first I thought he was going to see how badly she was hurt, but he didn't do that at all, he just bent down, picked up the bag, and got back in the car.'

'And then they drove off.'

'Fast. And then I went out to Stella. I took a cushion for her head, you know? But another car came along and the driver wouldn't let me use it. He said if she'd broken her neck I could have killed her, just moving her head.'

'I guess that's true,' I said. 'What happened next?'

'He stayed until the ambulance and police came. I went to the hospital with her and told them all her details, then the police brought me home. I couldn't stay any longer, I hadn't even locked the door.'

'The place was all right when you got back?'

'Oh, yes, the police insisted on looking all around, just in case.'

'Can you remember what make of car it was?'

'I'm not very good with cars, I don't have one of my own you see, so I don't really notice makes. It was dark blue and had four doors, I remember that much. I should have thought to get the registration but it didn't come into my mind.'

'Don't blame yourself,' I said. 'You were worrying about Mrs Johnson, a number plate is the last thing you'd be thinking about. How about the man who got out? Can you describe him?'

'I told the police everything I could, I don't see how it can help going over it all again with you. Forgive me, dear, but if the police can't find the car, how can you?'

'I have friends in the garage business who'd be more likely to talk to me than to the police, and that could make a big difference.' That was almost the absolute truth. I had one, very good friend, Charlie Fagan, and I didn't doubt he could lean on a few less reputable repairers if I gave him good enough reason. And Charlie owed me a favour.

'I suppose so,' she said. 'But I wouldn't want you to end up in trouble too. I wouldn't want that on my conscience.' I swallowed down what was left of my tea and sighed. Why is it that everyone feels they need to look out for me?

'A description of the man to go with the car would help. If I pick up any information I'll hand it over to the police,' I promised. And so I would – in my own good time.

'Well, if you're sure about that, I did get a good look at him, he had on a bomber jacket, you know the kind of thing, elastic at the waist, and it was beige with green inserts at the top of the sleeves.' She puckered her forehead up and did some more remembering. 'He'd be around five-ten, dark hair, really short sides and back and long on top. He kept his head down so I didn't see much of his face, but I would think, perhaps, middle twenties.' She stopped there and looked at me scribbling it all down in my little notebook.

'That's fine,' I said encouragingly. 'How about pants and shoes? Did you notice what he wore?'

'Jeans and trainers. The trainers were grey.' I wrote that down too.

'If he kept his head down you'd only get to see him in profile. Anything unusual there?' She shook her head. 'How about his ears?' I prompted.

She closed her eyes for a couple of seconds, then opened them and stared at me. 'I'd forgotten about the earring. Not a plain round one, or I wouldn't have noticed. His had something dangling from the bottom.' She sighed. 'I can't tell you what though, I wasn't close enough to see.'

I closed my notebook and put it away. 'Thanks,' I said, 'that's brilliant. I hope Mrs Johnson will be home soon.'

'Oh, so do I,' she said fervently. 'All the other neighbours work. It's really quiet without Stella. I think I'll go and see her tomorrow. Shall I tell her you've been?'

'If you feel you want to, yes,' I said. 'She knows I'm looking for Jeannie.'

She looked relieved. 'That's all right then. Would you like more tea?'

'No thanks, that's been lovely, but I have to get home.' I rose to my feet, put the cup back on the tray, and held out my hand. 'Thanks,' I said. 'You've helped enormously. I'm sorry, I don't know your surname, Mrs Johnson calls you Molly.'

'Molly will do very well,' she said. 'But my surname is Stansfield, and I'm sure if Jeannie knew what had happened to her mother she'd be home right now.'

'I'm sure she would,' I agreed.

Molly's head tilted a little as she looked at me. She was anxious again. 'You think she *is* all right don't you? Jeannie, I mean. She *will* be all right?'

I really wanted to tell her yes, I was sure of it, but the fact was, I wasn't sure of anything, so I told her the bare truth instead.

'I don't know, Molly,' I said. 'I really don't know,' and that kept both

26

of us quiet until we got to the front door, where she told me to take care before going back inside to think it all out.

I slid into the car and drove home sedately. Molly wasn't the only one with things on her mind.

5

I had hoped that Nicholls might come around and share a little knowledge with me, but that didn't happen. Such small disappointments are an irksome part of life. At ten-thirty I skipped *Newsnight*, took a shower, and had an early night, sleeping like a baby until a couple of cooing pigeons woke me at six-thirty next morning. Fifteen minutes later I was out on the streets taking in relatively fume free early morning air, keeping up an easy pace on the five-mile run that's part of my regular fitness routine. Taking care of my body is one of the few good habits I've picked up.

It was going to be a hot day, the sky already bright blue and heat haze distorting chimney tops. Halfway home a tongue-lolling dog loped along until he picked up an interesting scent and went his own way. I have a soft spot for dogs. Maybe one day I'll get rich and have a place big enough to have one around permanently. Maybe.

At eight-fifteen, showered and fed, I picked up my car from Dora's. Dora is a good friend and pushing seventy, although she seldom owns up to that. A retired school-teacher, she gave up her own car and took to cycling, working out that way she'd keep fit and save money, which worked out fine for me. The Victorian villa on Pindars' Run where I have my attic home is garageless, so now I rent Dora's empty space a hundred yards along and we're both happy with the arrangement.

Right now Dora has her hands full fostering a young teenager she helped rescue from the streets, and that seems to be working out just fine too.

It was still a little short of eight-thirty when I pulled into Charlie Fagan's repair yard, a walled enclosure that used to be a stables and farrier and still has a few bits and pieces of the old building left, renovated and re-roofed by Charlie. When I pulled up in front of the workshop he was already hard at work, and came out to greet me wiping his hands on the habitual paraffin rag. I swear they're so oily they just make things worse rather than better.

'Thought you'd be walking and keeping healthy on a nice day like this,' he said. 'Car all right?' He looked it over critically. Charlie's sideline is rebuilding old cars, not always with the same make of engine, and the hybrid I drive is one of them, an old Morris Minor with a BMW engine under the bonnet that makes it fly.

'The car is fine,' I said. 'I've come to ask a favour.'

'Ask away. I owe you a few.'

'I don't know if you can help me with this. I need to find a car involved in a hit and run five days ago. A friend of mine got herself hurt and the police aren't making much headway. I thought you might know a few places where that kind of damage gets repaired and not reported.'

'A few of them about, love. Make money where they can these day. Want me to ask around?'

'It'd be a real help. I'm looking for a dark blue four-door. The witness didn't know if it was a hatch or a saloon, and she didn't get a look at the driver, but the passenger got out and stole my friend's handbag. She got a good look at him.' I repeated the description Molly Stansfield had given me. Charlie wiped his hands some more.

'Think it was joy-riders?'

I shook my head. 'I think it was planned deliberately. The handbag held a letter and I believe they ran her down to get it.'

'Not nice.' He pushed the rag back in his pocket and spread his hands on porky hips. 'You getting yourself in bother again? 'Cos if you are, don't forget you've got friends.'

'Why else would I be here?' I said. 'How's Sidney keeping these days?'

'Want some help from him too?'

'If he knows anyone fairly local who makes enough to need some laundering.'

'Not the sort of thing you want to get into, that,' he said reprovingly.

'Hey,' I said. 'Help I need, advice you can put on hold.' His face took on a worry crease. The pony-tail he'd grown to make up for the lack of hair on top wagged.

'I'll ask,' he said. 'Don't agree with it but I'll ask. 'Bout time you let that boyfriend of yours do a bit of work.' He patted the hybrid. 'Sure it isn't giving you trouble?'

'Sure of it,' I said, getting back in. 'See you, Charlie.'

'See you,' he said doubtfully, and watched me drive away, the paraffin rag doing overtime again. I guess for Charlie paraffin rags take the place of comfort blankets.

I turned out on to Market Street and headed for the Inland Revenue building, a council-owned glass and concrete affair, built in the sixties as an ugly replacement for an architecturally blessed town hall that now serves mostly as a function centre. Whatever virtues the town fathers may have, a strong sense of historical continuity can't be counted among them, and from certain angles the local skyline makes Bramfield a place to pass by rather than visit. I manœuvred around the four-lane roundabout that adds a little spice to local driving lessons and pulled into my usual parking bay behind the offices. Up on the fourth floor Pete, my boss, was already hard at work. I tapped on his glass cubicle as I went by and got a half-hearted wave in reply. The trouble with Pete is, whichever area of his life you look at, cars, work, women, he tries too hard.

I settled down behind my desk and got on with a little work of my own, checking returns, verifying assessments, telling myself what fun it would all be in 1996 when citizens got to do all of that for themselves. Maybe I should retrain for something, like a manicurist or collecting the dole. I was still pursuing that thought when the telephone rang and Nicholls asked what I planned on doing for lunch. I told him eat. Fine, he said, he'd pick me up. I looked at the buzzing receiver and thought how nice it would have been if he'd mentioned a time. I put it back on its rest ungently. A second later it rang again. Nicholls said, 'Twelve-thirty,' and hung up without giving me a chance to argue. Maybe he'd decided it was time to be masterful; such notions afflict him from time to time.

At twelve-thirty I trotted down the outside steps and found him sitting in his car, his face non-committal. It was a look I recognised, one he wears when he has something to tell me that he knows I won't like. I climbed in beside him and buckled into the seat. 'OK,' I said. 'Let's hear the worst.' He slid into gear and cut into the traffic, weaving round a lorry, drifting across two lanes, and getting hooted at from both. If it was that bad maybe I didn't want to hear it after all. By and by he turned through the park gates on to a cinder square, sharing the space with three more cars and an ice-cream van. I wondered where the regular hot-dog stand was today. Maybe the weather was just too warm to slave over a hot stove.

Nicholls climbed out and I followed suit, pondering on what might be in the carrier bag fished out from behind the front seat. Not champagne and smoked salmon, I'd bet my boots on that. It's depressing the way I know his habits. He led me past the tennis courts at a brisk pace and stopped at a bench overlooking the deserted bowling greens. I arranged myself nicely at one end – he took the other and set the carrier bag between us. I said, 'I hope it's food you have in there, Nicholls.' He still didn't answer, just lifted out a flask of canteen tea and a neat pile of packeted sandwiches. I grabbed a cheese and pickle, getting in a couple of bites while he messed with the flask, filling up two mugs and handing me one. Finally he scowled a little and said, 'You're not going to like this any better whichever way I put it, and it's for your ears only, not to pass on to Jeannie's mother.' I stopped chewing and paid him some attention. 'Jeannie could find herself in trouble. A lot of trouble, but if she does it's because she's been taking pay-offs.'

'What . . . ?'

He held his hand up. 'Try, just for once, to listen. You saw the bank book, and you saw the balance, and that by itself amounts to a lot more than Jeannie could have saved out of her salary. It could even be she was into this kind of thing before she was seconded to NCIS. They've turned up an overseas account with a lot more than twenty-five thousand in. The kind of pay-off that's earned by turning a blind eye to something like money laundering. I know that isn't something you'll want to believe, but the facts are evidential.'

'Bet your sweet life I'll have trouble believing it,' I said. 'Offshore accounts can be falsified. Haven't you ever heard of computer fraud? Setting up an account in Jeannie's name would be child's play.'

'It isn't the only thing NCIS uncovered.'

'What else?'

'I can't tell you anything else, Leah, not yet, I shouldn't have told you as much as I have, but I don't want you falling into something you can't handle.'

'Where do you think she is?'

He shook his head.

'Does that mean you don't know, or you don't want to say?'

'I don't know where she is. That's the truth.'

'But you suspect,' I said, feeling a coldness despite the heat of the day. 'Nothing to stop you telling me that is there?'

'She could have asked for too much and run foul of the wrong people.'

I stared at him. 'I'm sorry,' he said. 'And before you ask, I talked to her old boss at Customs and Excise. He thought she was straight, but the evidence that's been accumulating says otherwise.'

'Where did this evidence come from? A helpful phone call? An anonymous tip? Or did you and NCIS ferret it out all by your little selves?'

'I can't tell you that either. Leah, all that loose money floating around can tempt anybody. Jeannie wouldn't be all that unusual if she'd cut herself in.'

'Would you put your hand out?' I said.

'No. But I'd expect to get caught – a lot of people don't think that far ahead.'

I stared at the sandwich. 'Shit, Nicholls, you really know how to take away a person's appetite. What are you going to tell Mrs Johnson?'

'Nothing – and neither are you.'

I said, 'You found the handbag?' He nodded. 'Was Jeannie's letter in it?'

'No, but it's possible the letter was her insurance, the old chestnut of if anything happened to her it was around to name names.'

'So how would they know where it was?' I said sweetly. 'Don't you think it a teensy bit more than chance Mrs J had it in her handbag at the right time? I mean if somebody hollered phone bug here I wouldn't argue.'

'We already checked the phone. No bugs.'

'Who checked it?'

'Technicians.'

'Right after the hit and run?'

'Does it matter?' he said uncomfortably.

'You know damn well it matters. If it wasn't done right away whoever put a bug in had time to take it out.' I shook my head. 'I don't believe any of this. Tell me something, Nicholls, the night Jeannie got picked up and brought into the station, what was it all about?'

'A fracas in a car park. That's all Jeannie would say, and it's all the pub landlord would say. And don't ask a fracas with who, I only know what I'm told.'

'Which pub?' I said. He eyed me stonily and stayed silent. 'Come on. Damn it, you know I'm better at wheedling than you'll ever be, let me talk to him, I promise I'll tell you every word he says.'

'I'd just as soon you got mixed up in this as I'd cut my hand off.' I was about to say something unkind when I saw his face. I ran my finger along his jaw.

'That's nice, but I wasn't planning on doing anything stupid.' He leaned over and kissed me and his aftershave smelled good. I got to thinking it was time I invited him round for cocoa after all, and when he pulled back I read the same message in his nice blue eyes. 'Sometimes,' I told him, 'you just have to trust in people.'

'Sometimes,' he said, 'you can do too much of it.' I didn't argue; it wouldn't be the first time he'd been right. My stomach got set to rumble. I picked up the sandwich and finished it off. Starving wouldn't do a thing to help Jeannie wherever she was. When we were through picnicking Nicholls dumped the waste plastic in a rubbish bin and drove me back to the concrete monster. 'Maybe she's found herself a safe house,' he said as I got out. 'It's as likely as anything else.' It was a nice thought to leave me with. I turned around and looked at him.

'I wasn't planning on anything but an early night. How about you?' He shook his head. 'That's good,' I told him. 'I'll get out the cocoa tin.'

It's really nice the way his eyes light up.

I skipped up the outside steps and took the lift to the fourth floor. There was a handwritten message on my desk from Martin, brief and to the point, giving his address and telephone number in Windermere, and saying his mother was well enough to transfer to a hospital near his home that afternoon. If I heard anything, anything at all, about Jeannie would I let him know?

I thought about the things Nicholls had told me, and knew there are some appeals that it's best to just ignore.

6

A couple of days later Jeannie turned up in the Aire and Calder Navigation Canal. One of the wandering homeless had seen two men dump what could have been an old carpet in the water, around two in the morning, only there'd been something in the way it hung between them that made him take a closer look. Luckily for him the men who'd just cleaned out their car boot didn't look around, and luckily for Jeannie the weeds didn't hold her down. The moon had been full, the itinerant had seen a hand, and what he thought was a face, and that had been enough for him to go in after her. And when he'd got her out, he'd had to run a mile and a half to the main road to flag down a passing lorry.

Don't ask me how lucky is lucky. Maybe when Jeannie woke up she'd be grateful – then again – maybe not. She'd been beaten, raped – God knows how many times –and collected enough needle holes to qualify as junkie of the year, and although she wasn't dead there must have been a lot of times when she'd wanted to be. Standing at the side of the hospital bed looking down at her, I couldn't work out how she'd held on.

Nicholls said, 'Is it her?'

'Same hair, same height,' I said woodenly. 'I guess it has to be.'

'I need a positive ID, Leah.'

'Why me?' I said angrily. 'How come her caring colleagues aren't doing that? Shit, Nicholls, all that swelling and bruising, her mother wouldn't know her.' I looked at him. 'Who's going to break the news to her family?'

'We haven't established identity yet.'

'Who else could it be?'

'A lot of people. How about birthmarks?'

'I haven't seen her in years – how am I supposed to remember birthmarks?' We stared at each other, both of us unhappy. 'I'm sorry,' I said. 'I guess you'll just have to ask Martin, maybe he'll remember a mole, or an appendectomy scar, or . . .' I trailed off there, and remembering something from way back, bared her left knee. There was a starry scar where Jeannie aged thirteen had run foul of barbed wire. 'It's her,' I said bleakly. 'Somebody really fouled up this time, didn't they?'

'Nobody fouled up but Jeannie,' he said. 'She didn't follow the rules.'

'Maybe she had good reason not to.'

'Meaning what?'

'Meaning whatever you want it to mean.' I looked at the bleeping, flickering monitors. 'What are her chances?'

'Not good.'

'Great,' I said, and walked out before the gravel in my throat got the better of me.

Nicholls caught up with me as I clattered down the stairs in preference to the elevator. 'I'm sorry,' he said.

'Not your fault,' I told him. 'You didn't set her up as an Aunt Sally.'

'Nobody did.'

'No?'

'No. You've heard the evidence, Jeannie was skimming profits, she knew what the risks were.'

'Stick with that thought,' I advised as I shoved open the bottom door. 'It must be a real comfort.'

It was half-past midnight when the telephone woke me, and the first thought I had was that Jeannie had worsened. I pulled up out of the night's first deep sleep and headed for the hall, trailing shreds of dream. Nicholls and I had been on a warm and quiet riverbank, and from the bit I remembered, fishing hadn't been a part of the storyline.

'I've got your number, bitch.'

A male voice in my ear, saying just that and nothing else before the line disconnected. I crawled back into bed and waited for the dream to restart. It didn't. Instead the voice replayed itself inside my head. Weirdos are a real pain. After twenty minutes of tossing around I gave up, heated some milk, added honey and nutmeg, and watched the end of the late film on television. At one o'clock the phone rang again. Same voice, same message.

36

I turned the switch to silent ring, put on some Bach, and fell asleep on the sofa. This time Nicholls didn't come into my dreams, only Jeannie was there, dripping water and screaming soundlessly, and when I woke at five-thirty I felt like I hadn't slept at all.

When I went to the hospital again to check on Jeannie, Martin was there, and so was Nicholls, with a thick-set, medium height man in his thirties, mid-brown hair tailored neatly, and a nose that would have looked good on Shylock. They weren't in the room with Jeannie, but in a fat stump of corridor, and Martin was looking good and angry. When Nicholls saw me he looked shifty, so I walked right up and listened in.

' . . . better explanation than I've been given so far,' Martin was saying when Nicholls cut in on him.

'Leah, if you want to go in, go ahead, but she's still in a coma.'

'Thanks,' I said, 'but I want to say hallo to Martin, and to meet your friend.' I stuck out a hand toward the unsmiling stranger. 'Leah Hunter.' For a second I didn't think he was going to respond, then he gave my hand a quick shake and let go.

'Geoff Lomas.' Just that, without any embellishments.

Martin's hands had balled into fists. He said savagely, 'Jeannie's boss, Leah, only he doesn't seem to have a good explanation for how my sister got into this state. Plenty of excuses, yes, but sod all answers.'

'We don't have answers,' said Lomas.

'You knew damn well she was missing.' Martin thrust his chin out pugnaciously. 'Why weren't all stops pulled out to find her? You knew the danger, you knew this might happen, but you let her get into it, and I want some bloody answers.'

'We didn't foresee the outcome.' His eyes slipped down to Martin's hands. 'The people responsible will be found.'

'They'd better be,' Martin muttered. Lomas turned his eyes on me, pale hazel and uncompromising.

'When rules are broken, things get out of hand. You know that from experience don't you, Miss Hunter?'

'Hey. Don't I though? Something I see every day. Make a mistake in your tax return, Mr Lomas, and I'll be right there in your office pointing it out,' I said. 'Or isn't that what you had in mind?'

'Not exactly.' He glanced at Nicholls. 'Keep in touch on this,' he said flatly, nodded at the three of us, and walked away.

'Why do I want to take him apart?' breathed Martin.

'Because it's your sister in there,' I said. 'And he doesn't exactly exude a warmth of personality.'

'He can't afford to,' said Nicholls. 'Emotion and clear thinking don't go together.'

I shrugged. 'Horses for courses I guess, but he isn't going to win prizes for likeability. How's Jeannie?'

Martin seemed to shrink a couple of inches. He muttered, 'I barely recognised her. God, it's . . .' He sought for a word he couldn't find and then, slump shouldered, went back to her bedside. I looked at Nicholls and his eyes drifted to a picture on the wall. There wasn't any need for me to ask just how bad things still were, that shift in focus said it all. He didn't think Jeannie was going to make it.

'The guy who saved her,' I said. 'I suppose he's back on the streets.'

'Social Services fixed him up with a bed-sit. He might be needed as a future witness.'

'After which public spirited piece of community service he gets booted back on to the road again? I hope he appreciates the depth of state generosity.'

'A fixed address gives him a chance to claim Social Security,' Nicholls said. 'It's up to him what he makes of it.'

'I'd like to drop by and talk with him.'

I could see the little wheels moving around in his head when I said that, trying to work out why I'd want to and thinking maybe I was planning to elbow in on his territory again. I can't think why he gets so hung up over things.

'Somebody ought to say thanks,' I said gently, pointing out something he'd most likely forgotten about. 'And maybe at the same time I'll pass on a few wrinkles about collecting his statutory rights from the benefits system.'

'I'll go with you.'

I shrugged. 'Suit yourself, but I'd have thought you had more pressing things to do than act as a chauffeur.'

He reddened, scribbled down an address and handed it over. 'Since he doesn't know anything useful it can't hurt,' he said. 'Advise him not to disappear.'

'If he doesn't know anything useful why would it worry you?'

'I told you – he's a witness.'

'Who can't identify anybody.'

'That isn't general knowledge.'

I stared at him. 'Shit, Nicholls, you're hanging him out. Shooting targets belong in fairgrounds.'

'He isn't a target.'

'Right!' I snapped. 'Maybe I'll give him advice on crossing roads too.' I turned around and followed Martin. He had a hold of Jeannie's hand and was stroking his fingers across it rhythmically and looking lost. 'I don't ever remember a time when Jeannie gave in,' I said. 'And she isn't going to do it now.'

'I don't know,' his thumb continued its movements. 'I can't think straight.'

'Have you told her mother?'

'Not yet.' His eyes lifted and fixed on me. 'It's going to knock her right back, she'll want to come and she can't. Her pelvis won't heal that fast, they've nailed it together but it takes time. When I came down here I hoped I wouldn't need to tell her, not right away, but the way things are going . . .' His head shook hopelessly. 'I didn't expect Jeannie to be this bad, it isn't just her injuries, or the canal water, it's the quantity of drugs pushed into her. We're talking brain damage, Leah, that's what they say. The coma could deepen, and if it does she won't come out of it.' Martin's eyes dropped. He said dully, 'I don't know . . . maybe, after what she's been through . . .' He stared at the hand he was holding and I knew what the words were that he had left unsaid. Maybe Jeannie would be better off if the coma did deepen and she drifted away without having to come to terms with her ordeal. I felt angry, at Martin, at Lomas, at Nicholls and at myself, but most of all at the people who had done this, and the anger made my voice sharper than I'd meant it to be.

'Martin, has your mother begun to talk about the hit and run yet?'

He looked startled. 'Some, but not a lot, she doesn't want to talk about it any more than she has to.'

That didn't surprise me. People tend to shove such things into some deep archive of their mind, like hiding a skeleton in a cupboard.

'When the police talked her through it,' I said, 'could she remember any details? Did she know the make of car or colour? Or anything about the men inside?'

'She said the car was big and dark coloured, and that's all she could remember. Why are you asking?'

'Interest,' I said. 'Will you still be here tomorrow?'

'As long as it takes.' His thumb went back to its rhythmic stroking, his shoulders rose and fell. 'God knows where the business will end up with all the time I'm taking off,' he said despondently, more to himself than to me, and since I couldn't think of anything that wouldn't sound like a platitude I squeezed his shoulder, said I'd be back the next day, and left him to worry it all through in peace.

7

From time to time knowing how to defend myself has proved very useful, and Monday evenings I'm usually to be found at the T'chai and Oriental Arts Centre on Pilkington Street making sure my ability to do that doesn't rust up. It's also a good place to pick up on other interesting things besides Karate. The truth is there's very little going on in or around Bramfield that Jack, owner and instructor, doesn't get to hear about, mostly because his clients are such a varied lot. It's no unusual sight to find bouncers and stick-thin weaklings eyeing each other up across the mats. That particular night I hoped Jack's information network might have picked up some whispers about a crime syndicate sufficiently sure of itself to order Jeannie's death. OK, she wasn't dead yet, but dumping her in the canal showed they'd intended her to be.

As is usual when I want to pick Jack's brains, I got there early and sat in his office for a while, snug behind the one way mirror, watching the hunks at play. A couple of months back Jack tried getting a mixed session going, but the big boys weren't having any. I can't think why – I mean we wouldn't have *hurt* them.

By and by they finished up and trooped off to the showers. I put Jack's kettle on to boil and got down the Lapsang Souchong.

'That's what I like to see,' Jack said, coming in as I warmed the pot. 'Always wanted me own handmaiden.'

I grinned and handed him the tea-caddy. 'Dream on. Who knows what might happen when you get to heaven?'

'Can't think how you got to be so hard hearted,' he said, levering off the lid. 'Must be in me karma.'

I squatted on a chair, heels on the edge, and hugged my knees, watching steam rise from the pot. 'I need to hustle your expert knowledge, Jack.'

'Oh yeah? What for this time? Something nice and straight forward like a tax fiddle?' He quit stirring the pot and sat in his desk chair. Round eyed, squarish faced, high cheek bones giving him the look of a wise Indian. 'Or is this you sticking your neck out again?'

'Maybe I've got some bad karma too. Some degenerates dropped a friend of mine in the canal, around two in the morning, and I'd like to find out who. They also did a few other things to her first that you wouldn't like to hear about. She's in intensive care.'

'What you planning to do if you find 'em? Call in the boyfriend or sort it out yourself?'

'Come on, Jack, I'm not stupid, I'd pass it on. Since when did I go looking for trouble?'

'Since forever. You know your trouble, should have been born with a cock, an' I don't know if I can help you.' He went back to the Lapsang, straining it into a couple of mugs, then coming back and handing one to me. 'One of these days you'll get hurt.'

'I already did,' I reminded him gently. 'So now I take more care. If you don't feel you can help, it's OK.'

'Didn't say I wouldn't,' said Jack. 'What I said was, don't know if I can. Depends on what you want.'

'Jeannie's Customs and Excise, Jack. I think she was on to some heavy kind of money laundering deal.'

'Not talking small fry then are we? How long's it going to be before she can speak for herself?'

'I don't know about that, the way things look maybe never. They filled her so full of drugs she's in a coma. It could be irreversible. I thought maybe one of the boys . . . ?'

'Could have picked up some info. Haven't heard any talk about it, but I'll ask around.'

I sipped the smoky brew and stayed silent.

'Have to give me a bit of leeway, love, can't work miracles.'

'I'm not asking for miracles, Jack, I just need a place to start. How's your knowledge of antiques?'

'What period?'

'I'm talking auctions.'

'Don't get to go to many, I'm what you'd call more of a modernist. MFI and all that. What's the connection?'

'An easy scam. Antiques purchased with unbankable cash get re-sold in Europe. Clean currency gets fed into offshore accounts and filters back into the system. Half the city lives on the back of illicit cash flow and I guess Jeannie got too close to one of the taps.'

'Not any place you'd want to get close to then, is it?' he said. The words raised goose-bumps. Too right it wasn't.

I took my pot over to the mini-sink and rinsed it out. Digging up information was one thing, tangoing up too close to the wrong kind of people was another, and not something I meant to get into. All I'd planned on was to come up with a few hints and names to pass on to Nicholls. After that he could do the heavy work. I passed that piece of information on to Jack and he nodded politely. Telling the absolute truth never gets me believed.

When I went out on to the car park, feeling limber and pleased after a good session, a Panda car was taking up space, its driver checking number plates. I opened up the hybrid's boot and stowed my gear.

'I thought it was your car. This where you build your muscles up?' I turned around. Since the PC was smiling I guessed I wasn't in trouble.

I patted the car. 'Me and it,' I said. 'Both unique.' A switch clicked in my memory. I remembered his face. 'You're the one picked up a friend of mine, a few weeks back. I was in the front office when you brought her in. Good looking, chestnut hair, raising a rumpus.'

'A lot of people do that,' he said. 'It's usually why we bring them in.'

'I don't suppose you remember her then? That's a shame. She's an old schoolfriend I lost touch with and I'd kind of like to meet up with her again. If she's fallen on hard times I might be able to give her some help.' I crossed a few fingers and hoped he didn't know the girl-friend I was asking about, and the near drowned woman in hospital were one and the same. If he did he didn't let it show.

'If you tell me the date,' he said, 'maybe it's in my book.'

I opened up the car boot again and hunted out my diary, flipping back through the pages. 'July sixth,' I said. 'It'd be around eight, eight-thirty.' He unbuttoned his top pocket and did some page turning of his own.

'Oh, that one!' he said. 'Yeah, I remember her all right, a bit early in the day for that kind of trouble.'

'What kind was that?' I asked innocently.

'Fight in a pub car park. Seems she didn't want to get in a car.'

'So how come you brought her in instead of him?'

'She'd used a bottle on him, nicked his cheek.'

'So I guess you'd get his name and address?'

'He wouldn't press charges, said it had been a misunderstanding and he wanted to get home.'

'You believed that?'

'Didn't have any reason not to. According to him she'd tried soliciting and got nasty when he told her to shove off.'

'Doesn't sound like the person I used to know.'

'You saw what she looked like when we brought her in.'

'Can't deny that,' I said. 'Have you seen her around the same place since?'

'There haven't been any more incidents if that's what you mean.'

'Is her address in there?'

He closed his book. 'That'd be against regulations.'

I dredged up what I hoped was a disarming smile. 'Do regulations stop you telling me which pub it was? Maybe somebody there would know where she is.'

He shifted around a little and gave it some thought. 'I probably shouldn't, but it's not as if you couldn't find it out for yourself. Royal Oak, out on the Doncaster Road, and don't tell the DI I put you on to it.'

I put a finger up against my nose. 'Not a word.'

'Better get on then,' he said, putting his book away. 'How about you? Going home now?'

'Supper and bed, that's me.' I relocked the boot and opened the driver's door. 'See you around.'

'Drive safe,' he said, and went back to looking at number plates. As I pulled out on to the road I wondered vaguely what he was looking for.

8

Instead of going directly home I drove to Clarence Street, on the west side of town, cruising slowly between red-brick terraces, looking for number forty one where Social Services had found Jeannie's rescuer a room in bed-sit land. At nine-fifteen he could be out and about, walking the warm streets or cuddling a pint in a pub, but somehow I thought he'd be home, savouring four walls and a television set before someone snatched them away again.

Bedsits tend not to have personal bells with neat little name labels. I pounded on the front door and hoped somebody might feel up to answering it. Somebody did. Late twenties, blue jeans, grey sweatshirt and Nike trainers, lean and hungry looking enough to be the guy I was looking for. I squinted at the name Nicholls had scribbled down and said, 'Don Simpson?'

'Top floor back,' he said, and disappeared into the ground floor front. I climbed the stairs and did some more knocking. Preconceived ideas are seldom right, Simpson looked nothing like the guy downstairs, no hollow cheeks, no bony wrists, just average height and build, eyes deep-set grey set off by dark lashes, eyebrows feathering close together above the bridge of his nose, and nothing to suggest he might be one of life's rejects. I could feel my eyebrows go up as I studied him.

'Don Simpson?'

'Yes.' The grey eyes settled on me with curiosity.

'You pulled a friend of mine out of the canal. I came by to say thanks.'

His face closed up and he shook his head. 'Take it as said,' he told me and began to close the door. I put my foot in the way.

'I'd like to talk with you. Can you spare a few minutes? It won't take long.'

45

He eyed me through the gap. 'How did you know I was here?'

'The police told me.'

'Seems funny they'd do that when they told me not to talk about the canal business.'

'Did they tell you why?'

'I didn't need telling why.'

'Hey, if I was an assassin I could have shot you through the gap. We're on the same side for God's sake. Here . . .' I fumbled in my bag and pulled out a card. ' . . . This is me.' He took the pasteboard in two fingers and read it carefully.

'Tax inspector?' He handed it back and eyed me some more. I tried to look friendly and unthreatening. He stopped pressing against the door and let it open. 'Better come in, I might never get to meet a tax inspector again. Itinerants don't seem to provoke too much interest.'

'Everything has its bright side,' I said, and stepped past him. As rooms go it was pretty spartan, but he had a screen to cut off view of the kitchen area, a television, and a couple of easy chairs that still had life in them. Compared to a cardboard box it was the Ritz. He sat on the edge of the single bed and watched me look around.

'How about sitting and telling me what you want?'

I turned one of the chairs so it faced him.

'Jumping into a canal takes a lot of courage,' I said. 'I wanted to thank you.' He nodded. 'I also wanted to talk about what happened out there. Jeannie is still in a coma, it could be a long time before she comes out of it enough to speak. Did you see what kind of car it was?'

He shook his head. 'I didn't take much notice of that. It was a dark colour but that's about all I can say. The moon was up and that kind of light changes things. You know what they say, all cats look grey in the dark. Same applies to cars.'

'Hatchback?'

'Yep. I saw the tailgate.'

'Not the registration though?'

'Not unless you want me to invent it.'

'Lucky you were awake.'

'I wouldn't have been except for the car engine and their voices.'

'Could you hear what was said?' He shook his head. 'No names mentioned?' I pursued.

'If there were I didn't hear any.'

'Could be somebody's got a vendetta against the family,' I said. 'Sounds like it could be the same car that ran Jeannie's mother down a few days earlier. It's a pity you can't remember anything that might help track down both car and driver.'

'I wish I could help you.'

'How about accents, could you tell if they were local?'

His head moved sideways. 'One of them had an earring. I caught a flash of light when he turned his head, probably a leather jacket too judging by light refraction.'

I stared at him. He smiled slightly. 'Am I spoiling your image of a workshy inadequate? Sorry about that. Have you seen the figures on graduate unemployment?'

'Pretty high,' I said. 'What's your subject?'

'History and Philosophy. Bad choice. Makes you wonder why they waste time and money educating clever monkeys when there's nothing at the end of it – except maybe a labouring job or the dole.'

'Sleeping rough is better?'

Simpson shrugged. 'Call it wilderness training,' he said. 'Time out. That's what I've been telling myself so far.'

'I guess from Jeannie's point of view it's lucky it worked out that way.' I got to my feet, and he held out the card I'd given him. 'Keep it,' I said. 'If you remember anything else, or you need any help claiming benefits . . .' He put the card in his back pocket and nodded.

'Looks like I'll be stuck here for a while,' he said. 'Who knows? Maybe some job or other will turn up.' I hoped it did, but openings for philosophical historians are thin on the ground. I said goodbye and went back downstairs and out to the car, turning it around and heading home, disappointed that I hadn't learned anything about Jeannie's attackers except that one had worn an earring and maybe a leather jacket.

Call in at any pub in Bramfield and there'd be at least one customer answering that description.

Maybe if I'd spent a little less time watching TV detectives asking dumb questions and getting helpful answers, I wouldn't find reality so frustrating. I tried to imagine Magnum coming away from that kind of interview empty handed and failed dismally. The truth is, life just fails to live up to the expectations imposed on it by fiction.

It was Wednesday before I got around to taking a close look at the Royal

Oak. It wasn't the first time I'd seen the place, I'd driven by it many times but never had an urge to stop. I guess that had something to do with the locale being bang in the middle of the local cat parade. The pub itself fronted the main Doncaster Road, islanded between two narrow streets that were being steadily emptied ready for demolition. To the right of it, a run down parade of shops was still open, and I trawled each with Jeannie's photograph, getting shrugs and zero interest until I went into the Royal Oak. Some pubs don't live up to their names and this was one of them. Stale beer, stale tobacco smoke and left over human rancidity gave the bar a certain pungency. Obviously air-fresheners were for sissies.

I hiked up on a scuffed leather bar-stool, asked for a cold Pils, and showed the photograph again. This time I was lucky. The barmaid took a casual look and said, 'Oh yeah, looks a lot different there, but I know her. Came in a lot, one time. What d'you want her for?'

'We were good friends, but we sort of lost touch.'

'Yeah? Well she's changed. Could be you might not want to know her now.'

'Why's that?'

She shrugged and slid her eyes away. 'Well, you know, when a girl can't get proper work there's always one thing to fall back on.'

'That's what she does?'

'Did,' she corrected. 'Haven't seen her in a bit, maybe she got a job. Donna's the person to ask, she'd know more about it than me, they room in the same house.'

'Donna's in the same business?'

'No, I don't think so. Always skint, but I haven't seen her offering it around if you know what I mean?'

I did. I also got to wondering if Jeannie had a double. Then I remembered the way she looked when she was hauled into the police station. I took a good long swallow of Pils while I thought about it. She was operating under cover, that much I'd got out of her, and according to Nicholls, NCIS hadn't known what she was up to. That was hard to believe too. Under cover or not, would she really go as far as picking up punters? I didn't think so. I didn't *want* to think so. I put off asking about the fracas in the pub yard and asked where I could find Donna instead.

'Cooper Street,' the barmaid said readily, then screwed up her forehead. 'Seventy . . . um . . . four. No! *Five.*'

'Seventy-five?'

'That's it.'

Jeannie worked for NCIS and Jeannie was a hooker. I felt like Alice disappearing down the rabbit hole. Things were getting curiouser and curiouser. 'Can I ask your name?' I said. 'Just so I can tell Donna where I got the information from?'

'Chloe,' she said. 'Just tell her, Chloe, down at the Oak.'

I drank up. 'Thanks,' I said. 'How do I get to Cooper Street?'

'Turn up past the chippy, and it's right by the school,' she said. 'Can't miss it.'

I said thanks and hoped she was right, trying not to listen to the voice of experience telling me can't miss it and needle in haystack usually mean one and the same thing.

9

On the right-hand side of the road a painted sign read, Sam's Fish Bar. A little further along a red and blue neon sign announced, Ocean Fisheries. I pulled up at the bus-stop and asked a waiting pensioner for Cooper Street. 'It's near the school,' I encouraged when he looked nonplussed.

'Ah, well, depends which school,' he said sagely. 'Now, up there's the nursery school,' flapping a hand at the turning before Sam's Fish Bar. 'And down yonder, up past that lit up chippy, see it?' I nodded. I was way ahead of him. 'Right then, well, up there's the junior school. Depends which one of 'em you're after.' I thanked him, and thought about turning around and going back to the Oak, but if I did that I'd probably waste as much time as trying both streets. I tossed a mental coin, remembered the pensioner's throw away 'chippy', and turned left at the neon sign. Idly I cruised a council estate and wasted valuable time. I guess there had to have been street signs around there once. Maybe now hub-caps were out of fashion there was a new mania?

By and by a kindly Brown Owl directed me back to Sam's Fish Bar. Cooper Street was right around the corner. Hey ho, life is full of such fun surprises.

I gritted my teeth and looked for number seventy-five.

As a street there wasn't much to commend it; grey, narrow and depressing, both sides lined with houses that were probably full of narrow, depressed people. Maybe when the sun came out from behind its cloud it would all look different, but somehow I didn't think so.

A lot of the houses seemed to want to be anonymous, and I guessed the postman must have a lot of fun keeping count as he walked along. I found the right house and parked out front. Across the street a couple of truanting males loitered, nonchalantly eyeing up the car and sharing a bent cigarette. The hybrid doesn't look like a joy-rider's dream machine but I locked up carefully and didn't take chances. Except for a clapped-out Escort there wasn't anything else around to tempt them.

Number seventy-five didn't run to a bell-push and the street door was locked. The downstairs window sported a free-art arrangement of empty lager cans. I pounded the door vigorously and watched a bubble of maroon paint, crisped by the sun, split open like a seed pod. By and by feet shuffled and the letter flap opened up. A female voice asked, 'Yeah? Who is it?'

'Leah Hunter,' I said. 'I'm looking for a friend.' I held up Jeannie's photograph so the eye could see it. 'I'm told she lives here.'

'By who?'

'Chloe, at the Oak.'

'What do you want her for?'

'Like I said, she's a friend. We've been out of touch for a while and it's time we did some catching up.'

'What's her name then?'

A good question, and one I could easily get wrong. If Jeannie hadn't wanted anybody she worked with to know about this place, chances were she wouldn't have rented under her own name. I shook my head at the solitary eye. 'Her name is Jeannie, but she might be calling herself something different.'

'Why would she do that?'

'Well . . . There's this guy she was with,' I said inventively. 'She wouldn't have wanted him to find her – you know how it is?' I smiled encouragingly. 'He'd probably have come round and beaten her again.' Obviously that was a situation the eye could appreciate. A bolt slid back, the door opened, and I walked into a hall empty of anything except a threadbare carpet and a mountain bike missing its front wheel.

'It's Ray's,' she said as I cocked an eye at it. 'Takes the wheel upstairs with him.'

'Wise precaution.'

'Yeah.'

We eyed each other. I guessed she was around twenty, pale complexion, long mousy hair, the side pieces plaited and caught back. Whatever other problems she might have, over-eating wasn't one of them. I said, 'Jeannie home?'

She eyed me. 'Sure you're a friend and not a snooper?'

'I'm sure,' I said firmly. Her scuffed black ankle boots shuffled indecisively.

'Better come on up then,' she said finally, and began to climb the stairs.

A little chill touched my skin as I remembered Jeannie's battered face. If there was somebody up there in a room I guess there had to be a double after all. If so I'd need to improve on the flimsy story offered so far. I worked on how to do that as I trailed along behind.

The brown paint on the handrail was dull and cracked, the greying cream walls depressing. Whoever he was, the landlord didn't go in for overspend.

On the second floor we turned down a stump of corridor and into a small back room. A narrow bed, nothing like as comfortable looking as that I'd seen in Don Simpson's room, sided one wall. Two tubular chairs *circa* the sixties flanked a Formica-topped table, and over in the corner a television set sat on a low cupboard. The only other piece of furniture in the place was a worn armchair minus a bottom cushion, bumpy springs pushing up against green velour. All the comforts of home.

I looked around. 'This is Jeannie's place?'

'Mine. Hers is across the landing. Doesn't call herself Jeannie though, told me she was Mo Allen.'

'Is she home?'

'Hasn't been here since the row.'

'What row?'

'I should have busted in,' she said. 'I know I should.' Her face creased into worry lines. 'It's just round here you sort of learn to keep out of things.'

'You're Donna?' I said.

'Chloe tell you?'

I nodded. 'What kind of things do you keep out of?'

She shrugged. 'Arguments. Mick's fault for letting them in, silly sod should know better.'

I sighed and straddled a tubular chair. 'Donna, we're not getting anywhere.'

She said, 'Everybody round here's DHSS, it's mind-your-own-business land. Can't wait to get some money and move out of it. That's what was best about Mo moving in. Somebody to talk to for a bit, you know?'

I nodded. 'So what happened? Who did Mick let in that he shouldn't?'

She shrugged. 'Two fellas. Shouting and banging around, you know? I thought – shall I go see – and ask Mo if she's all right? Only then they went, all three of them, before I'd made my mind up.'

'Mo went with them?'

'Yeah.'

'Did it seem like she was happy about that?'

She folded her arms, rubbing at them like she was cold. Her face furrowed again. 'I don't know. I asked if she was all right, but none of them looked round.'

'Did you go into her room?'

She hugged herself a bit tighter. 'Looked like they'd had a real fall out, chairs knocked over and stuff, so I straightened it up, thought it'd be better for her when she came back, not having to do it herself. Only she hasn't been back. Not yet.' I sat in silence and thought how it was just as well she hadn't butted in. 'Must have been the ex,' she said. 'The one you said hit her. I should have done something.' She unwrapped her arms and started to chew on a thumb-nail.

'Don't blame yourself,' I said. 'It wasn't you let them in, it was – what did you say his name was? Mick?'

'Yeah, he's downstairs.'

'Has he lived in this place long?'

'Not that long, 'bout the same time as Mo came. She moved out of her own place 'cos she had a fight with a man at the pub. Said she didn't want him coming after her.' She bit off a piece of nail and spat it out. 'Said she'd been picked up.'

'Picked up?'

'By the police. Pub landlord called them. I don't know what it was about, not properly. Mo didn't say much but Chloe said she'd used a bottle. Did the right thing if she was in trouble, men think they're bloody irresistible.'

'Who was he?'

She shook her head. 'Chloe said he wasn't a regular.'

'I expect Mo was upset about it?'

'She didn't talk about it.' The thumb-nail got another chewing.

'I'd really like to take a look in her room,' I said.

'Can if you want, I've got the key.'

I stared at her.

'Well what else would I do with it?' she asked. 'Give it to the landlord and have him let it out from under her? Wouldn't leave it empty for long would he? Not the type. Thought I'd wait and see if she came back.'

'I can see you had a problem. Maybe I can take a look? See if I can find a clue to what's happening. I don't want to give up on finding her when I've got this close.'

She peeled herself from the bed and retrieved a Yale key from the tea-caddy. 'Don't suppose it can hurt anything, not if I come with you.' Here was someone whose trust in her fellow men was about equal to my own.

I followed her across the landing and found Jeannie's room not much different from Donna's, its only improvement being a less tatty chair. I wandered around and wondered how people could stand to live this way. No personal belongings, no pictures, no photographs. It felt like a waiting-room, a place to pause before moving on, numbing in its bareness. Squatting, I peered under the bed.

The suitcase, when I pulled it out, wasn't any help, except it matched that in Jeannie's flat. Both were grey tapestry in an interwoven leaf pattern and there'd been a vanity case in the same fabric. I opened it up. The clothes it held – shirts, pants, a couple of cotton skirts, clean underwear – were as anonymous as the room. They could have belonged to Jeannie, but they could equally have belonged to anyone else. I checked the labels. Dorothy Perkins, Lee Cooper. Underwear courtesy of St Michael. Shoving the suitcase back something else caught my eye. Flattening on the carpet I reached a little further and retrieved a purple plastic lighter.

'Might be mine,' Donna said, eyes contracting, hand beginning to reach out. 'Could have dropped it when I was in here.' Reluctantly I let her take it. She turned it around and looked at the bottom. 'No, not mine. Guess it must be Mo's after all.' She polished it nicely and handed it back. For the life of me I couldn't decide if she knew the significance of her action, but she'd just cleaned off every damn fingerprint. I dropped the lighter in my jacket pocket.

'I guess she hadn't been able to break the habit,' I said casually. 'What was she? Twenty a day?' I moved to the window, grimy on the outside and overlooking the street. The truants had disappeared. I felt a vague gratitude my car was still whole. One small sideways step in the fight against crime.

On the outer windowsill, mixed up with pigeon droppings, decaying evidence of a smoker clung to the brickwork in the form of flattened dog-ends. I turned around and leaned back against the sill. 'What brand did she smoke?'

Donna's eyes moved around the room for inspiration. 'Uh . . . don't think she stuck to one brand. Silk Cut maybe, more than most.'

'That's what you smoke?'

'I don't. Smoke I mean.' Her eyes rested on my jacket pocket. 'I don't suppose Mo would mind you having that,' she said in a sad voice. Guilt filled me. Here she was, having locked the door against thieves, and now she'd let one in.

'Hey, I'm not stealing,' I said. 'It's just important I have this lighter.' I fished a pound coin out of my purse and laid it on the Formica table. 'If Mo comes back before I catch up with her, this will pay for a replacement.' She nodded without much enthusiasm, watching as I trawled the rest of the room, found nothing else of interest, and knew when to quit.

'What'll you do now then?' Donna said, following me out of the door.

'I guess I have to find out if Mick is home. Maybe he'll remember who he let in.'

'Maybe.' She locked the door behind us. 'I'll come down with you, he can be a bit funny sometimes, it'll be better if there's two of us.' She caught my look. 'I mean because he knows me,' she said.

'He doesn't like callers?'

'He doesn't like anybody, much.'

Just the kind of guy I needed to brighten a fun-filled day. I went downstairs briskly, and walked a couple of yards down the hall to a door with a drunkenly clinging, tarnished metal '1'. 'This is it?' I asked, and got a nod.

I gave a good hard rap. No shilly-shallying around with polite little taps. Donna winced, but fast results are always better than waiting around. A couple of seconds later Mick was in the doorway looking at me, five-eight, fortyish, unshaven, pallid eyes unreflective, face seemingly devoid of interest in why I might be there.

Donna said, 'Mick, this is Leah. A friend of Mo's. She's looking to find her.'

'Good luck,' he said, and started to close the door. I leaned on it.

'Five minutes isn't much out of a lifetime,' I said.

'I didn't know the woman, OK?' The door heaved against my hand. I leaned a little harder.

'Five minutes,' I said.

'What is it with you?'

'She's not a snooper,' Donna said. 'Not DHSS or Social.'

'Five, and that's it.' He checked his watch, then opened the door so suddenly I almost fell in. Donna didn't try to follow. I took a look around. Compared to this guy I was up for housekeeper-of-the-year award. A little mound of unclean briefs and socks sat on a tacky carpet by the bed. Aluminium take-away trays had been breeding on the table. He checked his watch again and said, 'Four.' I fished Jeannie's photograph out of my bag.

'This is the friend I'm looking for. Is she the woman who rented upstairs?'

'Could be.' The flat eyes were unfriendly and distant. Obviously helpfulness wasn't part of his nature.

'How about being a bit more certain?'

'Don't think I saw her more than twice. That it?'

'The men who came looking for her, you let them in? Can you describe them?'

'Yes.'

I waited and nothing happened. Mick was a real chatterbox. 'So go ahead,' I said. 'What were they like?'

'Pimps.'

'What?'

'Pimps,' he said. 'Know what they are don't you? Suppose she must have been giving them trouble.'

'How about names?' I said flatly. 'Occupations aren't necessary.' He did a quick recheck on time.

'I wouldn't go looking if I was you, you couldn't handle 'em.'

'Nice of you to worry but names and descriptions would be a bigger help.'

He shrugged. 'Suit yourself.' His eyes did a slow trip to my feet and back again. He leered, 'They got special ways of dealing with women. Still want to know?'

'Do I seem to be moving?' His wrist began to hover again. 'Nice watch,' I said. 'Came off the back of a lorry did it? Or did you save up for twenty years or so?'

He glowered. 'Ed Mulley and Rassa Ali. Thick-set yob with a flat-top, an' a poxy weasel with a pony-tail. Hung out at the Oak.'

'Thanks,' I said. For somebody who hadn't lived here long he seemed well acquainted with the low-life. Or maybe it was just the room he was new to and not the locale. 'Sounds like you know a lot about them.'

'Be hard not to, living round here. If I was you I wouldn't mess with them.'

'I'll bear that in mind,' I said. 'What would they want with Mo?'

He leered again. 'Depends.'

'On what?'

'On whether she was one of their girls or they was recruiting.' He opened the door. 'Time's up.'

'If Ed and Rassa are that mean,' I said, 'why let them in?'

'Do I look like a hero?'

'No,' I said candidly. 'I guess you don't.' Something vaguely like a grin moved his mouth – or maybe he had a toothache. He followed on behind me down the hall and watched me cross the pavement. 'I wouldn't go down the Oak looking for them, not if I was you,' he said. I nodded but didn't answer. I saw Donna come up behind him at the door. His lips moved. I started the engine. Donna said something in reply and Mick's face looked even less friendly. As I pulled away down the street the flat, lifeless eyes went with me all the way.

10

It was close on seven-thirty when I entered the Royal Oak for the second time, and Chloe was still on duty behind the bar, serving drinks to a couple of middle-aged men with pale faces. I climbed on to a stool and gave her a friendly smile. The place still didn't have many drinkers, but I guessed that in an hour or so things would start to hot up. I asked for a Pils. She set the glass down in front of me and wanted to know if I'd found my friend.

'Uh – no,' I said. 'Not exactly, but I talked with the neighbour you told me about. Donna?' She nodded. 'Well . . .' I leaned towards her confidentially. 'Donna told me my friend had a little trouble here that you'd know about. Some freak trying to get her into his car when she didn't want to go?' Chloe squinted down the bar, but the tubby landlord in the fancy waistcoat wasn't paying us any attention.

'Yeah, I remember. Bill there,' she jerked her head, 'called the police.'

'What happened to the yob?'

'Told the police it was her fault and took off. She seemed quite pleased to get a ride in a Panda. Expect I would too in the same circumstances.'

'What circumstances?'

'A couple of his friends had been bothering her earlier on.'

I took a drink of Pils. 'Did they leave at the same time?'

'Round about. I think they wanted to see what happened to her.'

'Seems to me their friend got what he asked for. Women get enough hassle without that kind of manhandling.'

'Isn't that the truth? I mean, even if . . .' she trailed off, eyes shifting again, which meant there was something I didn't know about. 'Even if?' I prompted. She polished a couple of glasses and twitched her shoulders.

I said, 'Why don't I buy you a drink?' She perked up a little.

'Rum and black all right?'

I put a five pound note on the bar and waited while she rang up the till and got her drink. 'Police seemed to think it had been a misunderstanding,' she said. 'But I think there was more to it. Not that I should tell you that. Tony – the guy – reckoned she'd led him on.'

'What do you think?'

Her shoulders seemed to have got into the habit of moving up and down automatically. I guess shrugging saved her having to come up with answers. She wandered off to draw a pint of bitter, giving a little girlish giggle as she set it down. Inside the cotton T-shirt her breasts jiggled like grapefruits. The punter appreciated it enough to forgo his change. She wandered back down to my end and leaned on the bar.

'I think he'd have liked to get even. Tony likes to be on top.' I wondered if that observation was from experience or just metaphorical.

I said, 'Sounds like a fun guy. He's a regular here?'

'Yes and no. He isn't local, I mean, he doesn't come from round here, he drops by when he has business.'

'What kind of business?' She clammed up again. 'Have another drink,' I invited.

'Ta, love.' She busied herself again. I looked at the paucity of customers and wondered when things would speed up. If this was the total throughput of trade they'd be bankrupt in no time. Chloe came back and leaned on the bar.

'You were going to tell me about Tony's business,' I said helpfully. 'What kind of line is he in?'

'Can't tell you that,' she said. 'Don't fancy having my face out the back of my head.'

I eyed her thoughtfully. 'If my tastes ran to something other than alcohol would he be the man to see?'

'His friends might,' she said.

'The ones he does business with?'

She nodded.

Certain things began to click into place. Like why Jeannie had found the Royal Oak so interesting. I said, 'The friends wouldn't be Ed Mulley and Rassa Ali would they?' I saw a glint come in her eye. As a tax inspector I've learned to read faces, it's an essential part of the job. Tax returns can hold so many lies it's unbelievable, and verbal statements aren't all that far behind, but eyes are a little harder to control. The glint in hers registered satisfaction, like I'd just saved her a lot of trouble. I guessed my line of reasoning was heading down the road she wanted it to.

'I don't know where you got their names from,' she said, 'but you got them right.'

'And being his buddies they'd be happy to help him settle accounts?'

'Don't know about that. Might do. Look, they're customers, I have to serve them, but it wouldn't break my heart if they dropped off the edge. Wouldn't break Bill's either.' She glanced at the landlord and dropped her voice. 'Having them come in here keeps a lot of people away. A lot of people don't want that kind of trouble, and they're the sort that keep a pub like this going. You know what I mean? It's really bad for trade.'

'I can guess,' I said sympathetically. 'Typical loud-mouthed bullies.'

'Well . . . that'd be right, but . . .' She shrugged again. 'Hang around for a while, they'll be here in a bit. See for yourself then.'

'Uh-huh. What do they drive?'

'Volvo, big one, tarted up with extra lights and stuff. Rassa drives, but the car's Ed's.'

'You mean Ed likes to look like he's Mr Big?'

'Nearly right,' she said. 'Except Ed doesn't *play* at it.' She left me to think about that and traipsed off down the other end of the bar again. I carried my Pils over to an empty table and settled down to wait. It worried me that so much information had dropped into my lap without much effort on my part. Almost like it was being fed to me in manageable bites. It was a new experience. Most times prising out the inside story on things is like milking a bull. All effort and no reward.

If I weren't so dumb and unsuspecting I'd have sworn Ed and Rassa were being stitched up, with me as the needle. I fretted a little. I hadn't exactly advertised my coming, so how come it felt like everybody but me knew their lines?

Paranoia?

'Come on, Hunter,' I muttered. 'Get on with it.' There was no way Mick could have known I'd be paying him a visit. Or Donna. Or, come to that, Chloe the friendly barmaid, and that being so a set-up wasn't on the cards. I sighed a little. An overly suspicious mind can be a terrible burden. Any minute now I'd be wondering what brought PC Willis to the club car-park, Monday night. Coincidence? Of course it was. Except . . . I explored other possibilities. Like Nicholls sitting back in his chair waiting for me to come panting by to put him on the right track.

Nicholls?

The most annoying thing about my lover is the way he tries to keep me *out* of trouble. The last thing he'd do would be encourage me to find it.

I stared unseeingly at Chloe. Not everybody shared his concern to keep me healthy. The barmaid's raised eyebrows and twitching head finally got through to me. I took a drink and eased around. Ed and Rassa, looking exactly the way Mick had described them, were heading for the bar and making like they owned the place. It didn't take an expert to see they were trouble on legs. Would Molly describe Ed's flat-top as long on top and short at the sides? I eyed their cute little earrings, finished up my drink and trotted out the door marked Toilets, hoping I hadn't guessed wrong about the layout of the place.

Ladies to the left and Gents to the right, propped-open fire door right ahead. I walked out into the car-park. Thunder rumbled, like the sky had indigestion.

Ed's Volvo 800 would have been hard to miss with its flashy spotlights and gleaming black paint. It looked totally over the top. I wondered if Rassa did the valeting as well as the driving. I walked around it critically, squinting in through the windows. Ed went in for sheepskins on the back seat, a throwback to the seventies. I wondered how often they got a wash. If I played the game and went along with what I was being told, the Forensic boys could be in for some fun. I dragged my mind away from what Ed might, or might not get up to on his back seat. Some things are just too gross to waste time on.

The sky rumbled again. I gave a little thought to the wisdom of going back inside the pub to find out if Ed and Rassa were as good at answering questions as everybody else. Somehow I didn't think they would be. I gave the idea a miss. I'd catch up with them another time when I'd done some more thinking.

I climbed into the hybrid and drove back to Cooper Street. There were another couple of questions I'd thought of that I'd really like to put to Donna, but this time when I knocked, there was no reply. Maybe I shouldn't have expected one, the singles scene had to be infinitely more appealing than a cramped bed-sit. I did some mental arithmetic, working out how long it would take her to change, put on a new face and do whatever else she wanted to do before heading for a more friendly environment, then I turned the car around and headed back to the main road.

Donna was at the bus-stop, white blouse, long, slim black skirt, and chunky heeled lace-ups. I wound down the window and called her name. She crossed the pavement without much enthusiasm. A bus crested the hill behind me.

'If you're heading into Bramfield,' I said, 'I can give you a lift.' She looked back up the road and then at the bus shelter. 'It'll save money,' I pointed out.

'Yeah, but there's three of us.'

'Fine, just so long as you sit up front. There are a couple more things I need to ask.'

She shook her head. 'I don't know . . .'

'Look. You liked Mo didn't you?'

'Haven't I told you I did?'

'So, get in.' She did some finger waving. The bus pulled up behind me. Two females headed for the car, three more and two males made for the bus.

'Tina and Amanda,' Donna said, and got in the front.

I turned my head. 'Hi! Everybody going to the same place?'

'Yeah. The Cellar. Don't suppose you'd know it, it's on Market Street.'

Whoo. Maybe I should head for the wrinkle cream. 'Cute doorman,' I said. 'If you like that kind of thing.'

They giggled.

'Tina does.'

'Shurrup,' said Tina.

'Fancies him rotten.'

Friendship is a wonderful thing. I let out the clutch. Donna said, 'There isn't anything else about Mo. I told you everything.'

'You're sure it was her on the photograph?'

'Yeah, I'm sure. I think I'm sure. Mind you she'd got more make-up and her hair was different, but she'd have wanted to look different wouldn't she?' I was going to ask why until I remembered the fist-happy boyfriend I'd so imaginatively created. Lies backfire so easily.

I said, 'I guess so,' and we drove a little way in silence. I negotiated a roundabout and worked on other things I needed to know.

'How come you didn't recognise Ed and Rassa?' I said brightly. 'I mean if you frequent the Royal Oak you must have seen them around,

Chloe told me they're always there.'

She screwed her forehead up. 'I don't know. It *could* have been them. I only saw their backs. If Mick says it was it must have been.'

'Has anyone else been around asking questions besides me?'

'What about?'

'Jeannie.'

'No.'

'Sure about that? The police haven't been around?'

'Why would they?'

'Following up on the car-park thing.'

She flushed and said, 'Mick said it'd be best not to say anything.'

'Why would he think that?'

'I don't know. Said it'd cause more trouble.'

'Was it before he let Ed and Rassa in?'

'Yeah, but she hadn't been at the house for a bit, away somewhere, you know? So I said she'd gone and I didn't know where they'd find her.'

'What else did they ask?'

'Same as you. When did I see her last, that sort of stuff.'

'They came just the once?'

'Yeah. They said had I heard about the fight at the Oak. I told them there wasn't anybody living round there that hadn't, and it wasn't her fault so why were they dragging it up again?'

'How long did she stay away?'

'Um . . . four or five days. I saw her on the Monday, before I went down to the shops, but she'd gone when I got back.'

'Did you and she often go drinking in the Oak together?'

'Never! It was just Chloe told me about the car-park thing, so when Mo moved in it was like hearing two sides of it, you know? So next time I saw her – Chloe I mean – I said, Oh, I know that one on the car-park, she's got the bed-sit next to me, and Chloe said, Well, fancy that.'

'Chloe hadn't known where she lived until then?'

'Shouldn't think so.'

I was silent again, crossing over the canal bridge and into the one-way traffic system. If Jeannie had rented it had to be because she'd needed to blend in with the natives, but that didn't mean she wanted her address made common knowledge. Chloe had said Tony had been looking to even scores, Ed and Rassa were his buddies. And from Chloe's whole demeanour when they came in the pub, she was shit scared of them.

Scared enough to let them know where Jeannie could be found.

I turned down Market Street and contemplated a new picture. One in which Jeannie's savage treatment was due to petty revenge by minor thugs and not because of her work with NCIS. If it was true, then Geoff Lomas could virtuously say she'd brought it on herself for stepping outside the guide lines.

Did I believe it?

I stopped the car outside The Cellar. Tina and Amanda got out but I kept a hold of Donna's arm. 'Two more questions. How long had she been back at the bed-sit when you saw her with the men?'

Donna looked scared. 'I don't know. Honestly, I don't. I didn't know she was back even until I heard all the banging. It could have been that same day. I don't know.'

'Is that what really happened, or it is what you were told to tell me?'

'It's true,' she protested, without much conviction.

'Like it's true she smoked?'

'I saw her with cigarettes.'

'Smoking?'

'Yes. No. I don't remember.'

I sighed and let go of her. 'Have a good time, Donna, but make sure you don't walk home alone.' She was three parts out of the car when I said that, and she turned around and put her head back inside.

'Why'd you say that?'

'With guys like Ed and Rassa around you can't be too careful,' I said, and eased off the brake pedal. She took her head back out. I reached over and closed the door. It seemed a shame to leave her standing on the pavement but at least I'd warned her what the score was.

What she did about it was up to her.

11

I couldn't believe that too much information could be as big a headache as too little. I drove home with all the little titbits I'd been fed swarming in my head like demented bees looking for a hive. Separating out facts from fiction wasn't going to be easy, and the impression that I'd been programmed to take a certain course of action stayed with me.

I climbed the stairs to my attic feeling peevish and out of sorts. It was late and I was hungry. Except for a chocolate snack I hadn't eaten a thing since lunchtime. I'd got past Marcie's door and half-way up the next flight when she stuck her head out and said if I hadn't eaten yet, then neither had she, and she could use some company. I turned around, gastric juices already flowing. 'It's only salad and quiche,' she said cheerfully as I went in the door. 'But Ben's tucked up in bed and fast asleep so we can eat in peace.'

I followed her into the kitchen and told her that eat was the best word I'd heard all day. She laughed and got down another plate from her cupboard. Marcie's slim and fragile looking, but in reality she's one of the strongest people I know. She was wearing a sleeveless cotton dress, lemon and long, with a dropped waist and flip-flops on her feet, the long silver earrings that were a part of her personality swinging as she moved her head.

'I'm starved of conversation,' she said. 'I've been pushing myself so hard on this last commission there hasn't been any time to socialise.'

'You've finished now?'

She nodded. 'Sent the folio off this afternoon. I've been rough-housing with Ben since then, I thought it time he had a little extra attention.' She looked wistful. 'Another year he'll be at school. It's going to be so quiet

67

when he's not around.' She talked about that for a while, then moved on naturally to other things, my stomach giving a little self-satisfied burble as it appreciated the food. 'You've got things on your mind too,' she said eventually. 'You're nowhere near as relaxed as you should be. Want to talk about it?'

'It isn't anything you can help with, it concerns a friend I haven't seen in years getting herself into trouble.' Marcie's interest perked up and wagged its ears. I told her the bit about Jeannie being fished out of the canal but didn't mention the rest of it. She put clingfilm over the salad bowl and slid it back in the fridge, coming out with a giant-sized black cherry yoghurt and spooning it into two dishes.

'What do you think happened to her?' she asked, sitting back at the table. 'A random attack, or someone she knew?' There was a note of anxiety in her voice, and I guessed she was remembering a relationship of her own that had gone bad.

'Part of her job, Marcie, was gathering information about the wrong kind of people. I think they probably found out what she was up to.' Downstairs, the front door opened and closed. I cocked my head and tried to remember if I'd locked it. Maybe not. Feet went by Marcie's door and on up to the attic. They sounded familiar. I stayed where I was and enjoyed the yoghurt.

Marcie said, 'Want me to come with you?'

I shook my head. 'Whoever it is can go away, it's too late for callers.'

'Maybe it's . . . um.'

'Maybe it is, but tonight I don't feel like that kind of company.' The upstairs bell rang a couple of times, then the door came in for a little pounding.

'Sounds determined,' Marcie said.

'Doesn't he though? Mind if I look out your front window?' I moved into the sitting-room and turned out the light, squinting down into the street. Nicholls' car was at the kerb. I sighed and went back to the kitchen. By and by he'd get tired and go home. Meantime his impatient attempts to get my attention upstairs were just too much of a coincidence. I settled down for some more conversation and waited for him to go.

Waiting Nicholls out didn't earn me all that much respite; when I panted home next morning from the daily run his car was back at the kerb. I banged on the roof as I went by and he hopped out like a jack-rabbit. He snapped, 'What time did you get home last night?'

I said, 'What are you? My mother?' and went on up the outside steps. When I opened the door he was right behind me. I picked up my milk and Marcie's and started upstairs.

'I was here until close to midnight.'

I put two bottles down outside Marcie's door and carried the third upstairs. 'There's a curfew?'

'Don't be smart.'

'Hey – if I were smart you'd be the other side of the front door,' I said. 'If you've got a problem come right out with it.'

'What were you doing at the Royal Oak?'

'Having a drink.' I marched into the flat and shut the bathroom door on him, stripping off and climbing in the shower. He gave the door a peevish thump and walked away. I stayed under the spray until my skin had soaked up all the moisture it could take, then towelled off and pulled on a terry robe. The smell of coffee told me he was still around. I padded into the kitchen and got myself a bowl of muesli. 'You still around?'

He fed bread into the toaster. 'The Royal Oak,' he said. 'Tell me about it.'

I shrugged. 'What's to tell? I called in for a Pils on a hot day. Is that so unusual?'

'Why that pub?'

'I was passing.'

'From where to where?'

'From where I damn well chose. Nicholls, if you've got a problem let's hear it, otherwise butt out.'

'You're the problem,' he said. 'You can't ever leave well alone.' I flopped on to a chair, scraped out another and put my feet up.

'So tell me about it,' I invited. 'What's wrong with the Oak? How come it's suddenly become a no-go area?' He reached up for the marmalade and slammed it down hard enough to crack the jar.

'Who did you talk to?'

'When?'

'Damn it, Leah! You know when.'

'The barmaid.'

'And who else.'

'That's it. The barmaid. Her name's Chloe by the way if you want to check up.' He glowered at me. 'It's the God-honest truth, Nicholls,' I said

69

virtuously, gratified that for once it was so easy to tell. 'And while we're on the subject it's high time you did a little explaining of your own, like how come you knew I'd been anywhere near the place?' He larded the toast with butter and put a half inch of marmalade on top. 'If you plan on having a coronary go away and do it some place else,' I told him tartly. He stuffed his face and didn't answer. I finished up my muesli, and poured more coffee.

By and by he said sulkily, 'You were seen there.'

'By whom?'

'We've been keeping an eye on the place.'

'Is that a royal we, or a we in general?'

'There's been a need for police surveillance,' he said carefully. 'Why, is something I can't discuss.'

'Uh-huh. Anything to do with Jeannie?'

'Why would it have?'

I got down to the last dregs of coffee, set the mug on the table, and got to my feet. 'Ever thought, Nicholls, that if you took the time to tell me the truth in the first place, I wouldn't need to spend so much time ferreting it out for myself?'

'Ever thought that some things are on a need-to-know basis and you're not on the list?'

'Works both ways,' I said darkly, and headed for the bedroom. When I came out fifteen minutes later, dressed and ready for another day's work, he was still sitting at the table and looking glum. 'Tell me one thing, Nicholls,' I said. 'Is there any reason why you *expected* me to turn up at the Oak?'

'No.'

'Sure about that? Sure you didn't lay a little trail that would guarantee me dropping into the bar so you could come here and ask me about it?'

His eyes narrowed. 'What little trail?'

'Having somebody feed me the information that Jeannie had been involved in a fracas there, the night she got brought into the police station?'

'Who told you?'

'Is it true?'

'Yes! Who told you?'

'That's my motto. I said I wouldn't tell.'

'Leah, I want to know . . .'

'You had your turn,' I said. 'Now it's mine. How long have you been watching the place?' He clammed up and his face took on a stubborn look. I sighed. 'How about a bargain? You tell me what I want, and I tell you what you want? It'll save us both a lot of grief.' He folded his arms and stared at me. I checked the time, dropped on to a chair, and faced him across the table. 'The Royal Oak,' I said. 'How long has it been under surveillance? Since Jeannie had trouble in the car-park?'

'No.'

'Since she dropped out of sight?'

'No.'

'Since she turned up in the canal?'

'Maybe.'

'OK,' I said. 'Get the next question right and you take home the jackpot. Were you expecting me to turn up?'

'Damn it, Leah, I'd have tried to stop you, you know that.' Worry clouded up his eyes. Nicholls is so honest it hurts.

'You'd better listen carefully then,' I said, 'because I don't plan to tell it twice.' And having got his full attention I told him about Donna and Mick, and Ed and Rassa, and the incongruity of dog-ends on a non-smoker's windowsill.

While he was busy digesting all that I gave him the lighter, told him there'd be zero prints, and left him to work it all out. I still thought that I'd been fed too much information too readily, but hey, what did it matter? As soon as Jeannie woke up she'd be able to put everybody straight. I didn't allow myself to think she might not win the fight, or that there were people around who couldn't afford to let her.

12

Naturally Nicholls started asking questions as soon as I shut up, and naturally I didn't let him. 'No questions,' I said. 'That's the full story and I'm late for work already.' I grabbed my bag and headed for the door. 'Lock up on the way out,' I instructed. 'I'd hate to have burglars. It seems these days Bramfield's finest are just too busy observing innocent citizens going about their business to worry over-much about thieves.'

He turned scarlet, stuffed his notebook in his pocket, and came after me. 'We need to talk,' he said, banging the door behind him as I made fast time down the stairs. 'There are things here that need explaining.'

'I had the same thought myself, and you know what? A couple of them kept me awake for a while. But I've done my duty and put the whole thing in your capable hands, which is what you're always telling me to do,' I reminded him. I turned around and gave him my sweetest smile. 'Working out what to do about it all is up to you, Nicholls. I'm too damn busy to play around being detective.'

'I wish I could believe that,' he snapped.

'Suit yourself,' I told him airily, 'but it seems to me if this relationship is going anywhere there has to be a little trust.' I watched him choke on that for a couple of seconds, then pecked his cheek and headed for Dora's. A couple of seconds later I heard him start his car and shunt it around. When he cruised level he lowered the passenger window and told me if we didn't talk now we'd need to do it later. 'Fine,' I said. 'How about the weekend? I'm pretty well booked up until then.'

'Tonight, Leah!' he barked, and spun off like a boy racer.

The little pep-talk I'd given him about trust kept coming back to mind as I worked my way through the morning. I guess the truth was, we were both so devious about things we got involved in, trying to keep the other one's nose out of our affairs, we behaved like a couple of dogs circling a good, smelly bone. Each of us so busy watching the other that any stray mutt with a good turn of speed could be away with it.

Maybe already had.

I stared at the columns of figures in front of me and didn't see them. What incentive would it take to encourage Chloe, Mick and Donna to recite a pack of lies? I took a step back, mentally, looking at it from a different angle. Maybe it wasn't lies, maybe it was the truth as they saw it, maybe they would have told it to anybody with or without a police badge who'd taken the trouble to ask.

As ideas go it was maybe a fraction less worrisome than the conspiracy theory I'd been carrying around since yesterday. I did a little more paid work and let the new idea take root. One thing was for sure, if the trail back to Ed and Rassa was for real, Nicholls was going to have a busy morning, and telling Jeannie, when she woke up, that the people who'd done that to her were behind bars, was going to make her feel a whole lot better.

I wished it could do the same for me when I called by the hospital at lunchtime and talked with Martin, his eyes red-rimmed from lack of sleep, and zombie voiced when he told me nothing had changed. Trying to persuade him he needed some rest got me nowhere. I kept the visit short, picked up a cheese sandwich from a nearby corner shop, and wolfed it down on the move as I headed to Charlie's.

When I turned into the yard he was eating fish and chips, paper wrappings in one hand, plastic fork blacked up with engine oil in the other. 'Was hoping you'd forgot all about it, Leah love,' he said, shifting sideways and making room on the lean-to's step. I parked my butt next to his, accepted a chip respectably far away from his fingers, and admired the amount of vinegar it had soaked up.

'How's Sidney?' I said. 'Still full of knowledge?'

He chewed around for a while, indelicately extracted a bone, and examining it minutely asked, 'How's your friend?'

'Mending.'

'Glad to hear that. That car you was looking for?' He squinted sideways and shook his head. 'Didn't bother with a body shop, love, did a torch job, this side of Emsall. Bobbies all over it from what I hear.'

How nice of Nicholls to let me know.

'Don't suppose anybody whispered who was driving?'

'Not a squeak. Don't suppose you'll be that worried about it now she's mending? I mean it's nasty but not as bad as you thought.'

I said, 'How about Sidney?'

'How about you put the kettle on while I finish me dinner? Got time for a cuppa haven't you?' I sighed. If Inland Revenue ever moved away from flexitime I'd be in real trouble.

Charlie's tap had its usual friendly airlock, sputtering water into the kettle and a good sprinkling over me. I cussed a little and put it to boil, hunting up a couple of mugs and getting another shower rinsing them out. Charlie's mug hygiene works on a simple principle, if there's no mould, it's not old.

I dropped back beside him on the step. 'Did you talk to Sidney?' He screwed up the paper wrapping into a greasy ball then sat with both hands drooping between his knees.

'Sidney reckons there's a bit of a war going on right now, doesn't think you should stick your nose in.'

'I appreciate Sidney's concern for my well-being,' I said. 'What kind of war?'

'Territorial.'

'Local?'

Charlie shook his head. 'Sidney reckons it's some outsider. Shut the locals down so he can bring his own stuff in. It's not a nice business to get into, Leah love. Looks like there's going to be trouble. They're trying to muscle in on Sidney too. Got his hands full.'

'Sidney doesn't deal in drugs,' I said.

'Has clubs though, and that's what they're after.'

'Charlie, if I can get a lead on the places they clean their money up the rest is up to our ever-on-the-ball police force.'

'Told him that, but he said as how bobbies and crooks being two ends on the same string, you got to end up in the middle whichever end you start.'

Since when did Sidney get to be so hot on philosophy? The kettle started shrieking. Charlie got up like he'd been shot and went to mess around with teabags. The screwed-up wrapper became a blackish-brown ball on his desk. I said, 'I hate to push but I really need some help this time. It isn't just the hit and run any more.' I watched him sniff a carton of milk. Charlie doesn't drink the stuff himself, just keeps it for visitors, and most of them decline politely. He squinted in my direction.

'So what's the problem?'

I told him about Jeannie and his face flattened out. He turned his back and hunted up a spoon. 'That's about as nasty as it gets,' he said. 'I'll sniff around, can't promise more than that.' He handed me a mug, dingy red with 'Kit-Kat' on the side. I turned it around so I didn't have to lick the thumb print.

'I'd still appreciate a hint from Sidney on the other business.'

'He reckons it'll get sorted.'

'Sorted how?'

'Don't know how, love. Didn't ask.'

'Charlie,' I reminded him gently. 'You owe me.'

'An' that's why I didn't ask,' he said solemnly.

I took a gulp of tea while I thought about things. For once it tasted surprisingly good, but right then something iced would have gone down better. The heat in the small lean-to was intense, its tin roof turning it into a cooking pot. I could feel sweat trickle in my armpits. I moved outside and breathed in some less oven-hot air. Friends are good to have around but sometimes they can be too mindful. I drank some more tea, then told Charlie I had to go. He stood in the doorway watching me drive away, looking a little forlorn. I guess being heedful wasn't easy for him either.

I spent the rest of the afternoon working diligently and pushed everything else out of my mind. On the way home I picked up a packet of stir-fry and two litres of orange juice, stuck both in my fridge, took a shower, and got ready for my usual Thursday work-out at the gym. Sometimes using up physical energy gets my brain into shape too. Jeff, the hunk who owns the place, was loitering in the training-room looking as good as ever. We chatted each other up while he kept an eye on a couple of newcomers, and between times told me how it was time I hiked up some weights. All of it innocent fun.

At nine-thirty I went home, took another shower, and cooked up the stir-fry. Luckily there was enough for two. Nicholls turned up soon after ten and bent my ear again. While we ate amicably I fenced off his questions by telling him the same things I'd told him before, and then asked if he'd picked up Ed and Rassa. He said no, they seemed to have got wind of things and were lying low. I told him that was about what I'd expected and he told me, huffily, that it wouldn't be long before they were found – with a car that flashy and every police patrol on the lookout it'd be hours, not days. I didn't try to contradict him. We shared a pint of pecan toffee ice-cream and then got cosy on the settee.

While we watched an old episode of *Magnum*, proving how easy it is to clean up a local crime wave, eight people died at a blues party in Chapeltown, Leeds, blown away by an Uzi. A mile away, and less than an hour later, a car carrying three males was rammed at a road junction and then ignited with a petrol bomb. I didn't know about either event until I caught up with the early news bulletin next morning, and I didn't learn that the car was Ed's, or that he and Rassa had been in it, until Nicholls told me, late that night.

13

Sometimes events seem to run away with things and this time they were doing it with all the heavy handed finesse of a B-movie.

I asked Nicholls how come if they'd been watching the Royal Oak so closely they'd managed to let Ed and Rassa slip between their fingers. He mumbled some excuse about surveillance on a building not being the same as a remit to follow villains around. 'Nice one,' I told him. 'Convenient. I guess now the two prime suspects are dead Jeannie's the only one who knows if they were guilty.' He started talking about witness statements, and I reminded him how I knew all about that, having heard Donna and Mick recite their version of events first hand.

I don't know why he gets so huffy.

The local papers were full of headlines about gang warfare coming to Yorkshire, and lengthy leader columns demanded tighter drug controls. Just how a drug-free Utopia could be achieved didn't seem to have taxed their brains any, but I guess it's always easier to demand action than think about consequences. The only newssheet brave enough to take a look at just how successful alcohol prohibition had been in twenties America, and see a sad parallel with current attempts to prohibit drugs by the same means, was a small underground paper with a mainly student readership. Which is not to say I support the idea of a drug culture – I don't. But it's a fact of life that any commodity in short supply encourages the growth of criminal networks looking to sell it for more than it's worth.

A week after Ed and Rassa were barbecued in Chapeltown, a dawn police raid on a terrace in the Hyde Park area around the University netted two dozen marijuana plants growing in a backstreet bathroom. I guess everybody felt really good knowing police resources weren't being wasted going after small-fry.

Meanwhile Bramfield CID were busy co-operating with their Leeds counterparts, and Ed's burned-out shell of a flash car gave up the skeleton of an Uzi. Everything fitted in nicely. According to Nicholls, four of the dead men at the blues party had been suppliers Ed did business with. Word had it they'd been ante-ing up prices so as to elbow Ed and Rassa out of the action. Such tactics can get a person killed.

Skirmishes between local drug dealers aren't all that uncommon in big cities, but up until now nobody in Leeds had used an Uzi to settle scores, and retribution had come a lot faster than Ed could have anticipated.

I held on to that explanation of things – the official police view has to be right sometimes – and tried to ignore a thought that nudged with pointy elbows.

'*Unbelievably* fast.'

Such subversive ideas didn't seem to give Nicholls much concern. He pointed out to me, with the same patience he'd bestow on any other doubting idiot, that as far as Bramfield CID were concerned, Ed and Rassa's demise had saved them a lot of legwork and the justice system a stack of money.

Whoo, but it was really nice of him to explain that so carefully! I dumped his coffee down the sink, tipped his Chinese take-away back in the little brown carrier bag, and opened the door for him politely. I was really glad he didn't argue. The weather was just too hot for civilised disagreement, one wrong word and the carrier bag could have wound up on his head.

Monday came around again, and I donned my little white pyjama suit and helped Jack rearrange the mats before we got down to the real business of throwing each other around. He told me his contacts in the local antique trade were mystified at the idea of a big spender. 'Truth is, love,' he said, 'there's most of 'em having problems keeping afloat. An' I don't think they're making that up, green-eyed monster'd have it out an' about in no time if there was anything.' I told him thanks and asked if he'd heard about Ed and Rassa. 'Have to be deaf an' blind not to,' he said. 'Little big-shots by the sound of it. Part of the same business were they?'

I dropped a mat and dust rose up in a powdery cloud. I said, 'I don't know for sure, Jack, but it's looking that way. The police think it was Ed and Rassa dropped Jeannie in the canal.'

'Got what they bleedin' asked for then, didn't they?' he said unsympathetically. I didn't answer that, it was something I wasn't too sure about. That they were local low-lifes I didn't doubt, but that Jeannie would have put herself at risk to entrap such relative small-fry was a different question. If she hadn't, the probability was some bigger fish had swum himself free.

Until Jeannie woke up.

The next thought I had was one I could well have done without; it ran along the lines of how inconvenient such an awakening might be for someone intent on remaining out of sight. And the prospects of Jeannie coming round were getting better. Her body was healing, bruises fading. She'd come off the life support machine, her coma had lightened. Improvement enough for Martin to risk a drive back to Windermere so he could catch up on the rest of his life.

Two days and he'd be back.

A lot could happen in that time.

'*Shit*!' I let go my end of the next mat. Jack's eyebrows went up.

'Thought of something uncomfortable?' I nodded dumbly and asked if I could use his phone; when his yes caught up with me I was half-way there.

Nicholls wasn't home. Is he ever when I want him? I tried CID and got told he was on another line. I said I was on my way and hung up, getting curious looks from the women in the locker room as I changed fast, palms sticky with sweat.

When I walked in on him Nicholls was still on the phone, elbows on desk, eyes down. I didn't let niceties of protocol deter me from voicing an urgent need for Jeannie to have a minder, some things are more important than others and he just had to realise that. Then he lifted his head and looked at me, and I saw his skin was limpid pale, with panda marks under his eyes and a look about him that said life had just kicked him in the teeth again. I turned around and closed the door quietly, standing with my back to it while what little sixth sense I had screamed that I should walk away and not ask what the bad news was. I didn't do that of course, instead I waited, and when he was through told him, 'You look like shit.'

He fixed his sad eyes on mine and said, 'Jeannie's dead.'

My heart turned into a lead ball and dropped down into my stomach. I sagged on to a chair, eyes pepper-hot.

'Judas, Nicholls. I don't understand that. How did it happen? Last I heard she was improving and getting stronger by the minute. How can she be dead?' He leaned back and eyed me silently, all the light gone out of his eyes. Conscience pricked. He didn't feel any damn better about this than I did. I said, 'Martin's going to blame himself for going home, he'll think if he'd stayed around he could have held on to her.'

'It wouldn't have made any difference. She went back into a deep coma and nobody expected that.' Nicholls' voice sounded flat, like he'd just run a long way and wanted to lie down. For some reason that made me angry, because he didn't have the right to do that. All kinds of fragmented thoughts moved around in my head, including one reminding me how easy Jeannie's death made it to hide everything under the carpet and close the file. Easy and convenient. No more awkward questions for Geoff Lomas to answer about how she'd managed to get into that kind of mess in the first place.

I said, 'I came here to tell you she needed a minder. I got to thinking about Ed and Rassa, and how Jeannie wouldn't have put herself at risk for a pair of local dealers everybody knew about – not unless she thought they'd lead her some place else, and we both know the drug business is too compartmentalised for that to happen. It hit me that with Martin gone she'd be vulnerable, especially if she'd already found out who the higher up was.'

Nicholls signed wearily, 'You've forgotten a couple of things, like the offshore account and the amount of money she'd banked. I know you don't want to face it, Leah, but the official police viewpoint is she was squeezing from both ends.'

'Official?' I said. 'Fine, I'll accept that. Now let's hear it from you.'

'It's a viewpoint I have to go along with,' he said. 'I'm a policeman. I have to judge by evidence.'

'Tell me about it!' I flared. 'Shit, Nicholls, she wouldn't be that stupid. She was set up and you know it.'

He threw his hands apart, as angry as I was. 'Fine,' he snapped. 'It's a valid argument. Now tell me by who?' We stared at each other, him struggling to nail the lid on an uneasy conscience, and me filled with a grief I didn't know how to shed. I thought how nice it would be not to fight. Maybe he saw something of that, I don't know, but he said abruptly, 'I put a WPC in with her this morning.' I cleared some gravel out of my throat and walked to the door.

'Nicholls,' I said without turning around. 'For some stupid reason I don't want to be alone tonight.' I didn't look back to see what his reaction was to that, I just toiled down the stairs and drove home.

At two a.m. the phone rang. I groaned and put the pillow over my head. Nicholls nudged me gently. I said, 'I hear it, it's rubbish, if I ignore it he'll go away.' It was the wrong thing to say. He rolled off the bed and padded out to the phone.

I guess when the crank at the other end heard the receiver picked up, and no reply, he thought it was me being coy.

Nicholls put him straight, then came back and demanded to know how long I'd been getting nuisance calls. Times are when he almost surpasses me in nosiness. 'It's just a harmless nut,' I said placatingly. 'Some weirdo who can't sleep. Look, he just latched on to my number by accident, OK?'

'How long, Leah?'

I said grudgingly, 'Since Jeannie got pulled out of the canal. Coincidence, that's all, it couldn't be anything else, could it, the case is closed.' I snapped on the bedside light and pulled on a wrap.

'What are you doing now?' he said suspiciously.

'Judas! I'm going for a pee. OK? And after that I plan to heat some milk.'

'Make me one,' he said.

'One what?'

'Cocoa.'

So I did, and while I wasted time and effort doing that, my knight in shining armour went back to sleep.

14

It was a clear bright summer morning, with a soft, purple haze softening the stark shape of tall buildings. It was a good day to be born on, a good day to make love in some quiet, grassy place, but it wasn't a good day for Jeannie, because Jeannie was dead, and the knowledge that she couldn't clear her name, point her finger at the real culprit, made coming to terms with her death even worse. I strode out, pushing myself, feeling the hard pull of effort in my muscles. Running is usually good for helping solve problems, I guess it's the combination of exercise and early morning air, but that particular day the formula didn't seem to be working and the problem giving me the most worry was the timing of Jeannie's death.

With a WPC watching over her it was hard to see how she could have been got at, but the suspicion persisted. Maybe the WPC had needed to go to the loo; bladders can be inconvenient things to have to carry around.

And then what? Some mini-dwarf with a pocketful of poison leapt out of a locker?

I shook my head. Nicholls' instructions had been that Jeannie shouldn't be left alone, and that meant she wouldn't have *been* left alone. Martin's not being there couldn't have made one whit of difference. A bit of my mind chased away inconsequentially. What the hell was a whit?

A milk float turned on to the street behind me, electric motor humming, bottles clanking just like they did on the television ad. Idly I thought how milkmen and postmen make the best saboteurs, nobody notices their comings and goings, they're an everyday part of street life.

Like nurses in hospitals.

Shit!

Who'd think twice about a nurse? And that was the difference between

Martin and a WPC. He'd been there so long he knew the staff, he'd seen shifts changing, knew the routine, knew the times of Jeannie's medications. A WPC would have to learn it all from scratch. I picked up a little extra speed and headed home, pounding up the stairs, breath gone when I got to the top. Nicholls was in the kitchen, showing off another of his talents. Coffee dripped slowly into the jug, the toaster sat loaded up with bread and waiting to be primed, while he beat a bowlful of eggs. I doubled over, hands on knees, trying for enough breath to tell him something he wouldn't want to hear.

When I did he eyed me like I'd just curdled the eggs.

I said, 'It's no use looking at me like that, damn it! You know it could have happened that way, the trouble is you don't want to believe it.'

'I wish you'd stop doing my job for me,' he said, and went back to beating eggs.

I turned around and took a shower, cooling off under the spray, the smell of coffee and toast waking up an appetite. I towelled dry, pulled on clean underpants and a long T-shirt and went to see if it tasted as good as it smelled. It did. Nicholls ate like there was no tomorrow, short on conversation and long on filling his fork. I watched him admiringly. Anyone who can put away that amount of food so fast deserves attention.

When he was through he didn't wait around, just rinsed off his pots like he was picking up my slobby ways and stacked them for later. I said, 'About Jeannie . . .'

'How about lunch?'

'How about we talk about Jeannie?'

'Lunch.'

'Maybe,' I said coolly. 'Who knows? A lot of things can happen between now and then.'

He sighed and picked up his jacket, feeling for the keys to his car. 'If you're not at the Crown I'll ring you tonight.'

'Fine.' I reached for the coffee-jug and poured a refill.

'Damn it, Leah!' he exploded, colouring up. 'Do you always have to assume I can't think up anything for myself?'

'No,' I said candidly. 'I'm good at my job, too, but sometimes a little help doesn't go amiss. I just don't want Jeannie filed away as a dishonest person.'

'That won't happen – unless she deserves it.'

I was glad he saw it that way, although I didn't like the added qualification, because the fact was that if he didn't prove her innocence I'd have to, and for the life of me I couldn't see where to start. I guess the reality was that Nicholls and I were starting from different points on the map, and what he saw as a possibility I saw as incontrovertible truth.

I said, 'Nicholls . . .'

What?'

'Thanks for coming over last night.'

He sighed and came back across the room with a look in his eyes I knew well. It was a real pity neither of us had the time.

Chip butties are not the healthiest of foods, but I work on the assumption that an occasional small sin can pass unnoticed. I sat in the Crown with Nicholls and chewed in amicable silence, but for once biding my time did me no good: the only piece of new knowledge I took away with me was that the landlord's daughter had got herself engaged. Uncharitably I wondered why she bothered when the baby was due any week now.

Times were when I'd have hassled Nicholls until I got what I wanted or he went off in a huff. Now I tend to take a more devious approach. As the saying goes, softly, softly, catchee monkey – which translated means that the time to get Nicholls to be indiscreet is when his mind is on other things.

I traipsed back to work and kept my nose fixed to the grindstone until mid-afternoon, at which time it got jerked away on to something unpleasant. An item of personal concern I would rather not have heard.

Most days Joe Public likes to raise lots of queries, which keep the desk phones ringing, so when mine buzzed at three-thirty I didn't think anything of it. All calls come through the switchboard and are rarely misrouted. I announced myself politely.

The voice in my ear said, 'I know everything about you, bitch. *Everything.*' And hung up. I slammed down the receiver and swore. This intrusion had gone far enough, it was sick that I'd got that kind of call at home, but shit! *Here in the office?* Maybe he didn't know that in this wonderful new technological age we live in calls can be traced.

I stormed into Pete's office and told him my problem. He came over all fatherly and sympathetic, which isn't easy considering he's only six years older than me. He also patted my knee. That's one more aspect of Pete's difficulty in life, he never learns from past mistakes. I patted him back and pointed out I was good and angry, not upset. He said he was glad about that because it meant he didn't need to let me go home early. Then he grinned and went out to the switchboard. Maybe he does learn the odd thing after all.

Most times I'm happy in my own company and being alone doesn't worry me any, although a lot of people think solitary and anti-social are synonymous. I guess a lot of my liking for solitude is down to the age gap between me and my big brother and sister. They were born pretty close together, but I sneaked in as an afterthought and surprised everybody, especially my mother. Most of the time when I was young she'd act like I wasn't there. Two she'd planned and two she raised, and my upbringing depended largely on Gran who was the best surrogate anybody could have had. If she'd still been around I would have homed in on her to shed some angst, but all I had left of her were crocheted afghans and bits of bric-à-brac, and that being so when I finished working out at the health club I called in on Dora instead.

When I garaged the car and peeked in through her kitchen window she was in there at the table, with her hands in a bowl of floury stuff. That's something she and Gran have in common, baking the kind of things shops don't sell. Maybe when I'm pushing seventy I'll be the same – who knows? When I tapped on the window she wiped off her hands and came to open the door, putting the kettle on to boil before she went back to her mixing.

'Haven't seen you for a while,' she said. 'Jude's out with her friends, but I told her to be home around ten.' I squatted down to scratch her big tabby's ear. His tail curled into a pom-pom end and he rubbed like we were friends. I knew better. There's no cat in this whole damn world as fickle as Oscar. Dora looked over at us. 'If Jude ever decides to leave I think that cat will go with her, he's like a leech when she's at home.'

I straightened up. 'She isn't talking about doing that?' The idea worried me. I'd put a lot of effort into getting Jude off the streets before Dora took her in, and I hated the thought of her sliding back.

'Not to me,' Dora said cheerfully. 'But I don't know what she talks about to the cat, and he's not telling.' She shook her head at me. 'Jude seems fine, Leah, don't worry, it's just me being foolish over an old cat.'

'Maybe you should give him a little competition,' I said. 'Let him know he's not the only pebble on the beach.'

Oscar arched his back and spat at me. That's another thing about him, his sense of timing.

The kettle boiled. I wandered over and washed my hands, getting down a couple of mugs. Dora clingfilmed the bowl and stuck it in the fridge. 'If you reach up for the blue tin,' she said, 'I just made the scones in there today.' Obediently I reached. Dora's scones are worth a little stretching. She brewed a pot of tea and swept off the table. I told her about Jeannie. When I got to the bit about the money, and how it needed somebody to prove her innocent, I got a sharp look.

'Leave it to the police,' she advised. 'Don't even think about putting yourself into jeopardy.'

'Leaving it to Bramfield's finest sounds good to me,' I said. Dora gave me a sceptical look. I shrugged. 'I don't have any problem with it, not unless the investigation winds up with her still looking guilty.'

'Have you stopped to wonder if she might be?' said Dora, effortlessly homing in on the one thing I'd been trying to avoid. 'I know it's hard to see friends doing wrong things but access to that kind of money must be a big temptation.'

'She wouldn't be dumb enough to leave a trail a novice could pick up on,' I said. 'The way I see it someone went to a lot of trouble to make her look guilty.'

'Got anybody in mind?'

'No,' I said ruefully. 'But setting up an overseas account had to take somebody brighter than Ed and Rassa. It needs financial know-how to do that kind of thing.'

'Something Jeannie had,' said Dora, probing the same sore spot. 'You ran into trouble before as I remember, letting friendship cloud vision.'

God, but I wished she hadn't brought that up. Death had sat on my shoulder twice now due to misplaced trust, and I could see Dora worrying I was about to make it three.

'What do you want me to do?' I said. 'Look the other way?'

'I don't want you to be any different from the way you are,' she said with a mix of worry and pain in her eyes. 'But I don't want you dead either. You'll do what you have to do, Leah, because that's the way you are. For some reason you can't make life easy for yourself.'

My mind rushed back to Gran, fitting a makeshift sling on my ten-year-old self before she took me to hospital. I'd climbed an old oak to show I was as good as any of the gang of boys I trailed around after, and come back down a little faster than intended. Gran's gentle fingers had been a comfort to my throbbing arm. She'd washed away dirty tears and asked why it was I never made life easy for myself. Now I brushed crumbs from my fingers and swallowed down remembered loss. Looking back I could see we'd had a lot in common.

I gathered up the empty mugs and plates and took them over to the sink. Jude bounced in through the back door and looked please to see me. We chatted about how school wasn't so bad after all, and talked about the new friends she had, and then I said goodnight to both of them and wandered home. The last dregs of day had drained from the sky and the cooling air hung in haloes around the street lamps. The house was in darkness except for the hall light, and I guessed that Marcie was having an early night. As for the downstairs neighbours, a couple in their thirties, I see so little of them I never have got to know their habits. Who knows? Maybe this is a *pied-à-terre* and their real lives are someplace else.

I climbed upstairs without adding to the electricity bill, there was light enough from the tall landing windows, and when I got inside the flat that was bathed in moonlight too. I left the curtains open and sat in front of the television watching *Newsnight* for a while, finding out the world hadn't improved any while my back was turned. People were still killing each other like the licence was about to expire. I switched stations, found Rambo taking out a few hundred Viet Cong, and hit the off switch. Sometimes entertainment is just too depressing. Fifteen minutes later, freshly showered and smelling pretty, I crawled into bed alone.

15

Since the human body manufactures insulin an added booster shot is hard to trace. The body tends to use it up fast, which is why in diabetes an insulin coma can impose itself so fast, and be rapidly fatal if no one is around to give glucose. Jeannie had been given enough to kill her twice over, which probably meant the dose had been calculated without medical knowledge. Either way, Jeannie's body had still been too weak to need much more than a gentle push. If the injected insulin had all been soluble and swift-acting instead of mixed with a slow-acting solution, forensic tests would probably not have shown up an excess in her body, but the killer had either not known that, or not cared.

According to Nicholls, the WPC had seen Jeannie given what she'd believed was routine medication, and had taken the opportunity to go to the loo while the nurse was in the room. When she came back the nurse had gone.

Since then she'd scrutinised every female face in the hospital, and said none of them belonged to the woman who'd come to Jeannie's room. That's the trouble with uniforms, anybody can get hold of one. I swallowed down an urge to point out the WPC's obvious intellectual failings. Who am I to throw stones?

Over the next couple of weeks I kept to my usual routine and tried to put Jeannie's death to the back of my mind. Such strategies are always impossible and this time was no exception. When a police officer is killed, all the stops are pulled out to find the perpetrators. Jeannie, attached to NCIS, was about as close to being a police officer as it was possible to get without being on the force. I expected that same kind of effort to be exerted on her behalf. I also expected, given NCIS's skill in intelligence gathering, that there would be some early arrests. But it didn't work out that way. Every lead Nicholls came up with faded away, and intelligence gathering began to seem like a very inexact science. Which was when I fell into butting heads with Geoff Lomas again.

I'd dropped by Nicholls' office on my way home and Lomas was with him. He didn't look over-glad to see me. I said, 'Hi. Lost any more team members yet?' and a little vein came up at the side of his head. Nicholls rolled his eyes to heaven and stayed quiet.

Lomas said if he'd had his way I'd have been charged with obstructing police enquiries, then pointed out it was only because of my personal relationship with Nicholls that I hadn't been.

'Hey,' I said. 'Forget about personal relationships. If you've got anything to charge me with go ahead and do it, it'll be interesting to see you get it off the ground.'

'I'd be delighted,' he said. 'Thanks to you we've lost ten months of covert intelligence work.'

'Thanks to me? Since when did I set foot on NCIS territory?'

'Since you took it on yourself to meddle, divert attention . . .'

'Balls,' I said rudely. 'If you're talking about the Royal Oak I didn't even have to ask for information, it was falling out of mouths. Don't tell me you gave up your *covert* surveillance because I bought a Pils.'

He scowled at Nicholls. 'I thought this was a private meeting?'

'I'm gone,' I said, and closed the door noisily on my way out. I couldn't decide how it was I disliked Lomas so much, but talking with him was like dragging my nails down a slate.

Later that night Nicholls called round with another little brown paper bag and a hangdog look. I took him in like I would any other stray, and when we'd eaten the Fu Yong and Won Tons he told me that against his wishes the search for Jeannie's killer was being wound down. For a while there I couldn't trust myself to speak, but when I pulled myself off the ceiling it turned out he'd been asked by both NCIS and Leeds CID to cool the investigation, because they were looking to net a drugs baron.

'I guess Lomas must fill his staff with confidence,' I said, 'looking after them the way he does.' I said thanks and sulked for a while, then Nicholls said whatever it was I was plotting, forget about it. I explained to him the difference between plotting and sulking, and then I sent him home.

* * *

Sometime during the night clouds rolled in just like Ian McCaskill had said they would on last night's weather forecast, filling up the sky with dirty yellow-edged cotton wool that hung in puffs like giant dolphin bellies. The air coming in through the open window smelled of rain and thunder, and breezelessly played host to a web of static.

I pulled on a pair of cut-off sweats and T-shirt and went out on the streets, kidding myself I'd get back before the deluge began. I almost made it. Almost. I carried the milk upstairs before it got washed away, dripping rain-water to mark passage. I hoped this exercise routine paid dividends, but it was a shame I had to wait twenty years or so to find out.

I breakfasted on muesli and felt virtuous. Thunder rolled around and the rain speeded up, bounding off the windowsills. I hunted out a waterproof and went out, hood up, hands stuffed in pockets. Such garments are ill-named. By the time I got to Dora's the damn thing had leaked in a dozen places.

I don't know why it should be so but some days going to work is hard. I was already frazzled when I sat down at the desk, and a succession of irritating telephone queries didn't help any. I got myself a cup of coffee. Geoff Lomas's charge that I'd fouled up his operation really rankled. I don't normally let such things get under my skin, but that, coupled with closing the file on Jeannie's death, was a major vexation. The hours prior to a death and the forty-eight hours after it are those most crucial in a murder enquiry. After that time clarity of memory starts to fade and evidence is harder to come by. It was close on a month since Jeannie had been pulled out of the canal, and two weeks since a fake nurse had overloaded her with insulin. If Nicholls put the investigation on hold now he'd never get it started up again. I'd seen Martin once since it happened and he'd been devastated, flagellating himself with the knowledge that had he been there he would have queried an unscheduled injection.

It wasn't right that he wouldn't even get the comfort of seeing the people responsible for his sister's death brought to justice, or that claims made about her lack of integrity should make the burden heavier.

I stared down at the mess of papers in front of me. If Nicholls hadn't been able to come up with any firm leads neither could I. Firm leads? What was I talking about? Every damn thing he'd followed up had led nowhere, he'd been working his butt off chasing duff hares. No one could complain he hadn't been kept busy.

Kept busy?

I walked around that thought. Too busy to stop and look at things from a different angle? It had almost been a perfect set-up, money in an overseas account, large bank deposits. If things had gone to plan Jeannie wouldn't have come out of the canal alive. When her body surfaced it would have looked like the final pay-off for a bent customs officer.

I extrapolated on that a little.

If the information trail I'd followed from the Royal Oak had been laid deliberately, not specifically for me, but for anyone like a bright DC doing a follow-up, then the neat story about Ed and Rassa dragging Jeannie away would have made their fiery exit look like rough justice. File closed on an episode best not made public.

It was all supposition of course and begged a lot of other questions, like who had enough clout to set that kind of thing up? If the inducement had been money then it wouldn't have been hard to find the right price to pay Mick, and Donna wasn't exactly living in luxury, but what about Chloe? She was more difficult. Had the idea of having Ed and Rassa permanently removed from the pub been enticing enough to make her co-operate, or had she only repeated what she believed to be true? I thought about the shiny engagement ring she wore and wondered why I hadn't been curious about the giver. And then I remembered how different the Donna I'd dropped outside The Cellar had looked from the Donna who'd let me see the room she said was Jeannie's.

Maybe Lomas was right, maybe my asking questions triggered what came after. It was an uncomfortable thought and one I couldn't be rid of.

It took me a couple of telephone calls to track down Sam Murray, a customs officer with the special investigation branch. I'd only met him a couple of times, and that over a year ago, but we'd sort of hit it off and he remembered me without any trouble. I explained about Jeannie and told him what I wanted to know, and he went quiet for a while. 'You're going to tell me to mind my own business,' I said. 'But I can't just let things stay as they are. The investigation is winding down without clearing her name.'

He said, 'I know about that. We've been liaising.'

'So how do you feel about it?' The silence came back again. This kind of thing seemed to be happening to me a lot lately. I said, 'Is there something else going on that I don't know about? Is that why you don't want to talk?'

'That's about right,' he said. 'Not much more I can add, we're all distressed this has happened to her.'

'Uh-huh. Somebody in there with you?'

'Fogerty's doing well, I'll tell him you asked.'

Fogerty! There was a man with a mean disposition. I said, 'Maybe you could ring me at home, later? You still have the number?'

'Getting together sounds good, Leah. I'd like to catch up on things too.'

'OK,' I said, appreciating the game. 'Name the place.'

'Um . . . Dolce Vita?' Murray came back slowly, acting like he was trying to remember. 'Isn't that the little place next to a furniture store? Yep, I guess I can be there for six-thirty.'

'Thanks Sam,' I said gratefully. 'You're a real friend.' We hung up and I got back to clearing paperwork. It didn't take a genius to know Nicholls wouldn't be best pleased if he knew what I was doing. But the way I saw it, if I hadn't been intended to play a part Providence wouldn't have pushed me into the affair in the first place.

Blaming Providence can be a real comfort.

I took an early lunch and dropped by Jeannie's bank, catching the manager just before he disappeared to some five-course feast of his own. He looked at my card and stared at me across the expanse of his desk. 'We don't get many personal enquiries from Inland Revenue,' he said. 'I suppose you have some other form of identification?' I fished out my driving licence and he compared the two closely. 'Seems all right,' he said, handing both of them back. 'What kind of help is it you're looking for?'

'A mutual client, now deceased,' I said. 'Jeannie Johnson.'

'You have the account number?'

'We don't have it on file,' I said truthfully. 'But I do know she banked at this branch.' He opened up the intercom and asked for the file to be brought in, then told me it was very irregular. 'I appreciate that,' I said, 'but I can't think of any other way round it. The fact is it's been brought to our notice that undeclared amounts of money are on deposit and that there is at least one offshore account too. Obviously since there are tax debts we need to be able to recover some monies.'

He shook his head. 'Shame death doesn't wipe it out.'

'A shame it doesn't wipe out mortgages too,' I said equitably. He looked back at me po faced and didn't answer that. By and by the file arrived and he opened it up and asked what it was, specifically, that I wanted to know.

'Specifically,' I said, 'how were these large deposits made? Over the counter in cash, or as cheques from some other party?'

'I don't see how that affects anything,' he said.

'You'd be surprised, Mr Warner,' I said. 'There could be third-party involvement. Large sums like that often mean someone else has things to hide. Do you have copies of the banking slips?'

He read some little notes and said irritably, 'The police have been asking the same questions.'

'You see?' I said blandly. 'Doesn't that prove we have cause to investigate?' He riffled through copy statements and other papers.

'The amounts we're talking of came in by bank transfer.'

'You have signatures?'

'The payments were made in Miss Johnson's name but the signatures were not in her hand.'

And of course the signatures weren't checked. Who cares about money going in? The hard part is trying to get it out.

'Cash?'

'Cash,' he said. 'No cheques.'

'And an offshore account could be fed by computer transfer? No need for name checks again?'

'Not necessarily, it would depend on the point of transfer.'

'Thank you, Mr Warner,' I said. 'You've been very helpful.' I stood up and offered my hand; he shook it cordially. As an afterthought I said, 'I suppose bank slips get handled by so many people it wouldn't be worth police time to run finger-print checks.'

He let go my hand, resting his fingers on the desk top. 'They'd be handled several times over at the bank of origin, then again at the destination bank – add to that this kind of enquiry and you're looking at a lot of people. Does that answer your question?'

'Almost,' I said. 'Except you didn't say if the police had run a check anyway.'

He came around and opened the door politely. 'I'm sorry I can't be more help, Miss Hunter,' he said with a smile that didn't crease his face. 'My advice would be to take up that last point with the department concerned.'

'Maybe I'll do that,' I said, stepping out and hearing the security lock slide home behind me.

And so I would. But not right yet.

Time enough to rattle Nicholls' chain when I had something better than a bank slip to do it with.

16

I got to the Dolce Vita a few minutes before half-past six, but early-bird Sam was already in there. I almost didn't recognise him in his casual outfit of jeans and grandad shirt, it gave him a totally different look from the lean-cut suits I'd seen him in before. 'You're looking good,' he said as I sat down.

'Thanks. So are you.' We eyed each other pleasurably for a couple of seconds until the waiter came and lived up to his job description. That's the trouble with the Dolce Vita, the food is good but they don't encourage loitering. I guess the place is so small they need a fast throughput to make it pay. We both of us went for pizza and a side salad, skipping the wine list in favour of cold Pils. The waiter flapped his little white napkin and looked like he wished he was back in Italy where good food is properly appreciated.

Sam grinned at me. He'd grown his hair a little, not long, but so it was bushier than before and made him look more youthful. He said, 'How's the romance, is it still on?'

'Mostly. How about you?'

He shrugged. 'She couldn't take the odd hours and absences.'

'I'm sorry.'

'Better now than later,' he said philosophically. 'I'm never going to be a nine-to-five man.' The grin came back but didn't look very stable. 'Let me know when you get bored with the DI.' I broke eye contact and knew this wasn't a good subject, it didn't take a diagram to guess the break-up had been recent. That kind of thing is shit when it happens, I'd been there myself, with Will, a guy I'd been planning to marry until a helpful friend happened to mention he already had a wife. These things really hurt. I could feel myself squeeze up tight, like a rolled hedgehog.

'Hey, come on,' I said uncomfortably. 'A good-looking guy like you doesn't need to wait around, I bet there's a queue already.'

He shrugged. 'Out of practice I guess.'

'How long was it?' I said unwillingly.

'Five years.' He leaned on the table and moved the conversation on to safer ground. 'How did you get mixed in with Jeannie?' Thankfully I loosened up and got my mind on to why I was there.

'How?' I said. 'How is the easy part, it goes back to being eleven-year-old drop-outs in a college for young ladies. I guess when you come right down to it neither of us changed. Ladylike behaviour just never appealed.' The waiter came back with two chilled glasses and set them on the table. I took a sip of Pils and gathered my thoughts, then I went back to the time Jeannie was brought into the police station and laid out everything that had happened since. He listened attentively, interrupting now and then with questions of his own. By the time I was through the pizzas had arrived and the waiter was hovering anxiously, worried we weren't eating. I picked up my knife and fork, took a mouthful, and nodded and smiled in his direction. Satisfied he left us in peace.

Sam said, 'That's pretty much the way we heard it, but there's a couple of things in there I didn't know before. The Royal Oak business sounds not quite . . .' he struggled for a word.

'Kosher?'

'As good a word as any, I guess. The truth is Jeannie had been keeping in touch with us all along, she wasn't happy with the way some things were working out, but she never mentioned the Oak, or trouble in the car-park, and that puzzles me.'

'The car-park incident is true, Nicholls vouched for that, but I'm not sure about the rest of it. I've thought all along that the information came too easy.'

He shook his head. 'Sounds weird.'

'You know about the money and overseas account?'

'We were notified.'

'Believe any of it?'

'Off the record, no. Officially, it's something that's had to be considered. Profit-skimming is a dangerous game and short lives aren't unusual.'

'As one professional to another, what was Jeannie's brief? If it entails money laundering I have a legitimate interest.'

He chewed for a while, mozzarella following his fork in long, sticky strands. The bread base was yeasty and cooked to just the right level of crispiness. I speared a cherry tomato and waited for him to come up with an answer. Finally he said, 'Anything I tell you stays unofficial. Right? If it ever comes up I'll deny every damn thing.'

'Understood.'

'You know Jeannie was an expert in antiques?' I nodded. 'That's why she was loaned to NCIS. A one-off arrangement because she knew the trade.'

'And antique dealers don't recognise dirty money,' I interrupted.

'Good, you know how it works. Well, Jeannie found out where the buying was done.' He saw my eyebrows go up in query. 'Country antique sales,' he said. I nodded, seeing in that an explanation of Jack's negative results from local traders. Sam carried on, 'What puzzled her was discovering the organisation behind it was smaller than expected. They handled drugs, but didn't import, and most of the dirty money came from illegal gambling and prostitution.'

I smiled at him and put a hand on his arm, easing my head closer to his. To a casual observer we must have looked like a cosy twosome. I murmured, 'The guy two tables over on your right seems very interested in what we're doing. Know him? He came in a couple of minutes after me.'

Sam patted my hand, nuzzled up to my ear and breathed, 'Times like this undercover work has its attractions.'

'This is serious,' I said.

'So am I,' said Sam, and straightened up. His napkin hit the floor. He turned a little to his right and bent to retrieve it. 'Don't know him from Adam,' he said when he straightened up, 'but his eyes look a little greedy.'

'Don't they though?' I raised my glass in Tom Peep's direction and smiled at him politely. His eyes dropped to his plate like they were marbles. Sam grinned.

'Maybe somebody gave you a bodyguard.'

'Which somebody? Nicholls? He wouldn't dare.'

'Don't bank on it,' said Sam. 'In his position I'd do the same thing.'

'That right? Then how about we finish up the pizza fast and have dessert at my place?'

'Dessert?'

'Cherry Garcia and coffee,' I said. 'Maybe if you're lucky I can find some ginger snaps.'

'That's the best offer I'm going to get?'

'Take it or leave it. I thought you said you were out of practice?'

'I'm doing all right?'

'Sam,' I said. 'With a different person and the same line, you'd be zeroing in like an Exocet.' He looked pleased. Maybe his heart wouldn't take that long to mend after all.

We split the bill and I was glad he didn't argue about that, some men can be a pain.

I'd left the hybrid in the multi-storey behind the new shopping centre, and it seemed like a good idea for me to pick up my car first, then take him round to where he'd parked on Market Street so he could follow me home. We scrubbed that idea when Tom Peep showed up on the same level. Cars have registration numbers and Sam wasn't over keen on having his traced. I took the down ramps fast enough for Sam to be gripping his seat when we hit bottom and turned out on to the road. Behind us an Astra did its best to keep up, but Charlie's handiwork did a lot better on corners. I swung through three back streets, then cut north and headed along the by-pass. Sam said, 'God Almighty, what have you done to this bucket?'

'What you hear,' I said, 'is pure BMW.' I squinted in the mirror and saw a flash of red, way back, that showed Tom Peep was still with us. It entered my head that if Nicholls had decided to give me a minder, the minder knew where I lived – but on the other hand – if Tom Peep wasn't on the side of angels I could be leading some miscreant home to my nest. The thought didn't thrill me. I said, 'Hold on,' and speeded up, braking hard at the roundabout to take the second exit into a mess of roads that made up Bramfield's newest and biggest industrial estate. Sam cannoned sideways into the door and swore. I swung another right and two lefts, checked the mirror, and turned on to the forecourt of a giant feeder warehouse, bursting out with oversize delivery trucks. I squeezed between two of them and cut the engine, hidden by the high sides.

'What the hell was that about?' asked Sam. I told him. He whistled a little tune between his teeth and shut up. I opened the door and crawled out through the twelve-inch crack. Sam eyed the space on his side and didn't bother trying. I could hear a hot engine in low gear, stationary but ready to sprint. Hunkered down by the truck's back wheel I peered under the chassis. The Astra lurked at a T-junction opposite, nose jutting out so Tom Peep could take a look both ways. While he dithered on direction a truck came up behind, horn busy. The Astra jerked and swung left, hesitating again at the next junction then going straight across and picking up speed. I hoped he'd taken special care to note the way he came in. The estate is a warren of identical junctions, roads and buildings, and if he didn't know the place it'd take him a while to get out. I eased back into the car and headed sedately for the north exit and the back streets that would take me home.

17

While Sam fingered his way through my little collection of CDs and vinyls, I headed for the kitchen to brew caffeine. When I came back with the coffee-pot and two dishes of Cherry Garcia he was comfy on the settee, flicking through *Marie Claire*, legs stretched out. Beiderbeck was playing quietly on the tape deck. I set the tray on a low table and handed him a bowl of pale pink ice-cream.

He gave me a long, slow smile. 'Thanks, Leah.'

Just so there should be no misunderstanding I seated myself primly at the other end of the settee. 'To get back to business . . .'

Through a mouthful of Garcia he mumbled, 'If this gets back to Fogerty I'm dead.' I got a quick rush of guilt. Maybe I was asking too much. Fogerty could be a real pain.

'I wouldn't want you hung out to dry.'

'What the hell?' Sam said, with a flick of his hand. 'We're after the same thing here, *sod* Fogerty.'

I licked my spoon and worried. 'You're sure about this? I mean just how confidential is this business supposed to be? Is your job on the line?'

'It's on the line every time the bastard opens his mouth,' Sam said grimly. 'One of us is overdue a transfer so ask away. It's OK,' he said, seeing doubt on my face. 'If things get too sensitive I'll clam up.'

'Thanks, Sam. What makes him so uptight on this?'

'He's just agreed to let things drop.'

I stared at him. 'You're kidding! Quit the internal investigation?'

'That's about it, everything's being covered up with a blanket and I don't like it.'

'Who gave the order?'

'Wish I knew.'

That made two of us. I thought back to where we'd been heading in the Dolce Vita before Tom Peep froze things up. Something Sam had said came to the front of my mind. 'Jeannie thought the operation she'd uncovered was too small?' I said slowly. 'That's what you said?' He nodded. 'Why small? What kind of set-up was she expecting to find? Obviously something bigger – but here? In Bramfield?'

'That's what worried her,' he said. 'The way everything turned back on itself and became localised. NCIS northern headquarters are here in Bramfield, but its intelligence activities cover five counties. Different teams of specialists work on different areas of investigation. You know that?'

'Basically.'

'Jeannie's team picked up some threads that led them north to Newcastle and Durham, but they didn't come to anything except a few local dealers pulled off the streets. Jeannie called them sacrificial lambs. It bugged her that every time she thought she was moving close to a big operation, her lead turned back on itself. She'd come up with the idea of a network spread like a spider's web, break a strand – i.e. take a dealer off the streets – and it didn't matter, the hole would be repaired.'

'And if a fly came along . . . ?' He stayed silent but that didn't matter, we both knew what happened to flies. I said, 'Did Jeannie believe she was being deliberately sidetracked, is that what you're saying?'

'It looked that way to her,' Sam agreed. 'Last time we spoke she said how sick she was of being fed titbits like some tame dog.'

'*Fed* titbits?'

'That's about it.'

'She didn't suggest who'd been doing the feeding?'

'No, she didn't, but Jeannie was a bit of a loner, always came good in the end but liked to be able to lay the whole thing out. I told her it wasn't a safe way to operate but she turned around and told me to mend my own house first.'

I squirmed a little, thinking of the number of times I'd said pretty much the same thing to Nicholls.

'Maybe she thought you'd bring her in too early,' I said.

'Maybe she did.' He flattened his lips, making negative motions with his head. 'God knows I've done the same thing, the simple fact is, as human beings we can't believe we're not immortal.'

'Isn't that a fact?'

We sat in silence for a while, drinking coffee and contemplating risk factors. The trouble is, once you start thinking on those lines you might just as well stay home in bed. By and by I said, 'How much money are we looking to be laundered?'

'Millions,' Sam said levelly. 'If we're thinking of the kind of set-up Jeannie talked about. That kind of trafficking doesn't get done by little men, we're talking about multinationals with all the logistics and infrastructure of big business behind them. The size of pay-offs is eye-boggling, and people who get too greedy disappear.'

'That's a lot of tax loss,' I murmured, half to myself.

'It works its way back into the system,' said Sam. 'Hot money tends to bounce around from place to place, fact is if all the dirty money were taken out of circulation world markets would crash overnight. Sobering thought.'

I did some more thinking. The money in Jeannie's bank, plus the offshore account, didn't exactly amount to a fortune. A reasonable nest-egg, yes, but not the kind of pay-off Sam had been talking about.

'This is crazy,' I said. 'Nothing fits. If Ed and Rassa were down at the bottom of the pile and expendable, and some unlucky people at a blues party were taken out to make it look like gang-warfare – where does that get us? What kind of organisation can have its finger on every button?'

'Think big business,' said Sam. 'Think area managers. The biggest difference in operation between a criminal organisation and a firm like ICI is in the way the criminal operation seals off levels of management. Lower levels are able to communicate with, but not name, the level above. Anybody trying to infiltrate would bang their head on an artificial ceiling.'

'They'd be able to go down – or across – but not up,' I said slowly. 'Every level with a fire door. Did Jeannie think there was a way through?'

'Not at that point, no.'

'You didn't talk with her again?'

'It wasn't possible – a big Hampshire bust came up,' he said, catching my look. 'Kept me away five weeks, and the Oak incident happened a week or so before I got back.'

'Did she tell Lomas what she'd come up with?'

'I don't know, he plays things pretty close to his chest. Maybe the new boy will be different.'

'What new boy?'

'You haven't heard? NCIS top brass have pulled the plug on Lomas's team. They're winding up.'

'When did all this come about?'

'News came just after I talked with you.'

'Lomas won't be happy. What happens next, do they put a new team together?'

'That's the way rumour has it – bring fresh minds in.'

'Or rid themselves of old leaks,' I said obdurately.

Sam poured us both a refill. 'Looks like we shared the same thought.'

'And really convenient to pile it on somebody who can't answer back. That's the reason Nicholls is supposed to wind everything up?' Anger came on me so suddenly I could barely speak, words coming out like they were constipated. 'It isn't good enough, Sam. Lomas and the rest get to go back to their old jobs and it's life as usual except one's richer.'

'Maybe you're right in that, you're the fiscal expert, Leah. I can tell you their bank accounts are clean but we both know sliding cash out of sight is a piece of cake.'

'Yeah. And we both know how dumb it is to leave evidence lying around to say "we've done it".' I picked up the empty coffee-jug and gave it a shake. 'You want some more? Sure about that? Well, maybe I won't either, I drink too much of the damn stuff.' I put the jug down again and said irritably, 'I don't think I want to hear all this negativism, it's too defeatist. It feels like I'm being told to forget the whole thing. Bury it. How come murder suddenly grew so easy to write off?'

'Politics.'

'Stuff politics,' I said rudely. 'You sure about those bank accounts?'

'Absolutely.' He got up and ambled over to the window. Leaning on the sill he eyed the scorched grass. My throat constricted. His action reminded me painfully of Jeannie doing much the same thing, and for a second her shape overlay his. Then he turned around and the impression went away. He said, 'Don't you have a street window?'

'Uh-huh.' I led him through the hall into the bedroom. The road out front was parked up nose to tail with neighbours' cars and daylight was fading into hazy blue dusk. As we stood looking out the standard lamps flickered into a soft glow. I slid up the window so we could get a wider view.

'There he is,' said Sam.

I angled my head and saw bright red, fifty yards away. For somebody playing at surveillance it was a lousy way to stay invisible. 'I guess he's going to trail us back to Market Street,' I said. Sam pulled his head back in. I straightened up and closed the sash. 'Maybe I should tap his window and tell him to go home.'

'Not all that good a policy when we don't know what he's up to.'

'Don't we?' I said. 'I thought we'd agreed on it being Nicholls' protectionism? Either way, Tom Peep knows my address, he sure enough didn't follow us home.'

'Is there a back way out?'

I nodded. 'If you're planning to leave on foot I'll draw a map. It's an easy walk but you need to know the right streets.' I moved back into the sitting-room and found pencil and paper, sketching out a rough plan of the area.

'If you're going to keep digging into this,' he said, 'don't get deeper than you can see.'

'You too.' I gave him the paper. He studied it and got back into his light jacket.

'Give Nicholls a ring and ask him to come round.'

'Why would I want to do that?' I said, puzzled.

'See if he knows about the Astra.'

Of course he knew. It'd be one of his own incompetents driving it. I started to tell that to Sam, then saw his thoughts weren't going the same way.

'OK,' I said, walking him downstairs. 'Maybe I will.' I let him out the garden door and locked up behind him. Then I punched Nicholls' buttons and invited him round. Half an hour later he was leaning on my bell. I led him into the bedroom.

He looked like the dog with eyes as big as saucers and it seemed a real shame to open up the window and point out the red Astra, its colour now almost indistinguishable under the street lights.

'Nicholls,' I said brightly, 'if you haven't set one of your minions to act as minder, that could be the guy you discussed crank calls with a while ago.' He banged his head and swore. A couple of seconds later the telephone pinged out in the hall. I stayed by the window and sent bad thoughts down to Tom Peep. By and by Nicholls came back and draped a protective arm over my shoulder. I snagged an arm around his waist. A mix of deodorant, aftershave and rampant pheromones drifted up my nostrils. He kept his eyes on the Astra. For once nobody could have complained about police response time, it took only three or four minutes for a patrol car to turn up the street, the only fault I could find was the way its driver had his blue light flashing all the way. Nicholls did a little more cursing and the Astra performed a near wheelie to prove how fast it could get to sixty.

Nicholls was still spilling out ungentlemanly words when the siren died away. 'Don't worry about it,' I said. 'I got the number.' He kissed the top of my head. I turned around and slid my arms up. Given the right encouragement I could do a lot better than *that*.

18

Nicholls left around midnight with things on his mind, like the neat way Tom Peep had lost the patrol car. Ten minutes after he walked out the door the phone rang. I wondered what he'd forgotten. I picked it up and said, 'Hi,' bright as a button, but it wasn't Nicholls. Instead a voice I was growing familiar with said, 'That was a bad mistake, *bitch*.'

'Hey,' I snapped back. 'You're early tonight.' He hung up on me. This was getting a real pain, maybe I should get BT to put an intercept on the line?

Tomorrow, I thought, and went to bed.

You'd think since sleep is a natural state of body and essential for good health, the act of lying down comfortably in a dark room would encourage its presence. Not so. Sleep stayed stubbornly elusive. My mind was a rabbit warren filled with boisterously fluffy scuts of ideas and half thoughts, that went nowhere except the next dark hole. Jeannie's shade haunted me. Gran believed in ghosts. Not wailing, chain rattling spectres, but unquiet spirits, unwilling to go through the gates until accounts were settled and justice done. The thought was disturbing. If Jeannie was looking for blame to be taken off her shoulders, and her killer found, then the way investigations were being terminated she could be earthbound a long time. I lay in the soft darkness, staring up at the ceiling, the clock hands showing three a.m., and had no clear notion of how I could intercede. Gran had died with debts paid and an easy conscience so as not to disturb anyone's sleep. She hadn't been ready to go and I hadn't been ready to let her, but neither of us got any say in it, and part of me would always regret the speed of her departure.

Around three-thirty I gave up on trying to empty my mind and shoved a load of dirty clothes in the washer instead. The hum of the motor was restful. Curled up on the settee with one of Gran's afghans and the television turned low, I watched *The Beat*, and finished the last of the Cherry Garcia, falling asleep as *Jobfinder* started scrolling up lists of vacancies. When I woke again at seven-thirty some clown was busy telling me how healthy I'd feel if I just cut down on coffee. I hit the off switch. Who needs advice at that time of a morning?

When I spoke to Sam on the telephone around ten-thirty he seemed surprised I was ringing him again so soon. I guess he thought I had to be coming on to him because he started talking about dinner. I said, 'That'd be really nice sometime, but right now it's business.'

'Story of my life,' he said, and sounded disappointed.

'What I wanted to ask is this, are Jeannie's team still around doing clear-up work?'

'It'll take a while to wind things up and get it tidied ready to hand over.'

'That's what I hoped. This next thing is kind of related to the bank account business. Is Fogerty there?'

'Not right now, there's a managers' meeting going on.'

'Great! We can talk without needing to worry. Sam, do you have their names and addresses?'

'I guess they'll be somewhere around, but it wouldn't help any if you started turning up on doorsteps, Leah.'

'I wasn't planning to turn up on doorsteps, I was planning to check tax records. Do they all have a Bramfield base?'

He went silent a couple of seconds, probably working out pros and cons, then came back: 'I don't see that can hurt, tax is your territory. When do you need it?'

'Right now would be soon enough.' He gave me a snitty laugh and said he'd get back to me soon as he could. While I waited for him to do that I got back to bread and butter work. It's really easy to get carried away and forget where the rent comes from. I sighed a little and got busy with the pen. I mean, how in hell could some guy think his wife's tights were tax deductible?

The phone stayed silent the rest of the morning and I began to think Sam had either drawn a blank or run foul of Fogerty. After a while I got to wondering what good it would do anyway. Chances were, since they'd all been seconded from other disciplines and widely diverse geographical

112

locations, they'd still be taxed at their original home base. Which meant there'd be no Bramfield-held files for me to pry into. The thought wasn't exactly inspiring. I wished it had come to mind before I got on to Sam.

A minute before twelve-thirty Nicholls pushed in through the double doors. When he saw I was still being industrious the anxious look disappeared. I wondered why it had been there in the first place. He made exaggerated eating movements and jerked his head. I tidied away neatly and wondered which budget bar we'd be visiting. Foolishly I hadn't put the police canteen on the list of possibles.

'This is nice,' I said, looking at the blackboard. 'It amazes me how many things they can do with chips.'

He said off-handedly, 'I need you to look at some photographs.'

'Uh-huh. Got them in your pocket? Postcard size from Paris? How come you didn't mention this before? You know what, Nicholls? You're sneaky.'

'It gets results,' he said equably. 'What are you having?'

'Fish,' I said. 'Minus chips. And a diet Coke. Why do you have to have the damn place in a basement?'

'Security,' he said briefly and didn't elaborate. I picked out a table as far removed from the greasy fug as I could get, and waited for waiter service. It was time Nicholls learned that some things have to be paid for.

'Is this to do with Jeannie?' I said when he'd unloaded the tray. He propped it up against the wall and got busy with the salt and vinegar.

'Yes and no.'

'What kind of answer is that?'

'The only one you're going to get.'

'Suit yourself, I'll find out when we get to the photos.' He ate stolidly and didn't answer. I said, 'You know, I really hate it when you do this. I mean, what's the point?'

He said, 'Leah, this is my job and my rules. Seen anything of the Astra today?'

'No, but I got another cute call last night.'

'I know,' he said smugly.

I put down my fork. 'How do you know?'

'I set up a monitor on incoming calls.'

'You bugged my damn phone? Nicholls ... let's establish something here, my life is private, get your stupid bug out of my telephone.'

'There is no bug,' he said, without missing a bite. 'The idea behind a

113

trace monitor is it records callers' numbers. I didn't think you'd mind.'

'Bet your boots I mind,' I snapped. 'It's an intrusion into my territory, and I mind like hell. Decide on who you are when you're in my bed, Nicholls, lover or policeman. You sure as hell can't be both.'

'Leah . . .'

'No "Leah",' I said. 'Come up with the wrong answer and you're out.' I pushed my plate away, food half eaten. 'Let's get on with the photographs.'

'At least eat your meal.'

'I lost my appetite. Look . . . you can eat if you want, I'll hang around upstairs.' I scraped back the chair and walked away. He got up off his a little more gently. If I'd embarrassed him it was tough, I couldn't remember being this angry with him before.

'Leah . . .' I didn't turn around, just kept up a fast pace and headed for the stairs. He caught up on the first landing and pulled me around so we were facing. A couple of PCs heading down turned their heads to get another look, caught Nicholls' scowl and picked up speed. I shook myself loose. Nicholls said, 'Now you listen to me. Remember Jeannie . . . did you like what you saw?'

I yelled, '*Shit*, that's a lousy question.'

'Is it?' he yelled back. 'Why? I'm a bloody policeman, Leah, in bed and out of bed, and loving you doesn't affect that.'

'Don't talk to me about love, damn it, I've been there, and it sucks!' I was still shouting, not much caring who heard. A whole mess of things were tangled up in my mind. Jeannie and Gran, and Will and Nicholls, and I couldn't separate out the emotions, all I knew was the casualness of his bugging my phone had got me fighting mad. He'd had no right to do that, motive didn't matter.

He said quietly, 'I'm not Will.'

I turned around and walked up the rest of the basement stairs, then started up the next flight. Neither of us spoke again until we got to his office. He went in first and made a bee-line for his desk, picking up a message sheet, reading it, and stuffing it in a folder before he sat me down with a fat collection of photographs and watched me turn the pages. The faces were all men's, head and shoulders snaps, most of them unsmiling. I wished I knew just who I was looking for, but when I got around to asking that all Nicholls would say was I'd know who if I found the right face. And I did find it. Three pages from the bottom Tom Peep looked out at me with the same long face and greedy eyes he'd had in the Dolce Vita. I put my finger on the snap.

'It's the Astra driver.'

'You're sure about that?'

'Of course I'm sure.' I checked my watch. 'Is that it? Can I go now?' He nodded. I got to my feet and moved out from behind the desk. He was still staring down at the photograph like it might come to life any minute and I itched to ask who it was, but for once I bit back on curiosity. I was half-way to the door before he realised I was leaving and said, 'Leah, not yet.' I turned back.

'What else?'

'I'm sorry,' he said stiffly. 'I should have asked.'

'I'm sorry too,' I said. 'And yes, you should.'

I felt sad as I went out the door, and I knew he felt exactly the same.

19

Sam got back to me around three that afternoon. Fogerty had been dogging him again and he was feeling hard done by. I listened to his gripes and made appropriate sounds of sympathy. Some days are like that, I guess it's to do with misaligned stars. When he'd finally got Fogerty down to pin size he said he didn't have much for me anyway. The addresses on file were those Jeannie's colleagues would return to when secondment ended. I guess it hadn't seemed necessary for any other department but NCIS to hold details of local billets. Oh-hum. Maybe if I asked him real nice Lomas would share the secret.

And maybe I could turn water into wine.

I sighed a little and told Sam not to worry. He made a couple of false starts the way people do when they're not quite sure if they should be telling you something, and then said hesitantly, 'Maybe you should talk to Francine Draper.'

'Good idea,' I enthused. 'If I knew who Francine Draper was I'd do just that.'

'She's a clerk-cum-typist-cum-dogsbody at NCIS and . . . Oh-oh,' he said hurriedly, 'Fogerty's bearing down, got a pen?'

'Yup.'

'Fifteen, Ventnor Way, and . . . um . . .' He quit speaking low and said loudly, 'No, it's the third time, if you don't fix it now I want a refund. Understood?'

'Understood,' I said. 'Thanks, Sam.' He hung up. I looked over at Pete in his glass cage with a new sense of affection. Compared to Fogerty he was a real pussy-cat.

At five I cleared my desk and beat the lift down to the ground floor.

Riding it at busy-time would be fine if I happened to be a person who appreciated the scent of ripe armpits. I went out to the hybrid thinking how helpful it would be to know more about Francine Draper than her name, address and occupation. I started the engine, eased out into the traffic stream and headed north. Three cars back, a bright red streak came with me. I swung on to a garage forecourt and watched it go by, a Honda Civic with a flash of grey hair at the wheel. I waved away a hopeful pump attendant and moved back into the traffic.

Ventnor Way is part of a new housing development, its builders famed for economy of size. Rustic and brick and neat front lawns sized so as not to overtax nail scissors. I guess it's a good way to ensure a neighbourhood of small families. More than two children and the walls would push out. Number fifteen had a white Nissan Micra filling up the drive. I pulled into the kerb and wondered if it were Francine's.

Conversations with strangers can be awkward, especially when you want to pry out information. I rang the doorbell. After a couple of seconds I heard a safety chain slide home. I guessed the job she did made her pretty cautious. The door opened around four inches. I saw part of an auburn bob and a grey eye. I said, 'Francine Draper?'

'Depends if you're selling.'

'I'm not selling.'

'Collecting?'

I fished out my ID, holding it up so she could see. 'Leah Hunter,' I said. 'Inland Revenue. I'd like to talk with you if that's all right?' She took the chain off and I got a good look at her. My age and maybe an inch taller and ten pounds heavier, her skin the pale alabaster that some redheads are lucky to be born with.

'Sure it's me you want to talk to? The only tax I'm due for is PAYE.'

I shook my head. 'It isn't tax I want to talk about,' I said. 'It's Jeannie. I heard you and she worked together?'

'Something wrong with that?'

'No. She was a friend of mine. That's why I want to talk.'

She stepped back. 'You'd better come inside. I guess it's all been as big a shock to you as it has to me. Did you see her? In hospital? I can't believe anybody could do that. It's sick. She looked so dreadful.'

'I saw her. The police needed an identification when she first came in. It wasn't pleasant, seeing what had happened to her.' She was leading the

118

way to the back of the house when I said that, and she turned around with a look of surprise.

'You? Why not her mother?'

'You don't know about that? Mrs Johnson was hurt in a hit and run while Jeannie was missing. Her son Martin had her moved to a hospital closer to his home. Didn't he tell you about that? I'd have thought if you introduced yourself as a friend he would have. I guess he'd be around when you visited.'

'I didn't see him, unlucky I guess. Fact is I made a couple of flying visits and couldn't bear to stay around. One time he was closeted in the office with a doctor, and the other he was taking a canteen break. I guess I should have made more effort to talk to him, but I didn't want to lay myself open to awkward questions.'

I followed her into the kitchen, surprised it was more than a galley. Pint-sized plots tend not to lend themselves to anything more than cramped up rooms. I blinked at the shine of it and said, 'What awkward questions?' She turned away and opened up a cupboard.

'I just made a pot of tea. Want some?'

'That'd be nice,' I said politely. 'Weak and black. You were talking about Martin?'

'Was I?' She got down a mug that matched her own, white china with trailing forget-me-nots. I bet the minute I left she'd wash up neatly and put them away. Such realisations should make me ashamed of my own slobby ways.

'I guess if I'm honest I didn't want to talk to him at all,' she said. 'I'm not good at offering comfort, I duck out of it when I can.'

I said, 'I know what you mean, the problem is nobody invented the right words yet.'

'That's it.' She threw me a pleased look. 'How about you? Did you talk to him?'

'Couldn't avoid it. Coming so soon on top of his mother's accident he was pretty choked.'

'Oh, I bet, but I didn't know about that.' Her forehead creased up like she was having some kind of internal debate, then she said candidly, 'It's no good, I'd have done exactly the same thing if I had, once a coward always a coward.' She opened up the fridge and reached out a plate of pre-cut sandwiches. When she lifted the clingfilm I noticed the plate had trailing forget-me-nots too.

I said, 'How well did you know Jeannie?' She looked like she was working out what would come next before she answered.

'Pretty well,' she said cautiously. 'We hit the night spots occasionally, did some shopping, flopped out at each other's place – the usual kind of thing. How about you?'

'We were at school together. After that I didn't see her for a while. We'd just begun to pick up the friendship again.'

She poured tea and pulled out a couple of stools, hiking up on one and indicating I should take the other. 'Hope you don't mind,' she said. 'I can't be bothered with a table. How'd you find out about me?'

Whoo, but she'd slipped that one in neatly. 'I've been asking around,' I said cautiously. She pushed the sandwiches closer.

'Tuna and mayonnaise. Try one. Asking who?'

I sighed. 'Look, I had to do some arm twisting here, and I promised not say. OK? I don't have any underhand purpose except to find out why Jeannie died.'

'I'd like to know that myself,' Francine said. 'Maybe we could pool ideas.' She bit into a sandwich with shiny white teeth and smiled. 'You first.'

I shrugged. 'You know more about her job than I do. Up to now it looks like an NCIS investigation gone sour. I'm pretty sure she started out by looking into some kind of money laundering operation, and it had to be some large-scale organisation doing it. After that I get a little confused. It *looks* like she ran foul of drug dealers, but how that occurred seems to be a difficult question.'

'You *have* been doing your homework,' she said. I sipped tea. 'It isn't any use expecting me to talk to you about NCIS, even if I knew anything it'd be confidential, and all I do is type reports, circulate memoirs, and make tea when it gets around to my turn.'

'Inland Revenue have an interest in money laundering activities too,' I said. 'Which means I know most of the clean-up methods. I wouldn't ask you to comment on anything that breached security rules.' I was eyeing the sandwiches, the smell of tuna setting taste buds tingling. Watching someone else eat when you're hungry can be a pain, but I didn't feel like butting in on a feast she'd prepared for herself.

'Oh for pity's sake!' She grabbed a sandwich and thunked it on the empty plate in front of me. 'Jeannie was just as bad, she'd sit there drooling before she'd help herself. What did they teach you at that school?'

'To be little ladies,' I said, devouring the neat triangle in two bites.

'Well, don't hold back, I have enough tuna to feed the five thousand. To tell the truth I'm getting sick of it, but aside from cottage cheese it's about the only thing that doesn't overflow with calories.' She eyed me. 'I don't suppose you need to worry about that?'

'I work out pretty heavily,' I said. 'If I stop I pile on the pounds. Look, I know you don't want to talk about this, but I suppose you know how Jeannie died?'

'She went back into a coma, that's what we were told. It shocked us all, it wasn't more than two days before that we'd heard she was improving.'

'That's all you were told?'

'There's more?'

I tried to remember how many people knew about the insulin. If it was supposed to be a secret nobody had mentioned that to *me*, and I hadn't exactly kept it under wraps. I'd told Jack and I'd told Charlie. There was no good reason, short of not wanting to worry them about their own risk factors, why Lomas would have kept it back from his own people. In fact I didn't see how he could have. Everybody knows about departmental leaks, and that particular news item would have spread like wildfire. I said, 'I don't think you're being totally honest here.' Her skin tinted, the flush spreading up from her neck.

'You know about it?'

'If we're talking insulin, I know about it.'

She said awkwardly, 'We were warned not to talk about it outside the office. How did you find out?'

Half lies are better than whole lies. I told her I had a hospital contact and left it at that. She seemed to accept it. I told myself that by saying that I'd protected Nicholls. Then I asked myself why I still thought I should do that. What did it matter to me if she reported back to Lomas that my ex-lover had a loose lip?

The 'ex' rattled around unpleasantly in my head.

I said, 'It's frightening anybody could just walk into a hospital and do that.'

'Isn't it though? And a policewoman there too. Must have taken nerve.'

'Or money.'

'Or both.' We stared at each other over empty plates. She shook the teapot. 'God, but this kind of thing plays havoc with a girl's diet.' She boiled up some more water and nearly tipped out a cupboard before she came up with chocolate biscuits. 'I *thought* I'd hidden some,' she said, breaking open the packet and stabbing it at me. I took one obediently. She nibbled hers really delicately, like she wanted it to last a long time, then gave up and swallowed it in one bite.

I said, 'Speaking of money. You heard the rumours?'

'You really don't miss much, do you?'

'If I did I'd be out of a job. Look, I'm going to be honest about this and I hope you will be too. I don't believe for one minute that Jeannie knew anything about the money she was supposed to have stashed away. She wasn't the kind of person to get into that type of thing. I think she was set up. How do you feel?'

'Pretty much the same,' she said slowly. 'I thought I was the only one. I don't know what the evidence is but it must have been fairly damning.'

'Suppose it was a set-up, do you have ideas on who might have done it?'

'Somebody we both knew, you mean? No. I can't think of anybody who would want to do that, and anyway, where would the money come from?'

'If they were on the take themselves and Jeannie was getting close . . . ?'

'Oh, I wish you hadn't said that.' Her eyes went big and troubled. 'No, I don't believe it. Everybody was cut to pieces when it happened. You know they're disbanding? They didn't feel they wanted to continue without her.' I shifted my gaze. Was that another little escape route or did she genuinely believe it? How much information were clerks given?'

I said, 'She never discussed work with you?'

'Well, you know, only in general terms, nothing specific, and I didn't ask her, that was understood. I mean I'd like to see the people responsible put away forever, and that really is the truth. I just don't believe there's anything you or I can do about it.'

'She was out of contact with everybody for a while, was she out of contact with you too?'

Francine flushed. 'I met her for coffee once. She said if she didn't get to talk with someone she could trust she'd go mad. And then when I met her she didn't really talk at all.'

'Can you explain that?'

'She had something on her mind. She had three cups of coffee and spent most of the time staring into space. I tried to get her to tell me the problem but she wouldn't. It worried me. She didn't look anything like her normal self, different clothes, different make-up, almost . . .'

As she struggled for a word I said, 'Tarty?'

'You mind-read too?'

'Not exactly. Someone else told me the same thing. Did she mention what she'd been doing?'

'No.'

'Or where she was living?'

'No.' She began to look distressed. 'I'm so stupid. I should have followed her.'

'It wouldn't have helped,' I said. 'For one thing Jeannie was bright enough to know if you were doing that, and for another you weren't to know now much trouble she was in.'

'Oh, I know, but it's just the thought of it. I mean, wanting to sit and drink coffee with someone just because she was so . . . upset.' She'd been going to say frightened, I could see it in her face. 'If I'd really thought about it, there must have been something I could have done.'

'There was, and you did it,' I said. 'She needed you to be there and anchor her. Not to gossip, and not to ask questions, just to be a positive force she could reach out to.' Francine put her mug down and began to cry softly. I could feel my own throat fill up. I got down off the stool and put my arm around her awkwardly. 'Hey, come on, this is the last thing she'd want.'

'I kn . . . know,' she wept. 'But I should have st . . . stopped her.' I sighed. If life just had a rewind button everybody would be happy. After a while she blew her nose vigorously and mopped her eyes. I took my arm away and stood awkwardly. Open shows of emotion always make me want to curl up. It isn't that I'm unsympathetic, it's just the feeling that one more tear will have me joining in.

I said, 'I'd better go now.' She nodded, put her wet tissues in the waste bucket and grabbed some more. When I started for the door she came with me.

'You really don't think Jeannie accepted that money?'

'No, I don't.'

'If there's anything I can do to help prove that . . .'

'There is one more thing I'd like to ask.' She looked expectant. 'Is there anyone you can think of, someone close to her, that she might have confided in?'

'Only Geoff,' she said.

'Geoff?'

'Lomas.'

'Lomas?' I sounded like a parrot. 'Why would she confide in him?'

'You don't know?' Francine said.

'Know what?'

'That they were an item? Almost from the time she first came. If he wasn't round at her place, she'd be at his. Everybody knew. She said he was sweet.'

I struggled to keep my jaw from dropping. Lomas, sweet? Maybe I'd misjudged him. Maybe that unfriendly exterior was blocking off grief. It was a new image to take away with me.

Lomas the lover.

20

It was coming up on seven when I left Francine, and I had no great wish to go home. If Nicholls was hanging around waiting to make up, then I didn't want to be there. Perversely, if he *wasn't* there I didn't want to know. Relationships can get really complicated at times. I drove back to Bramfield and then out again on the Pontefract Road, adding a little more pollution to the atmosphere.

The Royal Oak looked a little busier than usual. I headed for the bar, wondering how much of the extra custom was due to Ed and Rassa no longer being around to bring in their own kind of trouble.

Chloe had rinsed her hair pale plum and threaded bright pink and green floss into a swatch of hair. Her black T-shirt let everyone know she could get by without a bra and the shiny ring was still flashing. I hiked up on to a stool, leaned on the bar, and waited patiently. By and by she finished off what looked like a really scintillating conversation with a Neanderthal hunk in plaid shirt and Caterpillar boots, and got around to me. I ordered a Pils and asked where Bill was.

'Upstairs watching telly with his feet up,' she said. 'What do you want him for?'

'Just idle curiosity,' I said. 'The place seems busier tonight. I guess trade's looking up since Ed and Rassa stopped dropping by.'

She scrunched her forehead like she thought she ought to know me but didn't, then ironed out the creases and said, 'I've got you now. You're the one came in looking for a friend. Did you catch up with her?'

'Sort of,' I said, 'but it wasn't exactly joyful, she died two weeks ago.' She stopped wiping the bar and stared back at me with that wide-eyed look people get when they've just heard something unpleasant.

'Ooh, that's bad. I mean, you know, really bad. Didn't have anything to do with what happened in the car park did it?'

'Why would you think that?' I asked.

'Mmm? Don't know why. Just seems funny that's all. Coincidence.' She flapped the cloth out, refolded it, and started wiping again. 'Want anything else?'

I scanned the bar menu, looking for something unlikely to be loaded with BSE. Pizza seemed about the only thing available. She wrote down the order and slammed the slip of paper through the kitchen hatch. A couple of seconds later a hand grabbed it up. The hand was streaked with red. I did a quick re-check of the menu and hoped the staining came from redcurrants and not anything more sinister. On her way back Chloe served two pints and a shandy, then came over to me and said, 'Two fifty.' I gave her the right change and she fed the money into the till. 'What happened to her then?' she said, rubbing her hands on the bar towel. 'That friend of yours I mean. Was it an accident or what?'

I shook my head. 'No accident, somebody beat the shit out of her and dumped her in the canal.'

'*N-o.* Ooh . . .' She crossed her arms and hugged herself. 'I wish I hadn't asked, it's made me go dead goose-pimply. Who'd do a thing like that?'

'According to the police it was Ed and Rassa.'

She shook her head. 'No,' she said. 'Don't think that'd be likely. Might have got somebody else to do it, they were nasty that way, but they stopped doing their own heavy bit when they got loaded.'

My little ears pricked up. 'When would that be?'

'Don't know, six months back, maybe more. Hey, Jerry!' She raised her voice. 'When did Ed get that big car?' Everybody in the place looked round. So much for confidentiality.

The hunk said, 'Week after Christmas. Who wants to know?' She ignored that and turned back to me.

'Thought it'd be about then. They come swaggering in, flashing a roll, and big cheesy smiles. Said they'd cut a big deal.'

'What kind of deal?'

'Not the sort of thing anybody'd want to ask. Anyway, like I said, they didn't do their own heavy bit after that.'

I said, 'So how come they were bad for trade?'

'Don't know much do you?' she said smugly, exercising the right of superior knowledge. I refrained from pointing out the obvious. If I knew all I wanted to know about Ed and Rassa I'd be doing my eating in a different place. I smiled at her expectantly. She sighed and explained it to me patiently. 'What I mean is,' she said, 'suppose one of the girls got out of line, or some hero didn't pay dibs, they'd handle it, you know? Put 'em out of action for a while. Well, after they got the money they'd slip somebody else a pony and just sit around and watch. Trouble was it didn't stop them picking fights or getting their hands up every skirt in sight. That's what kept everybody away. Bill tried to bar 'em once and got a right working over. Hasn't been the same man since.'

'Didn't he report it?'

'What? So they'd come back and do it again? You must be joking.' Half a dozen men came in. She bounced off to serve them. I swallowed down some Pils and waited for her to come back. By and by the hand appeared in the hatch and slammed down a pizza. The stains had gone. A couple of seconds later Chloe brought the plate over. I sliced the pizza into quarters and bit into one unenthusiastically. The cheese was streaked with red too; this time I hoped it was tomato. I bought another Pils and, remembering her tastes, asked if she'd like a rum and black. She looked like it was the best idea she'd heard all day and rang up the cash.

I said, 'So you've no idea where the money came from?' She said it hadn't seemed advisable to ask. I could see her point; for someone with a less snoopy mind than my own such questions come second to avoiding trouble. 'Did it have anything to do with, um – I think you called him Tony? The guy my friend had a fracas with?'

'Might have. Before that he used to come in like he was giving out orders, you know? After Christmas it was more like they were equals.'

'Does he still drop by?'

'Only came back once after the bother.'

'Don't suppose you can describe him?'

'Didn't I do that already? Tallish, thinnish, dark hair, long nose.' She rattled it off like she'd said it so many times it was easy.

I said, 'I guess other people have asked the same question?'

'The police have. Got sick of them, coming in all the time. I mean you'd think they were setting up home. Don't believe they got their answers right in that Chapeltown business either.'

'Why not?'

'I told you,' she said, emphasising it like I was thick. 'Ed and Rassa didn't do their own heavy work any more, so why would they be in Chapeltown with an Uzi?'

'I don't know,' I said. 'I have to rely on what I read in the papers.' She took on a look of understanding.

'Oh, well, if that's all you're going by.'

I said, 'So what do you think happened?'

'I don't think anything,' she said. 'I'm getting married soon, and after that I'm out of here.' I could understand that too. I offered her a slice of pizza but she declined nicely. I nibbled a little more. Some more punters came in and she got ready to move.

I said, 'One more thing. Any idea where I might find Tony?' She shook her head. 'All I know is he didn't live round here.'

'How about his car? What was that like?'

'An Astra,' she said. 'Bright red.'

I almost choked. She reached over and patted my back. I pushed the pizza away and Chloe nodded understandingly.

'You should have had shepherd's pie, that's not bad.'

'Maybe next time,' I said, and slid off the stool.

'Going home now?' she said.

'I thought I'd have another talk with Donna, tell her what happened.'

'Oh my!' Her eyes got wide again. 'You didn't hear about that?'

The pit of my stomach bunched up, anticipating what I was going to hear. 'No,' I said. 'If it's that bad I guess I didn't.'

'Donna OD'd,' she said. 'Right after Ed and Rassa – you know, in the car? The police went round to talk to her, and there she was. Dead.' We looked at each other in mutual worry.

I said, 'I didn't think she had a habit.'

'Surprised me too. I mean she smoked, but she didn't hardly ever have a drink or anything.'

I touched the ring on her finger. 'When's the wedding?'

'Saturday.'

'I hope it goes well. Who's the lucky man? Don't suppose it's Bill?'

'Bill? You must be joking! Hey, Jerry?' The hunk looked up again. 'She thought I might be marrying Bill.' He laughed like it was the funniest thing he'd heard in years and thumped his chest.

'Me,' he said. I told him congratulations.

Chloe said, 'Why'd you think it was Bill?'

I shook my head. 'Just the way you seemed to worry about him, I guess.'

''Cos he's not back to his old self,' she said, 'that's why.' Somebody shouted, 'Hey, Chloe! Let's have a flash of your knockers!' Jerry got up and took a walk in that direction. Chloe said, 'He's really protective.'

I watched her head in the same direction and felt glad about that. The way things were shaping on the accident front she really needed it.

21

I left the car at Dora's, opening and closing the garage as quietly as I knew how, and trying to remember the last time I'd actively tried to avoid conversation with her. If there'd ever been a last time. Such deceitfulness isn't strange to me but it isn't something I practise on friends. The trouble is when we get together nine times out of ten she mentions Nicholls. He's sort of grown on her. I keep telling her he isn't exactly a permanent fixture in my life, but she just looks at me with a who-are-you-trying-to-kid expression on her face, and most times I give up trying. I guess at heart she's an incurable romantic. Dora has a daughter of her own, Susan, whose temperament is about as opposite as you can get, and it makes me wonder where she could have got her mistrustful nature. It could have been from her father, although to look at his picture you'd never guess, he looks every bit as placid and easy-going as Dora, who keeps his portraits and snapshots dotted about the house. Most of them are fading now, but his face is still clear, and she's still in love with him, which is why she thinks Nicholls and I are still going to be an item forty years from now. That's roughly how long it is since her husband was killed in the Korean conflict. When you come right down to it, there just isn't any excuse meaningful enough to validate making war.

After a while I gave up on trying to imagine what Nicholls would be like that far ahead – or what *I'd* be like come to that. The way things stood right then forty hours was a lifetime. I guess the truth is I've just grown to distrust dependency.

I walked home at an easy pace, still in no hurry to get there, the street almost as bright as day under the full moon, but bleached of colour like a monochrome movie. There was a space outside the house big enough to have held Nicholls' car. I told myself if he'd been hanging around, such busy-bodying was his own business.

I mean, it wasn't as if I'd just yawned through *Stargate* in order to avoid a possible confrontation, I'd actually wanted to see the boring movie. Bet your boots I had.

As I crossed Marcie's landing her door opened again. I pasted on a happy smile. She said, 'Hi. Everything all right?' I told her everything was fine, and how about Ben? She said Ben was fine too, and ducked back inside. I carried on upstairs, wondering why it was she looked a little guilty. Or maybe it was just imagination. Some days everywhere I look people wear the same face.

Including me.

I let myself into the flat, double-locked the door, and turned on all the lights. All in all I've been known to have better days.

I'd ended the night squatting in front of the television and pigging-out on a fry-up of potatoes, mushrooms, and sausages I hoped weren't too far past sell-by, hunger undistracted by John Wayne's hard riding to rescue a white girl from the Indians. Taking all in all, if I'd been in her shoes I'd have stayed with the Apache.

Around one in the morning I'd rolled into bed, tired enough to sleep on a rock, and dreamed of Jeannie driving around in a red Astra. I'd dreamed of other things too, but that was the one that stayed with me.

Thursday morning when I got back from exercising my feet, clouds were stacking up like dirty candy-floss, facing off a clear eastern sky. I told myself hopefully that maybe the sun would burn the clouds back, but all the time I knew they were too purposeful for that.

When I got upstairs the telephone was ringing. I turned the key in the latch and grabbed the phone. Nicholls said, 'We have to talk.'

'What's to talk about?' I said.

He went silent for a while, then came back, 'I'm glad you got home safely last night.'

'Why wouldn't I?'

He sighed.

'Don't sigh at me damn it,' I snapped. 'I resent it.'

'I'll buy you lunch,' he said. 'Neutral territory.'

'I'll buy my own.'

'Either way.'

Shit he was persistent. 'Where? Your canteen or mine?'

'I'll pick you up.'

'I'll walk.'

'Ring O' Bells, one o'clock.'

'Fine,' I said, and hung up.

When I got out of the shower the phone was jumping again. Sure it was Nicholls with some other little thing I snapped, 'What?' The voice said, 'Too bad you don't listen, *bitch*.' He was really good at emphasising that word.

'Hey!' I said, 'I'm listening.' But he'd gone. I wondered if Nicholls was still busily tracing calls, or if he'd got around to respecting civil liberties.

I ate a fast breakfast, and headed back to Charlie's. If Sidney wasn't so damn cagey about handing out his address, I'd bypass the middleman and go and bend his ear direct, but the fact is that after two years' acquaintance I still don't know it. I could of course pay a visit to a local massage parlour, and leave a message with Delia, but I didn't think he'd appreciate that.

Charlie bounced out of his office like a rubber ball. It looked like I'd caught him early, his hands were ungreased and the paraffin rag was missing. He said, 'Good to see you, girl,' and gave me a fatherly once over.

'I hope you mean that, Charlie,' I said, 'because there's a Tom Peep in a red Astra following me around and I'd really like to find out who he is.'

'What's the boyfriend doing about it?'

'He won't tell me a damn thing.'

'Thinks a lot about you, you know, that tame piece of fuzz. Chances are, if he's looking for it, he'll find it.'

'We're not exactly cuddle-bunnies right now,' I said severely, 'and there's a couple of things he doesn't know. Remember that friend of mine? The one who ended up in the canal? Some male in a red Astra tried to shove her in his car. I have this sneaky feeling it can't be just coincidence.'

'Have to say it doesn't sound good, love. Why don't you make up and move in cosy for a bit?'

'Charlie, what is it with you?' I said exasperatedly. 'How come it's suddenly so hard to get help?' He looked shifty. I stared at him suspiciously. 'Don't tell me you've been got at. It's Nicholls isn't it? He's done it again, he's been down here sticking his nose in.'

He shifted his feet. 'Only got your interests at heart.'

'Tell me about it,' I said bitterly. 'You know what? All this protectionism's going to get me killed one day.' I got back in the car and started the engine. His face got long and sad. He waved his hands at me like he was trying to stop a truck. I wound down the window and said, 'What?'

'Hadn't thought about that, love, could be right. I mean, if you don't know what to look out for you can't see it coming. I'll have another word with Sidney. Won't want you ending up like your friend.'

'You told him about that?'

'Came as a shock.'

'Came as a shock to me, too,' I said. 'It's lucky he didn't know her personally or he'd feel worse.' Charlie's eyes dropped to the bonnet. I softened my tone. 'I'm sorry, Charlie, it's Nicholls I'm mad at, not you. If Sidney asks, Tom Peep's name is Tony and he did some business with Ed and Rassa. Dark hair, long face, long nose. And . . . thanks, Charlie.'

He shook his head. 'Rock and a hard place, that's what. Best not tell the boyfriend or he'll have me credentials.' He breathed on the bonnet and rubbed with his sleeve. 'Give you a bell then, when I've heard something?' I told him that would be great.

When I drove out of the yard he was still looking unhappy. I felt a peck of guilt. Imposing on friendship can be really sinful. For a minute I felt like backing up and telling him not to bother. For a minute. After that the foolishness passed, and I turned the car's nose towards Market Street. There are times when even friendship has to be pushed to its limits.

The Ring O' Bells isn't usually Nicholls' first choice of eating place. For one thing it's pricier than town centre pubs, and for another the clientele isn't made up of people he's trying to keep an eye on. The building itself is eighteenth century but lacks the customary spaciousness of Georgian buildings. For some reason the original ceilings weren't much over six feet high and the management dropped the floor to compensate. I guess over the last couple of hundred years the pub's patronage has had a growth spurt.

To the left of what was still the original mahogany bar counter – raised up a little so it didn't break backs to stand there and have a drink – the eatery occupied a long, narrow room with a brightly lit steel counter at one end, hotplates well stocked with food. A help-yourself salad bar stood sideways on.

Down the long side wall, high backed oak settles flanked matching oak tables and formed mini booths. The rest of the floor space was taken up by circular tables and spindle-back chairs. Nicholls' eyes swept down the line of booths and his jaw tightened up when he saw they were all occupied. I guess he'd been hoping for more privacy than he was going to get. I made a bee-line for the hotplates and looked at the offerings.

I don't know why it is but in summer months meat doesn't hold much of a thrill for me. Come to that, what with all the documentaries on factory farming and soft-eyed veal calves, it's fast losing any attraction at all. I settled on spinach and ricotta lattice pie, with salad, heaping a giant helping of Waldorf on top of crispy lettuce leaves and adding a little colour with some marinated tomato. When I turned around a couple of men were stepping out of a booth. I put on a little speed and got there ahead of newcomers looking to corner it themselves.

Nicholls had gone for the mutton pie with new potatoes and carrots, overloading the plate from a big gravy jug. I noted the little wave that rose up and splashed over as he walked. When he sat down he started sucking his thumbs. 'It came out too fast,' he complained defensively.

I watched him go back for a napkin and run his eyes over the puddings. I knew darned well he'd want treacle sponge. I ducked my head and ate, appreciating the flakiness of pastry and combination of flavours. When he came back neither of us spoke for a while, I guess good food has that kind of effect. By and by he started throwing me slanty looks. I said, 'Why don't you come right out with it, Nicholls, instead of acting like some subversive?'

He said, 'You were in the Royal Oak again last night.'

'So I was, and I'm glad you brought that up. How come you didn't tell me about Donna?' He went sheep-eyed. 'Damn it, don't look at me like that,' I snapped, 'it doesn't work. You know what I'm talking about, another drug overdose for God's sake! How many coincidences can you swallow down, Nicholls? I'll be hearing next how Jeannie pumped herself full of insulin. And that's another thing – explain how that kind of investigation can be closed down without a fight?'

'I can't. I can't explain a lot of things. There are some areas of my life I can't share with you, Leah, just as there are areas of yours you don't tell me about.' He looked at me solemnly. 'That's where trust is supposed to come in, so why don't you have a little?'

Talk about a pot calling a kettle black.

I said stroppily, 'Speaking of trust, did you pick up on this morning's phone call?'

He dropped his eyes and pushed a piece of carrot around. 'He's ringing from call-boxes . . .'

'Surprise me!'

' . . . and using pre-recorded tape.'

'You've found one?'

He shook his head. 'Technicians pin-pointed tape sounds, the actual caller could be a paid courier.'

I thought about how great it was to know that. How come nothing was simple anymore? Why couldn't I have a plain simple heavy breather instead of a damn conspirator? Nicholls was still playing around with his fork like he was six. I speared a slice of tomato and watched the seeds stretch out and fall off. As far back as I remember I've been hooked on American crime series, and a faint memory of *Mission Impossible*'s opening sequence drifted through my head. There was always this one PI playing a tape in a telephone booth; when the tape ends the cassette blows up. I said brightly, 'I wonder why he doesn't go the whole hog and have the damn thing self destruct?'

'It isn't a joke,' Nicholls said.

'Who's laughing?'

We stopped playing around with food and looked at each other. Times are when Nicholls' eyes are so blue I can drown in them, but right then they were wintry. I wondered what mine looked like to him. He said, 'About yesterday . . .'

'I meant what I said, Nicholls, you can't ride rough-shod through my private life, that isn't the way the game is played.'

'Leah . . . People who go to this much trouble don't play games. All I want is . . .'

'I know what you want,' I cut in, 'and I don't appreciate it. Motive isn't important here, we're talking about the rights of decision. As a matter of record I was about to ask BT to run an intercept, but you waded in with your big feet before I could do that.'

His lips tightened up. 'Who did you think they were from?'

'What?'

'I said, who did you think they were from?'

'The calls? Since when was I psychic? Stop moving goal posts around. What's at issue isn't who they're from, it's the way you act like you own rights.'

'You want to know about the thought sequence? Is that it?' He pushed his plate away and leaned over the table, enunciating every vowel. 'In my desk is a folder, in the folder are forensic photographs of Jeannie: cuts, bruises, swellings, the lot! I see them, and I see you. In the same state. I don't like that, Leah, it scares the shit out of me. Now. Tell me again to stop monitoring incoming calls and I'll do it.'

He shifted his elbows and leaned back. A couple at a little island table eyed us interestedly. I started to move out of the booth. He said, 'Where are you going?'

'To get myself a drink. Want one?'

I didn't bother to wait around for an answer.

The bar was busy. I shouldered in. A dark blue suit with shiny teeth and a voice loud enough to reach both ends of the bar bawled, 'Step back and let the little lady through.'

'Sure thing,' I bawled back. 'Where the hell is she?'

I mean, what *is* it with men?

He shrugged and turned his back, which suited me fine. Right then anything in trousers looked better going than coming.

I got a couple of Pils and worked on what to say to Nicholls. I can't stand people who don't fight fair. When I slid back into the booth I said, 'Who's the guy in the Astra? And don't say don't know, you have him on file.'

He came up out of the Pils with white lip-liner, and said he couldn't tell me. Gran always used to say can't and won't are interchangeable. I told him that. He said he appreciated the point but the answer was still the same. I told him that was fine by me, I'd nearly run Tom Peep to earth anyway. It wasn't exactly the truth but I figure if someone is stonewalling it's best to throw them a curve. He got on his whipped puppy-dog look. I leaned my head back and stared at the ceiling.

He said, 'About the monitor, do you want me to stop?'

'Do you want to stop?'

'You know damn well I don't.'

I pulled up straight. 'Then do what you should have done in the first place. Ask. Give me the same privilege you'd give some guy at the bar.'

He said with stiff resentment, 'We'd like to monitor your incoming telephone calls if you have no objection to that.'

I waved a hand. 'No objection at all,' I said. 'Sounds like a good idea.' He swallowed down some words he'd thought better of and sulked for a while. By and by the scowl faded and he got around to asking what I'd like for pudding. I threw aside the principles of healthy eating and mendaciously told him the treacle sponge looked really good. He grinned at me like we were friends again.

Sometimes such small lies build big bridges.

22

Those heavy morning clouds had been encroaching east all day, and around three the rain started. No thunder this time, just a persistent heavy curtain running down the windows. Up in the office you could hear the sharp swishing noises of traffic on the road below, and the air felt noticeably cooler, like a foretaste of coming autumn.

At four o'clock Sam phoned and said how did I feel about eating out again? I made some non-committal noises. I'd skipped one workout session already, miss another and I was on the slippery slope. He said not to get too over-heated at the thought of a tête-à-tête since that wasn't what he had planned. Jeannie's team were having a farewell meal and a few drinks and had invited him along. He said, 'I thought you'd be interested, they're splitting up this weekend – starting to anyway, two of them go back to Northumberland.'

'Farewell party?' I said. 'Sounds fun, but where do I come in?'

'I asked if I could bring you along. I told them we'd worked together in the past and you were a good friend of Jeannie's. Nobody raised any argument.'

My mind raced down a track it hadn't expected to find. They'd probably be tight as clam shells with information, but if I passed up this kind of chance I'd live to regret it. A little voice in the back of my head murmured that 'live' was the operative word here. I ignored its downbeat implication and told Sam I owed him one. He gave me the time and location and said he'd meet me in the bar. I wondered how Lomas would feel about my intrusive presence. We really seemed to rub each other up. Such worry proved groundless. When I walked into The Feathers, Lomas wasn't there.

Sam got up from a table and came over to meet me. Everybody else was already there, and it didn't take a giant step of logic to guess that had been intentional. Such a ploy didn't worry me any, the way I see it whoever runs the party makes the rules and gatecrashers don't get a say. I collected a Pils from the bar and swapped first names. The looks I got were mixed, most faintly curious but two openly begging the question of why I was there at all. If as Sam said there'd been no active objections, I guessed that was simply because they'd kept quiet as a matter of politics.

For a while we sat around looking at each other and making inconsequential conversation, without once mentioning why we were all there. Then in the middle of a little lull I said brightly, 'How come Francine isn't here?'

The only other female said carefully, 'Francine? Why would she be?'

'I, uh . . .' Looking to Sam for support got me nowhere, he was too busy watching a fly. I spread my hands. 'I sort of picked up the idea she was part of the team.' Kath's eyes didn't even flick.

'How'd you meet up with Francine then?'

'I – uh, she dropped by the hospital a couple of times.' Never tell a lie when the truth works just as well. Kath accepted the implication and sank back into silence. A thirty-ish short guy next to her who'd so far said only the one word, Jake, muttered about how maybe they should have mentioned it to Franny. She snapped back that maybe they should have asked Ruby too. He said, 'Oh, for God's sake, Kath, there's a difference between Fran and the cleaner.' They stared at each other unkindly for a couple of seconds until she drained her glass and got up.

'I need another drink.'

She looped a long mouse strand behind an ear permanently bent in a question mark and walked to the bar. It worried me how easily I'd just managed to say the wrong thing. Sam said, 'What's got into Kath?' and we all had an awkward little silence.

Alan muttered, 'She had words with you-know-who.' Heads nodded, eyes studied drinks. Alan surreptitiously checked the time on his wrist, the ducking motion disclosing a difference in hair thickness. Men are really unlucky that way. From the front it looked like a robust brown thatch but appearances can be deceptive.

I shifted a little, uncomfortable with the role of spectre at the feast that I seemed to have taken upon myself. I took a long pull at the Pils and set the glass on its wet ring. 'Look,' I said uncomfortably, 'it's been really good meeting you guys, and thanks for letting me drop by, but . . .'

Alan said, 'How far back did you and Jeannie go?'

'Fourth form.'

'Sam tells me you'd been out of touch for a while. I guess that means you weren't all that close?'

I said, 'I wouldn't put it that way, addresses change, people drift, things like that aren't intentional and don't need to mess up a friendship. How about you? I don't suppose you knew her until she joined the team?'

'She grew on me.'

I glanced over to the bar. Kath was still busy bending the bar-keep's ear. I could see the attraction, bar-keeps get younger and better looking all the time. I said, 'I hope I didn't touch a soft spot in mentioning Francine?'

Jake stopped admiring dark depths of bitter and said moodily, 'What's irked Kath is Fran got a mortgage and she couldn't. Kath earns double what Francine gets and it rankles. She'll get over it.'

'Maybe Francine put down more deposit?' I suggested.

'Not the way Fran tells it.'

'Has to be luck of the draw then. Is that the only beef they have?'

'Nah, it's hormones pure and simple, like circling cats half the time.'

I said, 'How did Jeannie get by? Must have been hard work for her to stay friends with both.'

'Jeannie always acted like she didn't notice anything wrong,' Alan said. 'It worked for her and didn't do me any good at all.'

'She used to be the school diplomat,' I said. 'When we weren't busy subverting.'

'The way Sam tells it you haven't grown out of that.' Neil wore a smile when he said it, like he knew he was dropping Sam into trouble. 'The subversion that is,' he added. 'I gather you never were diplomatic.' I flicked another unkind look at Sam, but he was sitting there enjoying himself and not meeting my eye. I wondered what other kind of junk he'd been feeding them.

I said easily, 'Since when did you hear of subversive tax inspectors? Nine to five gathering money for the nation's coffers and boring as hell.'

Kath came back to us with smoothed feathers and a pleased look, and I was really glad she'd chosen to sit with her back to the bar, that way she wouldn't notice the way the bar-keep had moved in on a not-far-past-the-legal-age blonde. I dragged my eyes away from the pretty tableau and watched Alan's drift in the same direction.

Neil said, 'So how much of what Sam tells us is true then?' I sighed a little. How was I supposed to know what lies he'd been telling about me? I fixed him with an unfriendly stare. His ear turned prettily red but I didn't get his attention.

'Sam,' I said politely, 'I'd really like to hear what fictitious rubbish you've been feeding them. I don't appreciate being dropped down a bog by a friend.'

'All I said was you have a catch rate as high as theirs,' he said innocently. 'True or false?' Talk about Catch-22! Questions like that you lose out either way. I scowled at him a little harder.

'The mess up rate for amateurs is pretty high too,' Kath muttered. *Nice* one. I squinted at the bar-keep. The blonde had her head back and was laughing prettily. Maybe Kath and I should play musical chairs, that way she could keep an eye on things. I had trouble swallowing down such a kindly thought.

'Ignore her, the best looking men in her life are going back to Northumberland and she can't stand to see us go,' said Alan. From the look on her face I didn't think that was a problem at all.

'Kath told the truth,' I said. 'Amateurs mess up all the time. If they didn't do that my job would be a darn sight harder.' I smiled at her peaceably but she didn't smile back.

Over at the bar the pretty blonde's boyfriend had broken up the new romance and they were now head to head across a small table. Behind them, Lothario didn't seem to have taken it that hard; he was trying out his talent on a brunette ten years his senior but it seemed heavy going. I guess it was something of a relief when Jake interrupted and bought in another round. We all stared at the table again. Neil said into the little silence, 'To get back to Jeannie . . . Quitting before we nail the bastard sucks. I wanted you to hear that, Leah, so you don't think it's choice.'

'Sent home tail between legs and watched like hawks when we get there,' Alan said. 'Bang goes promotion.'

'How so?' I said.

'Top brass reasoning, that's how so, with Jeannie on the take the dirt rubs off on us. You can see the logic behind it, Leah, they've got solid evidence and there's nothing brass likes better. Up to somebody without past involvement to prove it now – one way or the other.'

Somebody new? My ears pricked up. I said, 'That's the new team's remit? Jeannie isn't just being written off?'

'Who said she was?'

'Lomas.' We had another little silence. They were getting really irritating. 'I guess he's mad at being sent home too?' I said.

'He'll still be here for a while, briefing the new boys.'

'That so?'

'Claims he has an open mind, so open you can almost feel the draught,' Jake said drily. 'It's a wonder he doesn't catch cold.'

'The ship may sink but Lomas walks on water,' Alan agreed, and everyone went back to table staring again. *Judas*, but this was some farewell party. Kath's eyes strayed over her shoulder. Lothario had run out of steam. She drained her glass, said, 'My round,' and was at the bar before anybody blinked.

'Never known her so eager to part with it before,' Neil said. He saw my eyes whiz over to Lothario and hooted. 'Money I'm talking about, not the other, although . . .' he did a little measuring of his own, ' . . . this time maybe it's a bit of both.'

Since they'd lightened up a bit, I bounced the conversation back to Lomas and him and Jeannie being an item. The way the temperature dropped anybody'd think I'd thrown a dead rat on the table. 'That's what I heard,' I said defensively. 'Tell me I'm wrong and I'll believe you.'

Alan got thirsty, Neil and Bill looked uncomfortable and Sam did some finger drawing.

The pub started filling up. A smell of mushy peas and hot pies drifted out of the back. I could feel my stomach getting ready to rumble encouragement. Kath came back from the bar, chat-up time ended in a rush of trade. A third Pils appeared and queued silently behind an almost untouched second. Assuming everybody had bought their own initial drink that made five more rounds to go. The hybrid's keys nudged my thigh. I decided the next round had to be mine, that way I could ease over on to tonics without fuss.

I wondered how much quinine I could take before the stuff put my heart into overdrive.

A plump woman with a too-tight dress and a little pinny came over and dumped knives, forks and paper napkins on the table. At The Feathers finesse is never on the menu.

Jake lifted his ale. 'To Jeannie,' he said. We all clunked glasses.

Sam said thoughtfully, 'It's funny I picked up the same message as Leah. We both heard the Jeannie investigation was being closed down.

Looks like there's been a change of heart.'

'NCIS decisions don't affect anybody else's investigation. Customs would have kept on looking,' said Kath.

'I know for a fact CID were asked to wind up,' I said. 'And they weren't happy about it. Look . . . didn't any of you know why she'd gone solo?'

'Might have mentioned it in pillow-talk,' Kath said. 'But she didn't tell me. Rest of you get to know anything?' Heads shook negatively. 'There's your answer,' she said. 'Played it close to her chest.'

'She knew it was dangerous,' said Alan. 'She'd have to have damn good reason to stick her neck out.'

'Twenty-five thousand of them,' Kath murmured.

'What?'

'Nothing.'

'So what was happening at the Royal Oak?' I said. 'What kind of surveillance?'

'Waste of time, we got nowhere,' Neil said. 'Local dealers like that can be picked up any time. What's the point photographing punters?'

'I don't understand how you missed seeing Jeannie. The place she rented wasn't that far away and she went into the pub. How'd she change her appearance enough not to be recognised?'

'Uniform carried out the surveillance, not us. I'm not making excuses, I'm saying none of them knew her, and we don't know if she was still around. If there'd been one of us on site it might be different.'

'Anybody'd think we'd killed an albatross, a proper failure, the lot of us.' Jake gloomed, then brightened. 'Food! Thought we'd cocked that up too.' He looked at me. 'Jeannie liked Feathers' pie and peas, told me she'd sneaked in under age tarted up in her mother's make-up.' He sniffed his newly arrived plate and waited until the plump woman moved out of earshot. 'Did you know some of her bruises were weeks old? Yes, that's right, weeks. Injection marks the same. Must have been shooting up all the time she was hanging around the Royal Oak for that to be right: up in that bed-sit you found. Has to be like that doesn't it, unless . . .' He stopped and cocked his head, waiting for me to catch up. I finished it off for him. It was really nice to have travelled around in full circle. The words hung in my head like recriminations of incompetence waiting to be voiced.

'Unless,' I said, 'she was never there at all.'

23

When the party ended I was the only one around still sober enough to drive. I left the males to their own devices and gave Kath a ride home. She informed me with exaggerated care that I wasn't too bad really – for a snoop, and then snored gently on the passenger seat.

The block of flats she lived in was council owned and newish. Up to now the housing people had been really picky about who they gave keys to and the place was practically free of graffiti. I say practically because although you can screen tenants you can't screen wandering jokers with spray cans. I declined to take up the suggestion thoughtfully left on the back lift wall and rode up with Kath to the sixth floor, waiting patiently while she proved how incompetent she was with locks. I took the key away from her and opened the door. She staggered inside and muttered about coffee.

'Just what you need,' I said grimly as she fell over the rug. I clicked on the light switch and shut the door. Kath sat on the floor and giggled. I left her there and went to find the kitchen.

Maybe I wasn't the world's worst slob after all.

I picked a pair of knickers off the percolator and dropped them on the floor. Then I scraped a couple of inches of mud out of its innards and started a fresh brew. While it burped and bubbled I went to find out what she was doing.

It looked like she'd given up on the idea of getting upright and decided to go back out the front door. Luckily she couldn't make it as high as the latch.

I got her on to her feet and propped her up. 'You just came in,' I said kindly. 'No point going out again yet.' She turned a pretty shade of green and I did a sharp left into the bathroom and left her to get on with it. She clung to the lavatory bowl like it was going up and down on a rough sea. I really sympathised with her. Tomorrow's headache was going to be a whammy.

By and by the bathroom noises stopped and the cistern flushed. I cocked an ear and heard water running into the handbasin. I moved bread, cornflakes, two empty take-aways and half a jar of jam off the kitchen table along with two mugs, a cereal bowl and a gunged up plate. Then I filled two clean mugs with coffee and went to find Kath. She was walking slowly along with one hand on the wall, holding her head as if she was scared it might fall off. I said, 'The coffee's brewed, can you make to the kitchen?' Her chin moved down a fraction and then stabilised. I guessed that meant yes.

I hung around watching the clock tick past midnight until I'd got two cups of coffee into her, and after that hoped she'd be sober enough not to throw up in her sleep and choke. I tipped what was left in the percolator into the mug in front of her and said I had to go. She mumbled that was OK, one hand still supporting her head, elbow on the table. I picked up my bag. She gulped down more coffee and moaned, 'God, what was I drinking?'

'Looked like just about everything they had on offer,' I said cheerfully. 'Shorts, lager, rum and coke, oh, and let's not forget two glasses of red wine and a couple of tequila sunrises.'

She looked at me with cloudy eyes. 'I feel like hell.'

'Want some aspirin?'

'No, it'll make me throw up again.' She closed her eyes and put out her free hand when I started to walk away. I stopped again impatiently.

'Look, Kath, it's after midnight. I need some sleep.'

'Something to tell you,' she said thickly. ''Bout Lomas.' I backed up a little; if I didn't hear her out now she wouldn't be anywhere near this talkative tomorrow. She popped her eyes open to make sure I was still the same person, then closed them again. I opened the blind and clicked off the overhead. The combination of reflected hall light and orange street glow made it into a different room.

I went back to the table.

'What about Lomas?'

'Don't *shout*,' she pleaded. 'And sit down – I can't see you.' I sighed and sat. 'If I wasn't so damn drunk I wouldn't be telling you this,' she said with self-perception. 'Wouldn't tell you now 'cept Jeannie was a friend. Right?'

'Right.'

'He's an arsehole,' she said inelegantly. 'Big – farting – arsehole. Him and Francine both. Arseholes.' She lapsed into silence again. I couldn't believe I'd almost missed such a valuable insight. I checked the clock, sighed, and thought how good it would be to roll into bed. She pushed the mug away and let her head fall on the table. When I eased up off the chair the damn thing squeaked. Kath mumbled, 'Arsehole. Screwing Jeannie an' she didn't . . .'

I hate it when people go to sleep in the middle of a conversation. Didn't what for God's sake? Want to do it? Know Lomas was an arsehole? I shook her a little and an eye opened. 'Come on, Kath,' I begged. 'Lomas was screwing Jeannie and she didn't what?'

'Know 'bout him . . . fucking . . .' the eye closed and the last word came out on a sigh I'd have missed if I hadn't got down to her level, '. . . Franny . . .' I listened to her snore and fought down an urge to do more shaking. At times like that it's really hard to let things be.

It was close on two when I rolled into bed and I was so tired I don't even remember doing it. I just fell down a black pit with no dreams, no thoughts, no nothing until I woke up too late to drag myself out for a run. I stood under the shower and waited for the spray to wash sleep out of my eyes. They felt heavy, like someone had filled them up with lead shot. I wondered what Kath's felt like. I also wondered if she'd remember letting me in on Lomas's sex life, or if she'd still been too drunk to notice.

One thing was for sure – if she hadn't made the whole thing up Francine hadn't been such a good friend to Jeannie after all. Which left me grappling with the problem of why Francine would tell me about Lomas and Jeannie in the first place. You'd think if they'd both been bedding the same male she'd have kept quiet about it. I only let that puzzle worry me for as long as it took to get a bowl of cereal and turn on the radio. Nice as it was to know I wasn't acutely brain dead, following such difficult thoughts was still a chore. I couldn't work out why I felt so hung-over when I'd been sipping tonics all night. Maybe alcohol was like cigarette smoke, breathe it in and you get the pain without the pleasure.

Such theories are interesting but not thinking at all was better . . .

Around ten Nicholls rang me at work to ask what I was doing. He

147

sounded cheerful. I explained the calculation I was busy with in minute detail, but for some reason that didn't seem to be what he wanted. 'Tonight,' he said.

'You didn't say that,' I told him. 'What you ask is what you get.' He said darkly if it was it had to be the first time, and how about if he came round with a take-away about eight. I tried not to sound too eager. After last night there were a few questions of my own I wanted to ask and it wouldn't do to raise suspicions. I said, 'How about making it nine? I have a few errands to do.' I swear sometimes such prescience scares me. We fixed on that and I hung up and tried to remember where I was at. I'd just about worked out what it was about that particular set of figures that worried me when Martin phoned up and asked if he could drop by the flat. I told him if he could make it around six-thirty we'd have plenty of time to talk. He sounded really down and my heart plummeted.

Knowing I have to share somebody's grief is a real burden; it's the kind of thing that makes me want to hide away in some distant place where nothing bad ever happens.

I tried to pull my mind back on to what I was supposed to be doing, but it kept wandering away down other paths, especially on to Lomas and the cheating way he'd been getting his jollies. If it was true. The problem is it's so easy to believe erroneous things about people you don't like. The temptation to telephone Kath was so great I had to keep dragging my hand back from the phone. If I hadn't known what a lousy hangover she had to have, I'd have succumbed.

My mind wandered on to troilism and played around with it for a while. How would Jeannie have felt about that kind of thing? Sometimes the nicest of people have the unlikeliest of sex lives, but I couldn't see Jeannie taking to three in a bed any better than I would – or knowingly sharing a lover.

My mind flicked back to Will and the pain of discovering his depth of deceitfulness. It had really knocked me out for a while. If Jeannie had experienced the same sequence of events, maybe dropping out of sight had been avoidance tactics.

When Pete touched my shoulder I jumped a mile. Talk about action and reaction. He took his hand away like I'd slapped it. 'That's jumpy,' he said, 'what's the problem?'

'No problem, Pete, I guess my mind was taking time out. Sorry about that.' I tapped the file in front of me. 'I'll have this back with you this afternoon.'

'Right,' he said, and stayed where he was. 'This garage you know about . . . ?'

'Charlie's Car Repairs. Having trouble?'

'Some,' he admitted. 'Where is it exactly?' I drew him a little map.

'Tell him you're a friend,' I said, 'and he'll work wonders.' Then I remembered how he hadn't got back to me yet about Sidney. 'On second thoughts,' I amended, 'tell him you're a high ranking tax officer and scare the shit out of him.'

24

I brewed coffee, made sandwiches and opened chocolate biscuits, piling everything on to a tray so all I had to do was carry it into the sitting-room when Martin arrived.

When he came he started out by apologising for being there at all. I told him it was good to see him again and I was glad he could drop by. He looked doubtful about that, saying when I'd heard what he was going to ask of me I might change my mind. He looked paler than before and seemed to have lost a little weight, but given the circumstances that didn't surprise me. What did was the fact that he wore a suit and tie on a day when humidity was climbing through the ceiling.

Maybe the greenhouse effect is for real, not a figment of imagination like the mini-ice-age. All the freakish weather patterns we've been having these last few years it has to be something like that.

I got busy pouring coffee. 'If you want to get rid of the jacket, feel free,' I said. 'There are hangers in the hall closet, or if you're not that picky just dump it on a chair.' He took a look at the open window and the busy electric fan I'd picked up cheap on the second-hand market and seemed to realise for the first time that it was hot. He shrugged his arms out of the lightweight grey worsted, folded it neatly and laid it on a chair, sticking a finger behind the knot of his tie and loosening it up before he sat down. The movements were automatic, like he'd engaged autopilot and wasn't back in his seat yet.

I handed him coffee and a plate. He put the coffee on the floor, and looked at the plate like he didn't know what to do with it. I helped myself to a sandwich and nudged the rest of the pile nearer to him.

'I . . . um . . . Coffee's fine.'

'Hey, come on,' I said. 'Eat. I bet you haven't had a bite since lunch-time.' I watched his hand reach out obediently. What was I? A nanny? Any minute now I'd be telling him to eat up his greens. After the first couple of mouthfuls he seemed to latch on to the fact that eating might not be all that bad an idea. I nibbled frugally and watched the pile vanish. Maybe I was wrong about lunch, maybe he hadn't eaten since breakfast. Heat and hunger make unhealthy friends. When his skin began to look a little less like he'd just fed a vampire I asked how his mother was doing. He lifted eyebrows and shoulders simultaneously.

'Talking about coming back to Bramfield.'

'Let me know when she does, I'll drop by and see her.'

'She'd like that, but I don't want her to move home for a while yet, she still needs sticks to get around with and I can do without the extra worry.' He looked awkward. 'Leah, it's been a hell of a day. You know they won't release Jeannie's body? I've been closeted with the coroner trying to get a firm date, but all he'd talk about were police investigations. I thought once there'd been a *post mortem* all that was done with.'

'There are all kind of good reasons why coroners won't sanction burial,' I said. 'For one thing, if the defence drag their feet when the culprits come to trial and then start demanding an independent *post mortem*, disinterring a coffin is distressing for the relatives. Coroners know that, so they like to work on the principle of least harm.'

'Couldn't happen to Jeannie anyway; when the time comes to do it we've decided on cremation. I think it's what she would have wanted.'

If he'd told that to the coroner he'd provided another good reason not to sign a release. I wondered if he realised that. I said, 'How did her father take it? Does he know what's happened?' Martin dropped his eyes and looked embarrassed. 'Forget I asked that,' I told him quickly, 'it's none of my business.'

'No, you're right,' Martin said, 'he should be told – should have been told,' he amended. 'But I can't think of the best way to do it. How much did Jeannie tell you about her home life?'

'I know things weren't right between your parents if that's what you mean, and that your father walked out, but I don't know any more than that. Hasn't he kept in touch?'

'*Christ*!' he said.

Me and my big mouth.

I started to apologise but he cut me short. 'That's what happens with

152

assumptions,' he said. 'I assumed you'd know the whole story without stopping to think it wasn't anything Jeannie would have boasted about. There were some things about her life she didn't even share with *us*.' Interest pricked. Sixth sense isn't exactly my strong point, but right then it stretched itself out of slumber long enough to tell me to listen good. I hung on his next words. He said, 'Jeannie and I have different fathers,' and kept his eyes on me, watching for a reaction.

'Relax,' I said. 'It's still a secret, nobody's going to find out from me. Want some more coffee?'

I busied myself playing hostess and worked on a way to ease out the name of Jeannie's father. Such delicate things need to be done diplomatically and diplomacy isn't a strong point either.

I poured us both a refill.

He said, 'If you want to hear the finer details it'd help to talk about it, and it can't harm Jeannie now. It might even help me come up with a way to break the news.'

Conscience is a terrible thing, it comes up and bothers me at the most inopportune times. I latched on to his saying it'd help him to talk it through and let that decide me – that and a sneaky feeling he'd meant to tell me about Jeannie's father all along.

I said, 'Is that the something you were hoping I'd do for you? Break it to him?'

His brows gathered up in a frown. 'What I came to ask was if you'd pack Jeannie's clothes and take them to Oxfam or somewhere. I've cleared out the stuff she left at home and I can't face doing it again.'

I did some frowning of my own. Go through Jeannie's things, handle her possessions? I remembered all that happening when Gran died. Everything looking sad, like it knew she'd never touch it again.

He said, 'It was a bad idea, I'm sorry.'

I made excuses. 'There might be all kinds of things you'd want to keep. Jewellery, family items I wouldn't know about.'

'If you could deal with her clothes I could manage the rest of her stuff. The only things I'd want to hold on to would be photographs. Anything else . . .' He shrugged. 'I could take the small things back to my mother.'

'She might want other things too, things that gave Jeannie pleasure. Have you discussed it with her?'

'Not in detail.' I didn't say anything. 'All right,' he agreed. 'I take your point, I'll come back down and take everything else back with me. The truth is I'm not a hoarder, if I haven't used a thing for a month I throw it out.' His shoulders moved dismissively. 'It's the way I am, excess baggage bogs me down.'

'Bogs me down too,' I said. 'But some things I plan to carry through life with me.'

'Look, I already said it was a bad idea, I don't want to push you into doing something you'd be uncomfortable with.'

'When does it need to be done?'

'The rent runs out at the end of the month.'

Some decisions are easier to make than others. I told him I'd clear out her clothes and leave the rest to him. It wasn't all friendship and altruism. Helping out Martin gave me a legitimate excuse to go over the flat again, this time without size nines running interference.

He nodded agreement and said, 'About Jeannie's father . . . The point is I've never met him, and Mum's in no fit state to do anything. In the circumstances I just don't know how to approach it. I mean, if I find him what do I say? I'm your daughter's half-brother, come to tell you she's dead? I'm useless at that kind of thing, Leah.'

Who wasn't?

I said, 'If it's an easy way you're looking for I don't think there is one. Where does he live?'

'I don't know, I'd need to find out from his solicitor.'

'You don't have an address?' He shook his head. 'So how about the phone book?'

'Unlisted.'

'If push comes to shove you could let his solicitor break the news. It'd be easier.'

'It wouldn't make me feel too good about myself though.'

'Did Jeannie and her father know each other?'

'Not until after my dad walked out; when that happened Mum told her the truth. It explained why the person she'd always thought was her father never liked her over-much. I found out about it at the same time, and it was a shock for both of us. Jeannie asked for her real father's name, and a couple of days later played hookey from school to go looking for him. She was gone three days and Mum was frantic. When she finally turned up on his doorstep he sent her back in a limo with a chauffeur.'

A chauffeured limo? Who was this guy?

'So Jeannie knew where he lived, but she didn't tell you?'

He looked embarrassed again. 'Jeannie's known all along where he is but she didn't even tell Mum. It's the way he wanted it. Some kind of game with him, I guess.'

'I couldn't stand that,' I said candidly. 'I'd be just too nosy not to track him down.'

'Ever tried following a limo on a bicycle?' he said drily. 'Jeannie saw me through the back window and said if I did it again she'd leave home.'

'How did your mother feel about the visits?'

'She trusted him. I think she was pleased for Jeannie, and as far as Jeannie was concerned he made up for all the snubs she'd had from my father. She used to say, "If I'm ever in trouble I just have to crook a finger. He'll be there so fast air will burn." '

I wished to hell Martin hadn't told me that, like I wished her father hadn't made promises he couldn't keep. Such things always lead to disappointment. I said, 'It sounds like they grew close. Your mother never got jealous?'

'Why would she? Jeannie didn't come out of a one-night stand,' he said with defensive vigour. 'I wasn't all that old when it happened, but I remember Mum being really unhappy. I didn't know it at the time but Dad was working overseas and not writing home. He'd do that, disappear on a job and only money coming into the bank to let her know he was alive. She'd be crying all the time, and I'd wonder if it was me.'

'Some men have thoughtlessness built in,' I said. 'You still see him?'

'Now and then. He remarried when the divorce was made absolute and it puts me in a difficult spot. I didn't like the way he treated Mum, but he was good to me.'

'Sounds like they should have married different people.'

He squinted at me. 'Mum still has a photograph of her and Jeannie's father, taken when they were dancing together. She was slim and pretty and he looked like he could eat her. They look – *right* for each other. It lasted three or four months until Dad came home, and then ended.'

'But they kept in touch?'

'No. He found out about Jeannie when a mutual friend let the cat out of the bag. Of course Dad knew all along she wasn't his, he'd been away more than six months and he could count. He wouldn't give Mum extra money for baby things, so when Jeannie's father said he wanted to provide for her, Mum let him. I mean he could afford it, and it was the only way she could be sure Jeannie got more than the bare minimum. He paid her school fees and backed-up her university grant. It must have seemed a real irony when she went into Customs and Excise.'

'Why's that?' I said. 'Don't tell me he's a Customs dodger?'

'No, he owns a string of casinos and gets richer by the day, but I hear he has less legal interests too. If Jeannie knew about those she kept it to herself, but you can see why her going into a branch of law enforcement seems ironic.'

I nodded, picking up signals. 'That isn't all that's worrying you though, is it? There's something else about her father.'

'When he hears what happened to her he'll want to know who's responsible.'

'Seems like a father's natural reaction.'

'Except that he'll try to deal with it himself. Aside from dodgy business interests he's a good man, Leah. I don't want him in trouble, in jail, or dead. If I chicken out long enough there'll be an arrest.'

'Maybe you're mixing up priorities,' I said. 'It sounds to me like he can look after himself, and the important thing is he knows about his daughter. I mean for God's sake, suppose he reads it in the paper?'

He looked weary.

I said, 'You knew I'd say that, didn't you?'

'I needed the extra push. Don't worry about it, Leah, it's my problem, I'll talk with his solicitor Monday a.m.'

'Maybe if I had his name I could come up with an address faster. Want me to ask around?'

'Dealing with Jeannie's stuff is help enough,' he said, and got up abruptly. He seemed uncomfortable at having told me so much and I hoped he wasn't regretting it. He gave me keys to the flat and said he had a long drive ahead of him. I told him I'd let him know when the flat was cleared, and any time he wanted to drop by and talk he was welcome. He thanked me for the coffee and sandwiches and got back into his jacket. I knew his anxiety to leave had a lot to do with the things he'd told me about Jeannie's father. I guessed he'd suddenly begun to wonder where my job ended and friendship began.

A lot of other people have the same problem, and on rare occasions I even worry about it myself. Not then though. Jeannie's father was out of bounds. I told Martin that and he loosened up again. I waited for him to tell me the name I'd been waiting to hear, but we got to the door without him doing that.

I said, 'Martin, trust me, it's like waiting for the other shoe to drop; if I'm going to sleep tonight I need to know the name of Jeannie's father.'

He dithered in the doorway for so long I felt for sure he'd leave without telling me. Then he let out a long sighing breath and said, 'Sidney Vincent.'

For a couple of seconds the name meant nothing – and then it did. I said, 'Oh, *sh-iit!*' and knew why Charlie hadn't got back to me. Hot drops spilled out of my eyes and dripped uncontrollably.

Martin came back inside and folded me up in his arms and that just made things worse. It took a while for me to dry up enough to tell him he didn't need to worry about contacting Sidney Vincent's solicitor, thanks to my stumble-footing around Sidney knew all there was to know about Jeannie already.

And I'd been the dumbo who'd unwittingly sent him the news.

25

Between Martin's leaving and Nicholls' arrival I spent a long time soaking in the bath. Crying has never enhanced my appearance. Swollen eyes, coupled with a red and bulbous nose and a persistent sniff fail to make an attractive picture.

When I'd accumulated enough wrinkles I dried off and powdered nicely, pulling on a shortie top and white cotton mini that would keep Nicholls' mind from functioning at optimum level. Such subterfuges are a necessary part of life.

I cleaned out the coffee machine, loaded it up again, and dealt industriously with the two days of washing-up stacked in the sink. Doing that chore got my brain bored enough to come up with a neat pile of questions to ask Nicholls. I arranged them in inverse order of importance. Getting information out of him is something that has to be approached systematically.

He came five minutes early, looking a little anxious, and examined me with wary blue eyes. I watched the look fade into something different as he took in my neat little outfit. I could almost hear the thought sequence tumbling over itself in his head. I took the brown paper carrier-bag out of his hand and hipped prettily towards the kitchen. He closed the door and came right after me. Sometimes I wonder what I'll do when I'm fifty and that kind of thing doesn't work any more.

I slipped the first question in as he tried out the wine I'd picked up on the way home. It was a real easy one just to get him started.

I said sweetly, 'I suppose you picked up Tom Peep already?' He put the glass down and got the wary look back.

'Not exactly.'

Not exactly? What did that mean? He had the guy's photograph for pity's sake. I hung on to the smile. 'I – uh, guess he's gone to ground? Left town or something?'

'Not exactly.'

I could feel the smile stretching itself out, any time now it'd turn into a grimace. And I'd tried so hard to start off on the right foot too.

'Maybe I missed something?' I said.

'Not . . .'

'If you say "exactly" once more you're out of here,' I snapped.

He said, 'He won't bother you again.'

'You killed him?' He got a set look and put his head down; concentrating on food is something he's good at. 'Nicholls, I have a right to know, I'm the one he was following.'

'It was a mistake, can't we leave it at that?'

'No, we damn well can't.'

Whoo! Whatever had happened to my master plan? I let out a little slack.

'I didn't mean this to turn into a fight,' I said sadly. 'It's worrying not knowing why somebody's been following me around . . . especially after Jeannie . . .' I let my voice trail off. He looked at me suspiciously. I blinked a couple of time.

'His name is Alders, and Lomas put him up to it. He wanted to know what you were up to.'

'Lomas! Lomas had me followed? That guy's a pain in the butt. You know he was sleeping with Jeannie?' This time he stopped in mid-swallow, juggling the food around the level of his Adam's apple before he let it go.

'Who told you that?'

'Doesn't matter who told me, it's a fact, and now I come to think of it he's probably been making the crappy telephone calls too.'

'Just because you don't like him . . .'

'Don't like him? Sometimes, Nicholls, you're really good at understatement. The only nice thing about him is he won't be here too long.'

'What you haven't thought about, Leah, is how badly he wants to pull this out of the fire.'

'And what you haven't thought about,' I said, 'is how easy it would have been for Lomas to have nudged it in there in the first place. I know for a fact every other team member had their bank account checked. Did somebody take a look at his too?'

'Come on, Leah, you know that kind of check never turns up anything but a moron.'

'Really? Jeannie was a moron?'

'Leah . . .'

'Eat your food, Nicholls, it's going cold.'

'It can go in the microwave. Shut up, and listen to some little things Lomas has on you.' I folded my arms and watched him tick off fingers. 'Gaining illegal entrance, interfering with evidence, harassing witnesses, disturbing police surveillance, obstructing investigations and probably, for all I know, withholding evidence.'

'Hey,' I said. 'You've got four fingers left – keep counting. Don't forget being rude to police officers.' We glared at each other. 'Going to charge me?'

'Lomas would like that.'

'Bet he would.'

'There's a warrant in my desk.'

I stared at him. 'Why'd you take it out?'

'I didn't take it out, I had it stopped, and it wasn't easy. You're not a law officer, Leah, you're a tax officer and I won't always be around to bail you out.'

'Who got the warrant?'

'Don't miss the point.'

'I won't.' I shoved food around my plate. 'Martin came by today, he wants me to clear Jeannie's things out of the flat.'

'Why?'

I shrugged. 'He's got a lot on his shoulders. I've got the keys just in case anybody complains about me breaking and entering.' I looked across the table and saw he wasn't smiling.

'It isn't funny, Leah.'

'I'm not making a joke.' Neither of us said anything for a while. I guess we both were wondering where it was all taking us. I said, 'He's really been getting under your skin hasn't he?'

'Who?'

'Lomas.'

'Lomas is doing his job,' Nicholls said flatly. 'He's a first rate police officer, on a difficult secondment, he outranks me, and he's under a lot of pressure. In theory if he says jump, I jump.'

'Aren't there rules about sexual relationships with subordinates?'

'Don't get back on to that again.'

'It's the truth. I think that's why she cut out. The relationship turned sour.'

'Where'd you get the information?'

'Are we calling a truce?'

'Depends on the terms.'

I drank up my wine and poured another glass. I wasn't sure how we'd got to this point in the conversation, but somewhere along the way it had slipped away from me. I'd asked a simple question about Tom Peep and it'd got down to battle lines. There was a sick feeling in the bottom of my stomach. I didn't like where we were going, and from the look on Nicholls' face he didn't like it either. Collisions are never pretty and we seemed to be doing it a lot lately.

I said, 'When I went to the Oak, Jeannie wasn't dead and her mother had asked me to find her – which is also why I was in her flat.'

'I know that.'

'I also told you about Donna and the bed-sit upfront – you didn't have to drag it out of me. OK? That being so I don't see how Lomas has a beef.'

'And the bank?'

'If you remember, Lomas had already told me the investigation was closed. I didn't plan to leave Jeannie carrying somebody else's guilt.'

He played around with his fork and didn't look at me. 'That's everything?'

Shit! How much did he know? Sometimes I swear he can read minds. I sorted through the things I hadn't told him and filed a couple away out of sight. Then I told him about Sam, and The Feathers, and taking Kath home. What I left out were Francine and Sidney. Sidney had no place in Jeannie's death, and it was up to Kath to break the news about Francine. If her mood stayed anything like last night's she wouldn't need much persuading.

'That's it?' he said.

'That's it.'

He got up and put his take-away in the microwave. I took that as a good sign. If he'd been in a real peeve he'd have sulked a little first, and if we'd really been on the rocks he'd have been half-way down the street.

I spent a couple of minutes examining that possibility. It was the second time in a week I'd been forced to think about Nicholls moving out of my life and it didn't fill me with joy. It wasn't that I couldn't do without him – I'd been doing fine before he came along, and I value the single life – it was just that as relationships go I knew ours wasn't worked out yet, and I hate to give up on a thing before it's ended.

I filled my glass again and looked at the bottle. There wasn't much left which meant Nicholls wasn't going to get his fair share. Life can be tough. The microwave pinged. I put the bottle down. It made a little thud on the table.

Nicholls brought his plate back and looked at the wine level. He fished out his car keys and left. Fine! If that was the way he felt. I stalked to the microwave and did some warming up of my own. Maybe when I'd cleared my plate I'd eat his too, anxiety always makes me hungry.

I was still thinking about that when he came back. He set a fresh bottle of wine on the table and started eating again. I came back to my seat and examined the label. 'Good stuff,' I said. 'How come?'

He shrugged, prised out the cork, and said, 'Celebration.' There's nothing like a good smooth wine for mellowing the mood.

It was a long time later before I brought it up again. We were tangled up the way people are when they've had good sex and are too spent to move. I played around with his hair and felt a little energy flowing back.

'Nicholls?'

'Mmm?'

'Why'd you leave the wine down in the car?' He eased his leg a little and didn't answer. I bit his ear.

'Ow!'

'You're pretty vulnerable,' I pointed out. 'Think what happened to the Babette guy.'

He came up on his elbows and said he'd left it there because if I hadn't told him about Sam and the other stuff he'd have walked away, and I knew he meant for good. I didn't try for a flip answer. What was the point? He was only telling me what I'd known all along. He needed me to trust him. Uneasily I remembered Francine and Sidney, neatly filed away. Guilt blew through me like a hot torch but I still couldn't give that last inch.

Maybe if he didn't know about it, it didn't matter.

Self-deceit never works.

26

From a security point of view habits are a real let down. Saturday mornings I extend the length of my run, pacing myself over the bypass and down to the park, where I join other early morning health freaks on the perimeter path. Going the same time every week you get to know familiar faces, people run along with you for a while and exchange snippets of news. That Saturday was no different except the humidity was so high it slowed everybody down. We sweated along and complained about the weather, and I wondered what a lot of people would find to talk about if we suddenly stopped having any.

I completed two circuits and turned out on to the road, heading for home. A lot of park runners get there by car, so when I heard an engine start up behind me I didn't think anything of it. It cruised along and ran by the side of me. Big, black and shiny. Up ahead a milk float coughed and rattled. Except for me, the float and the car, nothing else was on the road. The black shape pulled ahead and its driver got out, mid-thirties, big and beefy. I eyed him warily, keeping close in to the park wall and feeling my heart pick up speed. He pulled open the back door and waited for me to get level. What was this? I performed a neat turn and sprinted across to the other side of the road. A window whirred like an electric insect. I squinted over my shoulder. Sidney's head was framed in the bare space. I stopped running and he said, 'Got a minute, love?'

I crossed back slowly and wished Charlie hadn't passed on the message. The driver still had hold of the nearside door. I climbed in and sat down, sweaty-hot and fuming with BO. Sidney didn't seem to notice. He said, 'Good to see you again, Leah. You wanted help, and I didn't give it. I'm sorry about that.'

He was sorry? My throat dried up. I cleared it. 'Sidney – I . . .'

He nodded. 'Didn't think it'd take you long to find out. Don't worry about it. Are you still having trouble?'

I shook my head. 'Nothing I can't handle.'

'Seen anything of Jeannie's ma?'

Some questions come wrapped up in barbed wire. Had Charlie told him about the hit and run? Probably. Had I linked the hit and run with Jeannie. I couldn't remember. But if Sidney didn't know Stella Johnson had been hurt, telling him about it now would make things worse. Shit! I stared wildly at the back of the driver's neck looking for inspiration. Sidney said, 'Let's hear it. Something's happened to her as well, hasn't it?'

'I – uh – she's getting better.'

'Better from what?'

I turned around so I could look straight at him. 'A hit and run.' His eyes flickered ever so slightly. If I hadn't been looking I'd have missed it. I guessed he used to play a lot of poker. 'It happened before Jeannie.' There, I'd said her name. The world hadn't exploded and the devil hadn't come to get me. Maybe like some of my other sins, the carelessly brutal sharing of knowledge would be forgiven. Or maybe everybody's sins are forgiven and it's just they can't forgive themselves.

Sidney took in the new piece of bad news and sat statue still, absorbing it. His face looked older and harder, a man it would be unwise to cross. I hadn't seen that face before and I wondered what would happen if he found Jeannie's killer before the police. The worry must have shown because he smiled and turned into the Sidney I knew, dapper in a three-button polo and linen golfing pants. Not someone to buy insurance from, or trust your mother with, but someone who looked after his friends.

He said, 'Did you know you had a tail?'

'What?'

'Stuck to you like a second skin. Neat little blue shorts and a headband. Didn't know which side he was on so it seemed best to let him have a little sleep in the summer-house.'

'How'd you spot him?'

He tapped his nose. 'Experience. This hit and run. Any connection?'

'There might be,' I said cautiously, and told him about the phone calls, and Jeannie's letter.

'Know who's doing it?'

'I don't even know why, Sidney, never mind who.'

'I found that red Astra. Turns out he was one of the blues. Didn't call him Tony though. Think I should send him a few flowers and a sorry note?'

'You didn't . . . ?'

He shrugged. 'His own fault, it's nothing permanent.' I was glad to hear him say that, and I wondered why Nicholls hadn't mentioned it the previous night. It seemed like he was still holding on to secrets too, and that made me feel a lot better.

Sidney said, 'Still going out with your policeman?'

'If you mean Nicholls, we're still friends.'

'Bit more than that from what I've heard.'

'People love to talk.'

'Thought he might have told you where CID was heading.'

'He has this quaint idea that what I don't know can't hurt me.' I eyed him. 'If he was close he'd tell me, but things keep going wrong.'

'What kind of things?'

'How much did Jeannie tell you about her job?'

'Her being strictly on the side of the law you mean? Enough. She was chuffed working for NCIS, gave her a chance to make things up with her mother.'

I said, 'That was your doing wasn't it, Sidney?'

'I gave her a bit of encouragement in that direction, she didn't need much.'

'Martin came to see me yesterday. That's when I found out you were her father. He'd been trying to find a way to get to you without going through solicitors. I couldn't believe how dumb I'd been.'

'Use your head, love. How are you supposed to know if nobody tells you?' He went silent, busy with his own thoughts.

I said, 'He was planning to contact them Monday.'

He turned his head. 'You know how it is with me, Leah, I don't give out my home address. Make more enemies than friends, that's my problem. There's a few right now I'd be glad to be rid of but that's beside the point.'

'Jeannie found you.'

'Yes, she did. Had a lot in common with you. My girl. Set her mind to find something and she found it. Probably got her killed.'

'Sidney, I . . .'

His eyes hardened up again. 'I've lost a daughter, don't go the same way through stubbornness.' I stared at him. 'You're scared I might get

167

there first,' he said flatly. 'Don't be. Put me in the picture and show a little trust.'

Trust! There was that word again. I did a little mind editing. I'm getting good at that. I left out Lomas, and Jeannie's love life, and told him the rest.

'Somebody's cleaning up as he goes along,' he said when I was through. 'And I don't like the sound of these phone calls.'

'Nicholls is handling it,' I said. 'I'll be fine.' I squinted at my watch.

'Be worrying about you, will he?'

'You worry about your own private life,' I said. 'I don't have one, the whole damn world knows my secrets.'

'Hear he cooks too.'

I put my hand on the door. 'Better go, or like you said, he'll be getting itchy.'

'Drive you back if you like, drop you out of sight?'

I looked at the sagging tree leaves and the limp milkman, and told myself a cool ride was better than a hot run. I said thanks and leaned back. 'You've changed your driver,' I said. 'What happened to the last one?'

'Got put out of action a month back.'

I shifted round again. 'What kind of trouble have you got, Sidney? Anything I can bully Nicholls into helping with?'

'Just some outsiders persuading me to retire.' He grinned and gave me back my own words. 'Nothing I can't handle. Sent the wife on holiday and pulled up the drawbridge. It's yourself you need to worry about, Leah. Terrible Twosome. Ring a bell?'

School nicknames die hard, and with Jeannie gone it was a onesome. I could feel my face drop.

He said, 'You haven't told me everything. Jeannie used to get the same look. Keep back what she didn't want me to know about and act innocent. It was a game with her like it is with you.' He shifted a little. 'I want a favour, Leah.'

I nodded. 'It's what I owe.'

'If you get there first – *tell me before Nicholls.*' He was leaning across the seat, years stripped away to the man he once was, hard and handsome, and someone not to mess with. Nothing of the Sidney I'd known up to then was left. It was the second time I'd seen that change of face.

I shivered and he drew back.

A couple of minutes later the car stopped. I put a hand on the door handle. He said, 'Take care.'

I said, 'There's another Astra, Sidney. Red. Jeannie had some trouble with the driver, and like I told Charlie, his name is Tony and he did business with Ed and Rassa. I don't know what part he played in subsequent events, but I do know he had one.'

'If he's around,' said Sidney, 'I'll find him.' I nodded and started to get out. He said, 'Stay safe.'

'And you, Sidney. Any messages I get I'll pass on through Charlie.' He shook his head and gave me a card embossed with his name but no address. On the back he'd scribbled a telephone number.

'Twenty-four hours a day that,' he said. 'And somebody ready to go.'

I watched the car reverse and drive back the way it had come then picked up a little speed myself. Nicholls puts together a mean breakfast but he gets really impatient when I keep him waiting.

I didn't give thought to the sleeper in the summer-house until Nicholls asked which way I'd come home. His voice had a weeny note of anxiety and the two things connected together in a flash of enlightenment. I didn't let Nicholls know that. I told him I'd come home the back way for a change, rumpled his hair, and asked innocently why he'd asked. He loaded up a piece of toast with marmalade and said curiosity. I guessed the sleeper had made good time to a telephone when he woke up, which probably meant he didn't have too bad a headache.

I felt a vague regret that I hadn't got a peek at the neat little blue shorts.

27

Nicholls left early to put in a little honest work while I lazed around and tried to read the paper. For some reason such a leisurely occupation failed to grab my concentration. Around ten I shoved the keys Martin had given me into my handbag and drove to Jeannie's flat. It looked much the same as it had the last time I'd been there except that the bankbook had gone. I guessed that was in a plastic bag somewhere lined up as police evidence.

I found a roll of bin liners and tore one off, emptying the fridge and freezer and adding opened packets of food out of the cupboards before I took it down to the bins. When I'd finished with the kitchen I moved to the sitting-room, riffling book pages and trying to think where I'd put something if I didn't want it found. Such tactics were a waste of time, the police don't overlook obvious hiding places, but I felt impelled to try. By twelve there was a ragged line of black bags in the hall, and I'd come to the conclusion that whoever went through the flat in the first place had found what he or she was looking for. And if they'd missed out on anything Nicholls' crew had found it. Somebody had made a half-hearted attempt at hanging clothes back up in the wardrobe, and I left those until last, feeling around in all the pockets before folding the garments neatly and stowing them in a sack, hoping the roll didn't run out before I'd finished. I was down to the end of the rail and flagging when I found the pink receipt. Jeannie's pocket habits had been no better than my own, and a sad pile of tissues, sweet wrappers and odd coppers sat at my feet to prove it. I guess the police had been too finicky to pay them much attention. I smoothed out the pink paper. The date in ballpoint was July fifteenth, and beneath it a scribbled 35mm/C/24'. Printed in one corner was 'RBP'. I tucked it in my back pocket and cleared out the last of

Jeannie's stuff, carrying the bags downstairs and piling them in the car until it looked like I was doing a rubbish run. It gave me a weird feeling, driving it all away.

I gave Oxfam a miss – Saturdays the roads around there are so parked up I'd be running back and forth like a demented hare – and pulled up outside Barnardo's on double yellow lines. The woman inside looked at the black plastic sacks like she'd had rubbish dumped there before. I smiled at her encouragingly and went back for more. By the time I got back with the second load she looked happier. I finished emptying the car and backed off from her thank yous, saying I was doing it for a friend.

I cruised around hopefully until someone pulled out of a restriction-free parking spot. I swung into the empty space, locked up, and took a short cut through Boots, coming out almost opposite a shop window stuffed with cameras and photography equipment. Richard Black Photographics had been there as long as I could remember, the shop unchanging but the cameras increasing in price and complexity. I fished around in my back pocket for the pink photographer's receipt I'd found at Jeannie's, and handed it in. It took a little time to locate the processed prints. I waited patiently. The shop's only been there a few decades and I guess they need a little more time to get organised.

All the time he was rooting through boxes, the assistant kept up a monotonous whine about the length of time people leave things lying around without paying. I bit back the sharp retort that came to mind. If I antagonised him now it could take even longer.

By and by he came up with the right packet and asked if I'd like to check them out. I told him winningly that I just knew they'd be the right ones and paid over the money, tucking the packet in my handbag and leaving him to tidy up. By then there were another half-dozen people clutching pink slips and looking unhappy so I guessed it would take him a while.

Half way back to the car my stomach started yelping about emptiness. A greasy smell drifted up the street. I quit counting calories and headed into the market café, loading up a tray with tea, bread and butter, and crispy fish and chips. Being Saturday the place was pretty full. I eyed a table with only one occupant and beat a beer-belly to it with time to spare. I was so damned hungry I didn't even look at who I was sharing with, just started eating before the rumbles embarrassed me. When I finally looked up Kath was watching me like I had spots. Don't tell me coincidences like that don't happen, they do, all the time. I swallowed down a hot mouthful and said, 'How's the head?'

'It's fine.' She chewed on a chunk of cod. 'Did I say thanks for taking me home?'

'A couple of times. It wasn't a problem.'

'Did I – uh, say anything else?'

'About what?'

'You know, things I shouldn't blow my mouth off about.'

'That's hard to say when I don't know what sort of things those are. We talked about Jeannie a while. Most of the time I was busy getting coffee down you.'

'Can't think why I drank so damn much, must have made a fool of myself.'

I shook my head. 'It didn't really hit you until you got outside. Except for trying to grope the bar-keep you behaved beautifully.'

She groaned. 'I didn't.'

''Fraid so. He strayed out to collect glasses.'

'I can't believe it. God, I'll never dare show my face in there again.'

'Hey, I don't think he minded, he probably does a lot of it himself,' I said reassuringly.

'Jake keeps waving his butt at me.'

'Guess he's hopeful.'

'Wouldn't tell me why he was doing it, the bastard.'

I grinned. 'Next time, give him a little pat, it's a sure fire cure.'

'Experience?'

'You bet.'

'Seriously though, did I hand out trade secrets?'

I shovelled food for a couple more seconds. 'You mentioned about Lomas being no gentleman.'

She eyed me warily. 'Clarify.'

'About his sleeping habits.'

'Jeannie?'

'Among others.'

'Don't pass it on,' she said.

'I already did. Not about Francine, that's none of my business, but Jeannie is different. If she was in that kind of relationship and it went sour, it could have contributed to a lot of things.'

'Great minds think alike,' she said. 'Who'd you tell?'

'Nicholls.'

'Is he doing anything about it?'

I shrugged. 'He knows Lomas and me rub each other up the wrong way so he'll probably check out his facts with you. Depends if you want to confirm it or not.'

'Why not, won't have to work with him much longer. You didn't mention Francine at all?'

'No. If you want to blow the whistle it's up to you.'

She finished up her meal and moodily watched me eat. 'I wasn't too pleased when Sam brought you along,' she said. 'I didn't see why we should have an outsider listening in.'

'I gathered. If it's any help I'd have felt the same.'

'I mean it's not as if you were actively involved.'

'Definitely not.'

'So why were you there?'

'Busybodying.' I handed her the plain unvarnished truth and she didn't believe me. If I'd told her a lie she'd have swallowed it whole.

'No,' she said. 'Honestly, you must have wanted something?'

'I thought one of you might have some extra bit of knowledge about Jeannie. But I was wrong.'

'Funny business, that bed-sit. None of us knew a damn thing about it until you turned it up.'

'I don't think Jeannie was ever in that place.'

Her eyes widened. 'She had to be, there were her fingerprints.'

'On what?' I took hold of her cup, then her knife and fork. 'Take them home,' I said. 'They'll prove I've been in your place. Bet there weren't prints on windowsills, doors . . .'

'There were prints on the door handle,' she protested.

'Handles come off.'

'What about the girl? Donna?'

'Donna saw a female who looked enough like Jeannie to be mistaken for her.' I drew a pattern on the plastic tablecloth with the fork handle. 'I gave her a lift into town later than night. She was waiting at the bus-stop with a couple of girl-friends and I dropped them off at The Cellar. I'd have sworn she wasn't on drugs so how come she died of an overdose?'

Kath said, 'I don't like that.'

'Makes two of us. And there's something else too. Did Jeannie smoke?'

'Hated the things.'

'The bed-sit Jeannie smoked. There were dog-ends on the outer windowsill and a purple Bic lighter under the bed. It had rolled behind a suitcase and I guess she didn't notice it was gone. The case was Jeannie's, I know that, it matched two others in her flat, and I guess the clothes were hers too, but it'd be easy enough to get both if they had her keys. They could have left the bankbook on the dressing-table at the same time they got her clothes.'

'Shit! What happened to the lighter?' She was staring at me as if I'd just said the place was on fire.

'It wasn't any help. I passed it on to Nicholls but Donna had polished the prints off. She was just too quick for me.'

'I'm here for two more weeks yet,' she said, leaning on the table. 'Anything else I don't know about?'

'Only guesses. Chloe at the Oak told me Ed and Rassa didn't do their own rough work anymore, but if Tony had offered enough money I think they'd make an exception. It looks very like they got what they deserved but for the wrong reason. Jeannie coming out of the water alive meant they'd fouled up. I don't know about the blues party, so don't ask. I don't even know who the third man was in Ed's car.'

'I can help you there,' she said. 'Mick Collins from the bed-sit. Snug in the boot with a bullet in his head. For an amateur you're not doing bad.'

'I was raised on a steady diet of cop shows.'

'Lucky you! Mine was James Last and *Little House on the Prairie*. Talk about censorship.' She laughed. 'Just goes to show – something or other I guess. Any more wild guesses?'

'None.' We looked at each other soberly, each of us busily replaying things we knew. She said. 'Are you thinking what I'm thinking?'

'Depends.' I said. 'If you're thinking there can't be two women running around in fancy dress, then yes, I am. If there was a bogus Jeannie at the bed-sit, and a bogus nurse at the hospital . . .'

' . . . We have to find one nasty lady,' she finished up for me. Her eyes had paled out and the skin around them looked tighter. She slung her bag strap over her shoulder and got up in a hurry.

'I'll come with you,' I said. 'I haven't heard your side yet.' She shook her head and backed off.

'Not now . . . Not yet . . . I'm sorry, Leah, I can't – not here, it'll have to wait.'

'Till when?'

'Tonight,' she said, picking up some speed. 'My place – eight o'clock?'

I drank up the near-cold tea and followed her out more slowly. Something was shaping up at the back of my brain like a sea-fret ghost. I couldn't quite see its form yet but if I just waited long enough it would become visible.

28

I got home around four and started up another coffee brew. Sometimes my own predictability worries me. I was about to settle down with Jeannie's snapshots and a mug of caffeine when the nuisance caller phoned to let me know I wasn't forgotten. Maybe he'd got tired of spending the money, this time all he said was, '*Goodbye, bitch.*' I'd miss him like I'd miss a thorn in the foot. I wondered how long it took from picking up the phone to Nicholls hearing the latest offering. Then I thought there were other things goodbye could mean too, and checked out security.

Closing up windows in scorching weather about equals sitting in an oven with the door shut. Heat rises, and there'd been times in the hot spell when it felt like I'd got the whole street's. So the windows stayed open. For pity's sake! It'd take a cat burglar to get up that high – or a window cleaner – or somebody less imaginative using the fire-escape.

The fire-escape is a sore point. I guess when the place was converted someone got their sums wrong. Getting on to the damn thing from my place entails standing in the bath – and that's the easy part. The hard bit is finding foothold so you can get out of the window. Ingress would be easier – which is why it stays closed. Like it was then.

Good grief, I wasn't that stupid!

I went to look anyway; there was nothing in the bath save a couple of stray pubic hairs. I swilled them down the plug-hole in case anybody sensitive should drop by.

Since when did a crank in a phone booth make me so jumpy? I padded back to the coffee-pot feeling foolish. It'd be really sick if it turned out to be Lomas after all.

I flicked through the prints. The first few showed the office party. Paper hats and half-eaten mince pies. Kath kissing Alan, Neil holding up the mistletoe. Jake half-heartedly pecking Francine's cheek. Jeannie and Kath puckered up either side of Neil and everybody looking happy. I set them aside together with more in the same vein, guessing Martin would be glad of them. One, I kept back. Jeannie with Lomas, and nothing half-hearted about their clinch. I wondered if Francine had been looking on like a good friend.

The next snaps were domestic, taken at her mother's home. Mrs Johnson hanging out the wash, peg-mouthed, waving Jeannie away. Molly laughing, yellow forsythia rampant behind her. I passed through that bunch quickly, like an interloper.

From the passage of time, Jeannie's photography had been spasmodic. It looked like the camera stayed forgotten unless she had something she wanted to record.

Parties, family, and Ed and Rassa outside the Royal Oak. What was it about that place? They were in the car-park, close up to Ed's Volvo, talking to a dark haired male. I wished she'd had a zoom. I got up off the kitchen chair and hunted out a magnifier. I hate to think I'll need one all the time someday. It worked wonders for clarity. The dark-haired guy was handing something to Ed, but even with the magnifier I couldn't make out what. Drugs? Money? A ticket for the peep-show? I checked out the male. Taller than Rassa, but not so tall as Ed, dark hair, late twenties. He didn't have Tony written across the back of his shirt, but I guessed that's who he was. I looked at the little dangly earring in his left ear and wondered how long the fashion would last. It isn't that I have anything against men wearing earrings – they can hang the damn things off their noses if they want to – it's just when half the male population wear them, they're not much good as identity indicators. The reflective glitter Don Simpson saw when Jeannie was dumped in the canal could have come from any of them. I followed the thought. Rassa driving, and Ed and Tony making sure she sank.

Some ideas are so unpleasant it would be nice to let go of them, but they tend to be the kind that are tenacious, like the thought of Jeannie calmly focusing a camera on the instruments of her destruction. The next print was almost identical to its fellow, except that Tony and Ed had shifted some and I could see more of Tony's face. Both photographs had been taken from the same vantage point and I tried to work out where it was, picturing the environs of the Royal Oak in my mind and walking around them until I fell over the Telecom box. It was the only accessible point that would have shown Ed and his buddies doing anything but chatting, and Jeannie had deliberately put herself in jeopardy to get it on film.

Why?

I put the magnifier down, topping up the cooling coffee and carrying it over to the window. A pair of cabbage whites played chase-me-Charlie across the lawn, dipping and sweeping and having fun. By and by one tired of the game and the other flew away. I watched the left-behind settle on a geranium leaf and throb gently. Humidity was dropping by the minute as the sun flexed up and got ready to end its sulk. I wished I believed in omens. The second cabbage white came back looking for its friend and they both flew away together.

I worried at a familiarity in Tony's face until the right memory button sent me rooting through a bunch of old newspapers in the hall closet. I don't hoard such things *per se*, but if there's something I might want to flick back to, it goes in the closet. From time to time when I feel energetic enough I dump a pile in the paper bank.

Luckily I hadn't done that for a while.

I spread the local broadsheet, eyes skipping from Ed and Rassa to the faces of those they supposedly mowed down at the blues party. Third from the left was Tony. I refolded the paper carefully and put it back in the closet. It looked like somebody was doing an awfully good job of tying up loose ends and the efficiency of it scared me. I thought about Jeannie and her spider's web theory. Maybe she'd been a lot closer to the truth than Sam thought. A spider's web is so sensitive that the spider knows instantly the slightest touch of the smallest fly, and that had to be what was happening here. She'd collided with an organisation that reacted with instant savagery to such things, and to do that they had to have an intelligence set-up NCIS must envy.

Sea fret came back into my mind with a dark swirl of whispering ghosts. Uneasily I blocked them out and moved back to the kitchen. The brew in the filter jug had waited around too long and tasted bitter. I drank it anyway, and looked at the rest of the prints.

A tall, good-looking guy, climbing out of a Porsche. I didn't recognise the locale but it was somewhere a lot more upmarket than the Oak. I grabbed the magnifier again, but the Porsche's plate remained indecipherable. I set the print down and looked at the next. Mr Porsche and Tony deep in conversation. Shit! Jeannie had really played with fire. It didn't take much of an intellect to know she'd hung a tail on Ed's friend from the Oak to this other place, wherever it was.

The final print was blurred, the way you get with a camera shake. Tony was peering right, getting ready to swing the wheel of his Astra. I could read the number plate on that beautifully. Behind him the Porsche was still in its parking spot. I felt a prickle of excitement, like I was on the verge of something.

How come there hadn't been a camera in the flat? Because Jeannie had it with her when she was picked up, that's why. She'd left this roll of film at the photographer's and never had a chance to pick up the prints.

I cleaned out the filter machine, rinsed the mug and stripped off the bed, cramming the covers inside the washer and measuring out the powder. Water hissed into the drum. I hauled out clean bedlinen, swearing at the duvet as it rolled in a hump, occupying my monkey-brain so the rest of it could wrestle with other things, like why Jeannie hadn't shared her knowledge with anybody – not even Kath.

Or maybe she had shared it, but with the wrong person.

Sam said she'd always been upfront and bided by the rules, never put herself at unnecessary risk. People in her line of work have to play it that way. A wild card puts everyone in danger.

I hauled out of my clothes and dumped them in the wash basket, standing under the shower waiting for enlightenment. There were too many contradictions. Uncertainties swarmed in my head like hover-flies. Dressed like a hooker or not I'd had no trouble recognising Jeannie, but it would be easy with the right make-up and the same clothes to fool Chloe.

And Donna?

It's a sad fact that some people can be bought for the right price. Donna was hard up but had new clothes to go to The Cellar. Probably reciting an untrue story and getting paid for it wouldn't seem like any great sin – or maybe she'd just been paid to recognise the photograph and thought the rest of it was fact. It'd be safer to do it that way, create the illusion Jeannie was still healthy when the opposite was true.

According to Alan her work for NCIS had involved antique sales and antique shops, checking stocks and watching for high bidders. Knowledge of other levels of the intelligence operation were sealed off from her. That being so, why would anybody beat the shit out of her when she had no helpful information? What other thing could she know that someone might want?

I turned off the water and towelled dry, scenting up the place with Anaïs-Anaïs body spray before hunting out clean underwear. I stepped into panties and hooked on a bra. Some ideas are so outlandish they have to be true, like the one that told me I'd just shifted on to the right track. I pulled on jeans and a Rainforest T-shirt, pushing my feet into canvas lace-ups. I didn't know how it all fitted together yet, but I thought I knew why Jeannie had taken the risk.

I checked my watch and dialled Kath's number. She said, 'Hi, what's up? Can't you make it?'

'No problem, I just wanted to verify something with you. Did you ever get to look at Jeannie's personal file?'

'I – uh, took a sneaky look after she died. It was out on Lomas's desk one day and I didn't see it could hurt. Why?'

'Did you notice any birth details? Father? That sort of thing?'

'I saw his name wasn't Johnson,' she said cautiously. 'Why do you ask?'

'I'll – uh – tell you when I get there.'

'Is it important?'

'Not to anybody but her father,' I lied. 'Are you sure about Lomas and Jeannie?'

'She didn't come right out and say it, and neither did he for that matter, but they sure got into a clinch at the Christmas party. I tell you the place could have caught fire.'

'One drink too many maybe? Or putting on a show?'

'Who am I to judge? I still have a hangover from Thursday. Anything else?'

'How about Lomas and Francine?'

'That's a solid fact, I've seen them at it. That good enough? Advice from a friend, Leah, trust Francine like you'd trust a viper. You still coming tonight then?'

'Sure thing. Eight on the dot. Kath – one last thing, when I mentioned the lighter you looked like it meant something. Want to tell me what?'

'Not right now, maybe later. Whoops, there's the doorbell. That it?' I told her that was it, and we said goodbye and hung up. I moved back into the kitchen and tidied up the table, hunting around for a safe hiding place.

What happens to colour prints if you stick them in the freezer? There are gaps in my knowledge I'm ashamed of.

I did a three-hundred-and-sixty-degree turn, questioning the validity of hiding the damn things anyway when nobody could get into the place.

A small voice demurred.

Possibly fire-escapes aren't all that good an idea for people with my nervous disposition.

I carted the prints downstairs and asked Marcie to look after them. Sometimes simple solutions work best for simple minds.

The frontage to Kath's flat was pretty parked up. I could have wedged between a Toyota and a Nissan, but it didn't seem worth the trouble when I could pull in around the corner without effort. I checked the locks and walked back along the pavement in the half dark, crossing a patch of shadow before I stepped into the bright entrance. The lift still bore its interesting salutation and I wondered how long it would be before someone got around to cleaning it off. I rode smoothly up to the sixth floor, turned left, and pushed through the fire-door, picking up sounds of partying on the other side. Kath's place was three doors along, and hers stood slightly ajar like she knew I was on my way up. Lights were on inside. I knocked and pushed, and called out, 'Hi!' She didn't answer but music was playing, so I went on in and found Billy Joel singing to an empty room. The rest of the place stayed quiet.

Maybe she was visiting a neighbour and left the door so as not to seem rude?

In 1995?

In the middle of a council estate?

Who was I kidding?

I moved towards the kitchen, my feet in no mood to hurry, and found that Kath was home after all.

29

A corpse of any kind is not the best thing to find on an empty stomach. A squashed hedgehog can turn me green. A dead human can do a lot more – especially when it's someone I know. I finished throwing up in the bathroom and went back to take another look at Kath. If this were fiction and not real life I'd have picked up the knife already and got my fingerprints all over it. I left it on the sisal rug and belatedly felt for a pulse. There wasn't one, but her skin was warm enough to make me think whoever used the knife hadn't been gone long. The skin at the back of my neck prickled. Gone? I eased back gently on to the balls of my feet. Of course he was gone, why hang around when you've just killed somebody?

The answer to that was simple; because some other idiot came by before he could leave, that's why. I soft-footed to the kitchen door and peeked out. The bedroom door was shut tight and it was really sensible of me not to look inside. I squinted around for a weapon, heart speeding up.

Times like that a mini fire-extinguisher isn't near as comforting as a sub-machine-gun, but it was the best I could do. I got ready to ram the button and kneed open the door – that's about the only advantage lever handles have, you don't need hands to use them. I felt a little silly crouching there like Rambo when there was no one in the place but me.

I lowered my weapon and glanced around. Death doesn't leave any secrets. Now everyone would know she wasn't tidy. I wondered if that would matter to her. I moved around the room carefully, putting off the need to re-enter the kitchen. The knowledge that I'd talked with Kath less than two hours ago reminded me uncomfortably of my own mortality. I let the extinguisher hang at my side and looked around. There wasn't any place to hide out except a wardrobe that might have accommodated a good sized dwarf, but not much else. I guessed that except for clothes, knick-knacks and a mug-tree hung with chain-store jewellery on the dressing-table, none of the stuff in the room was hers, and I could see why she'd wanted to buy her own place.

Or maybe she'd liked Bramfield enough to plan on staying here. The irony of that was almost too painful to contemplate.

I carried the extinguisher back to the kitchen, clipping it into its holder. Billy Joel sang emptily and I was half minded to turn him off. I never did like his music and after this I'd like it a lot less. I toyed with the idea of Kath's killer sitting around relaxing when she set it to play, biding his time like Judas, waiting for her back to turn.

The tap dripped noisily. A broken bottle of Nescafé spread coffee and glass shards across the floor, and the kettle was still hot. Kath had let some person she trusted into the place and started making coffee, that much was obvious. Then what? He'd eased a knife out of its slot in the block, maybe made a joke of it, tested it on a thumb saying it was sharp? No struggle, no panic, no fight for life. Certainty settled. Kath hadn't sensed a threat or she'd have fought back tooth and nail, not just stood around waiting to die, and outside of people she worked with, who would she trust that well?

I hunted up the phone, punched in Nicholls' number and told him all about it. He said to lock the damn door and not let in anybody but him.

I hadn't intended to.

I got home around midnight and knew I wouldn't sleep. Nicholls tailed me back and stalked around like he was a cat sniffing out mice before he'd go home and leave me in peace. For once I didn't argue. It didn't matter who came knocking at my door, I wasn't going to let them in. By my reckoning the death count had just reached fourteen and I didn't plan on upping the ante.

I stripped, putting everything I'd worn in the wash, liberal with the powder, then stood under the shower scrubbing off the miasma I'd brought home with me, my mind all the time re-running the night's events.

Nicholls had got to Kath's place five minutes ahead of Lomas, and I'd just about finished telling him the score when sour-face walked in and started acting like I was prime suspect. It didn't take more than a second to point out that in my book the spot was already taken. He mouthed off for a while and Nicholls told him to either cool it down or take a walk until he felt better. Lomas took a shot at pulling rank but Nicholls can get really mean-minded when he has to. There are times when I appreciate his being on my side.

I pulled on a long T-shirt, brewed some coffee and hunted out half a tub of toffee-pecan. I guess that kind of comfort habit isn't all that different to drug dependency, except in the damage it does. The late film on ITV was half-way through, but I watched it anyway. Seeing Al Capone put away for tax evasion never fails to give me a buzz; it has to be about the only time IRS ever got to play the good guys.

Around two-thirty I crawled under the duvet and closed my eyes. When I opened them again the sun was up. I did my usual morning run with ears pricked for following feet and eyes watching out for strange cars. Such a state of alertness spoils the pleasure of a thing. I got home still wired up and nothing much to vent steam on but a bowl of muesli.

Never having woken up at Sam's place on a Sunday morning I didn't know if he slept late, but I rang him anyway. Eight-thirty is late enough even for a laggard.

I counted ten rings, two more and if he didn't pick up I'd put the phone down. On eleven he picked up, grumpy like he'd just crawled off the sleep express. I said brightly, 'Hi, Sam, sorry if I woke you. Did Nicholls or Lomas talk with you yet?' There was a long pause. I supposed he was getting his head together. He came back clear voiced like he'd shaken the sleep away.

'About what?'

'Kath's been killed, Sam. Last night in her flat. She hadn't put up a fight so I guess she knew him.'

'Him?'

'A her is possible, but women don't usually use knives. Too messy.'

'It's a bad thing to happen when she only had one more week to do. I'm sorry, Leah, I'm not thinking straight yet. Do they have a suspect?'

'No, but I guess they'll be interviewing everybody who knew her. Judas, but I'd like to put Lomas on the spot.'

'You really dislike that guy,' he said.

'It's mutual. Did Jeannie ever say she was sleeping with him?'

He said cautiously, 'Private lives didn't come up for discussion, not in that much detail. Who told you she was?'

'Francine.'

'She'd be in the best position to know.'

'Yeah. All sisters together. From the way Kath told it Francine had the hots for him too.'

'Am I missing something here? You've been talking to Kath?'

'I picked up that bit of gossip after The Feathers. Sam, I feel awful, she'd invited me round to her place last night and I got there just too late.'

'What were you going to talk about?'

I stared at the hall door, puzzled. Was it me, or was Sam giving out the wrong responses? 'I – uh, girl talk I guess. What else? Look, did you hear what I said? Ten or fifteen minutes earlier and I could have stopped it.'

'There's another alternative,' he said evenly. 'Nicholls could be looking into two deaths instead of one. Be glad you didn't walk in on it, Leah. I am.'

'It's nice of you to say so, Sam, but it doesn't make me feel better. Odds of two-to-one would have evened it up a bit.'

He said, 'I'd better get in the shower and then start ringing round to find out what's happening. Are you all right over there or do you want some company?'

'I'll be fine, Sam.'

'If you think of anything else, call me.'

'Thanks. I'll do that.' I got ready to put the phone down.

He said, 'Did Nicholls find the Astra?'

'False alarm, it was one of Lomas's hirelings. Having him up against a wall would be real fun. I'll catch you later, Sam.' We said goodbye and hung up. I couldn't work out how it was that nobody but me could see through Lomas's skin.

I went down to pick up the photographs from Marcie and got talked into sharing her breakfast toast. One thing led to another and by the time we were through talking it was close on eleven. I climbed back up to the attic and got out the magnifier again, but there just wasn't enough of the Porsche's number plate visible to help me any. I took the print over to the window and looked for some other helpful clues.

Gold lettering on a black hotel board behind the stone wall announced 'Dinner; Dancing; Function Rooms; Casino' and obtusely failed to indicate name or place. The entrance had a dark blue canopy and two windows matched.

I turned my attention back to the word Casino. If Sidney had told Jeannie he was being hustled out of business and she'd seen a connection between the hustlers and the syndicate NCIS were trying to bust, it would explain her decision to work alone. Protecting Sidney would have headed her agenda, and she'd have closed her eyes to the extra risk.

If her personnel records hadn't named Sidney as her father she might have got away with it, but confidential information rarely stays that way. Anyone determined enough can hack into a computer or pick a lock, and if they can't money will buy a man who can. Add to that a mountain of personal information held in databases and suddenly no one has secrets anymore.

When Kath saw the file on Lomas's desk and read the name Sidney Vincent, it meant nothing, because Kath wasn't on the syndicate's payroll – but someone was – and that someone had seen Jeannie as a lever to use on Sidney. Except that they hadn't known where to find him, and Jeannie wouldn't tell.

And it had all gone too far.

I found the card Sidney had given me and spent minimal time debating the rights and wrongs of what I was about to do. If Mr Porsche had had dealings with Tony, he wasn't exactly on the side of the angels, and I'd just have to trust Sidney not to do anything too dramatic until he knew the score.

I sat on the hall floor and dialled the number. Sidney picked up on the second ring. I said, 'Hi, Sidney, that was quick.'

'Coat pocket, love. Got something for me?'

'Somebody it'd be helpful to find. Black hair, five-ten, fortyish, drives a Porsche. I've got a photo of him taken outside a hotel-cum-casino, a place with blue canopies, big car-park and a stone wall. Does it ring any bells?'

'Could be a lot of places, love.'

'Play fair.'

'He sounds familiar but I'd have to see the photo. How about I send somebody round?'

'I'm about ready to go out, Sidney.'

'Won't take him long,' he said, and hung up. I put the photo in an envelope and sealed it up. The front door bell rang before the adhesive was dry. I shoved the envelope down the back of my leggings and went downstairs. A blond guy around thirty, broad shoulders and a pony-tail, smiled nicely and said, 'You've got something for Sidney.'

'I said, 'Sidney who?' He fished in his back pocket and gave me another pasteboard card like the one I had already. I handed over the envelope and watched him walk away. He got into a white Daihatsu a couple of hundred yards up the street, and accelerated out as soon as the engine caught. As he went by he gave me a little wave. A black Metro did a U and went after him.

It was really nice to know so many people were watching my door.

30

I changed into jeans, white T-shirt and lace-ups, and drove out to Francine's, hoping she wasn't in the middle of cooking some elaborate Sunday roast while Lomas put his feet up. Did anybody do that any more?

Her car was in the drive so I took that as a sign she was home and leaned on the bell. I heard a scuffle of sound as she came to peer through the fish-eye, then the door opened a crack. She mumbled, 'It's not a good time right now,' and sounded like she'd lost all her teeth.

I said, 'Francine? Are you OK? I need to talk.' She mumbled some more and opened the door, keeping out of my line of vision. I went in sideways, ready to duck back out if anybody was in there looking for trouble, but the only person around was Francine. I felt my lips edge up at the sides and fixed my eyes on a Mondrian print. Green-faced, Francine looked like she'd just landed from Mars. 'I'm – uh, sorry,' I said. 'How much longer has it to stay on?' She held up three fingers and moved down the hall, waving me into the kitchen and beating a retreat upstairs. Face-masks can be a real pain to get caught out in.

I guess she didn't know what a snoop I was or she might have thought twice about leaving me alone. I peeked in the nice neat cupboards, and slid open drawers. Maybe she had a cleaning lady. When the water sounds stopped I got back on my stool and started looking through a cookery book. I was really engrossed in the thing when Francine walked in a couple of seconds later. She said, 'I don't know how it is, if I have a mask on somebody calls or the telephone rings.'

'It's always the case,' I said sympathetically. 'It's the same when I'm in the bath. Sometimes I think the damn phone does it on purpose.'

'Uh-huh.' She gave the kettle a shake and plugged it in. 'You said you wanted to talk. What's it about?'

'You heard about Kath?'

'Drinking too much?'

'She's dead.'

She reached up for mugs and knocked the salt cellar over. Sweeping the salt into her hand, and throwing it over her left shoulder, she laughed nervously. 'Superstitions are a pain but I can't seem to break out of them. What did you say about Kath?'

'I said she's dead. Somebody went into her place last night and used a kitchen knife on her.'

'Oh – my – God!' Francine plumped down on to the other stool and held on to its sides like it was the only stable thing in the room. 'Who?'

'I don't know, they haven't arrested anybody yet. She'd invited me round and when I got there she was on the floor. I guess it had to be somebody Kath knew, it looked like she was making coffee.'

'Who'd do it?' she said.

I did a mouth shrug. 'Somebody who thought she knew too much about them. I hoped you might have some ideas. Did she seem worried when you saw her Friday?'

'Apart from a hangover she didn't act different from any other day. I mean she never liked being in the office, it made her moody, she said it was the lights.'

'Lights?'

'Neon. They buzz. Kath said it gave her a headache but everybody else got used to it. I think she just liked to . . .' She broke off and spooned instant coffee. 'Don't mind do you? The other stuff takes too long.'

'Instant is fine. Kath just liked to what?'

'Uh? Oh. I was going to say, liked to have something to complain about, but I'd forgotten about – you know.' Francine stirred so vigorously coffee slopped over on to the work surface. She ripped off a paper towel and mopped up. 'Who knows about it?'

'Lomas. He came round to see for himself, soon after the police got there.' I watched her face closely, but the worry lines over her nose stayed the same. 'I thought he'd have told you.'

'Why would he?' she said sharply. 'I'm not part of his team, I just do clerical work, I thought I told you that.'

'You did,' I said equably. 'But I heard you and he were close.'

'Who told you that?'

'Kath.'

'Right, well we . . . had coffee together a few times but that's all.'

'I got the impression it was a bit more than that.'

'Look, if that's what Kath told you she must have got the wrong idea. It was Lomas and Jeannie.'

'The way he's been down on her recently it doesn't seem like he had the time of day for Jeannie.'

'Upset I guess.'

'Funny way of showing it.'

She got out an ashtray, put it on the work surface and left the kitchen. When she came back she had a pack of Benson & Hedges. 'Hope you don't object? I've cut down, but after that kind of news I feel like I need one.'

'Go ahead. It's your kitchen.'

She stuck a Silk-Cut in her mouth and flicked a Bic lighter, drawing the smoke deep. I swallowed down too-weak coffee and tried to look like I was enjoying it. She said, 'What else did Kath tell you?'

'Not a lot, Francine. Where do you suppose she got the idea about you and Lomas?'

She was pulling so hard on the cigarette the red tip looked like a mini volcano. She put the tip of her tongue out and picked at it with one finger, eyeing the nail as she drew in more smoke. 'I don't know,' she said, without looking at me. 'I'm a tactile person. You know, hand on shoulder, touching arms. I guess Kath must have picked up the wrong idea.'

'Uh-huh. Did you talk to her yesterday?'

'It was Saturday, I don't work Saturdays.'

'You could have met in town, used the phone, dropped by. Somebody called by around six-thirty.'

'Who?' She stubbed out the cigarette and lit another.

'I thought you were giving up the habit,' I said. 'Why so nervous?'

'I'm not nervous,' she snapped. 'I'm upset. Jeannie, Kath . . . I didn't expect . . .' She broke off without telling me what she didn't expect so I finished it off for her.

'It'd get this rough? Is that what you were going to say?' She stared at me sullenly. 'Some people just aren't fit to do business with,' I said.

'I don't know what you're talking about.' She eyed her watch uneasily, like somebody was coming and she wished I'd go.

191

I said, 'Donna's dead too.'

Her eyes flicked. 'Donna who?'

'Donna who might have recognised a woman who'd been passing herself off as Jeannie.'

'I don't know what you're talking about,' she said again.

I shrugged. 'I guess they don't tell you much after all.'

'I already told you that.'

I got to my feet. 'Thanks for the coffee.'

'Thoughtful of you to let me know about Kath.'

Wasn't it though?

When we stood up we were almost eye to eye with the extra inch in her favour. Same height as Jeannie, same nose, same colour eyes. With the right make-up on and a wig, nobody but a friend would know the difference. I wondered how she looked in a nurse's uniform.

She walked me to the door and took another peek at her watch. I stepped outside and turned to face her.

'There's one other thing I guess no one thought to tell you, Francine. The woman renting next to Donna smoked Silk-Cuts.' Her hand dropped to her pocket like it was magnetised. I turned around and walked away.

Sometimes mistakes can be costly. If I hadn't told Kath about the lighter she wouldn't have connected it with Francine – or confided in someone else. It had to be Lomas, who else would she tell that kind of thing to but her boss? I felt sick with shared guilt.

I hung a left, and then two more, pulling up at the end of St Helier Avenue, able to see across open-plan front gardens to Francine's drive. I cut the engine and waited, hoping no neighbourhood-watch hawkeye was looking through a window. Unknown people in unknown cars sitting around residential areas are likely to attract suspicious notice. I'd hate to have a Panda pull up behind me before Lomas joined his girlfriend, and from the way Francine had been eyeing her watch I didn't think that would be long.

Five minutes went by before the front door opened and Francine came out lugging two suitcases. She'd loaded one in the boot and was hefting the next when a green Mondeo pulled up, blocking the drive. She slung the second case in with the first and slammed the boot, half-way to the offside door before she got hauled away and dragged across the pavement. From the way she was struggling I guess she didn't want to go. I watched her being shoved discourteously into the Mondeo through the driver's door, making her hump across the gear console. A couple of seconds later the car spun off.

I wondered why Nicholls wasn't there too, but his absence didn't worry me, it was enough to know that Sam had worked it all out and knew Francine's culpability. The rest would follow. I started up the engine and turned on to Ventnor Way, telling myself it was all over bar the shouting.

Which just shows how stupid I can be.

The Mondeo turned right, crossing the light Sunday traffic. I cruised down to the junction and went after it. Unless he knew a short cut Sam was heading away from Bramfield, and I couldn't work out where he'd be going. I watched for a left indicator, but after three miles without turning I knew he wasn't taking Francine to visit Bramfield's Best. My stomach knotted up. *Sam had worked it all out how?*

If Kath guessed who'd owned the bed-sit lighter, who would she confide in? Not Lomas, that was for sure, not when she'd seen him and Francine 'at it', and she couldn't be sure about the rest of the team. Possibly she hadn't even been sure about Nicholls. But Sam would have seemed safe, Sam wasn't even involved, she'd have felt confident telling him – *and it had probably been him ringing the doorbell while I was on the phone.*

My palms were sweating on the wheel. I didn't want to believe any of this, but Sam and Francine were on the road in front of me and there was only one way to find out if I was right.

I trailed the Mondeo out along the Aberford Road towards Leeds and followed it off the roundabout on to the M62, keeping a wide distance. Once out on the motorway Sam picked up speed, swinging out into the fast lane. I checked the petrol gauge and cursed not having a full tank. At junction twenty-five he moved into the exit lane and came off. I shortened the distance and hoped I didn't lose him. He moved into the right hand lane. With nobody coming up behind me I stayed left until he entered the roundabout. A low black car came off the M62 behind me. I took the roundabout slowly, peering down exit roads for a sight of Sam's car, not particularly caring if I held anybody up. I saw the flash of it heading towards Mirfield, stuck behind a thresher. I crept up to a safe distance and sat there. On a straight stretch of road the Mondeo pulled out to the right. I took its place behind the thresher and fumed half a mile until it turned off. Sam was out of sight.

Shit!

The road serpentined.

I took it speedily, hoping nothing big and fast was coming the other way, leaving the final curve on a down gradient and seeing the Mondeo's back-end disappear around another bend at the bottom. The road quietened through a cluster of houses and shops, clear and straight for a mile ahead, and the only car on it mine. I dropped down to crawl and eyed both sides of the road, noting a branch library with minimal opening hours and a boarded up chapel.

On the left, a wood and brick building that looked like it had been an old school was signboarded, SALEROOM – ART, ANTIQUES, AND BRIC-À-BRAC. The Mondeo was parked to the right of it next to a Porsche and both were empty.

How clever – owning its own saleroom meant the syndicate could launder money and make a profit at both ends. I wondered how much they'd had to spend to buy Sam. Sam the good, the brave, the trustworthy. A guy to rely on in a tight corner – only don't turn your back! I felt sick with anger that his perfidy had cost Kath and Jeannie their lives.

I backed up and reversed into a minor road by the chapel, locking my bag in the boot. A black Jaguar cruised by sedately, following the road to I didn't know where. I wished I'd bought a mobile phone, I'm just too stingy with things like that. I fast footed back to the library and looked at the notices. Hedgeley? I'd never heard of the damn place. Five minutes' fruitless hunting for a BT box drew a blank. It looked like Telecom hadn't marked Hedgeley down as a profitable enough location.

A cluster of telephone wires dissipated themselves among the buildings. I supposed if push came to shove I could always knock on doors.

I went back to the saleroom and gave the front door and cars a miss. Sensor alarms can be real giveaways. Multi-paned windows to the left were too high to reach, and the panes had been painted yellow. Around the back were more windows and an oversized door that'd need a battering ram. I checked out two five-lever locks and a Yale and gave up on it. It looked like the only way in was the side door. I kept in to the wall watching where I put my feet and, giving the cars as wide a berth as I could, eased up three stone steps and tried the door. When it opened I hesitated like a watched cat, checking for cameras and angles of vision. This was stupid, nobody knew I was there.

I moved inside, finding myself in a stone-floored corridor that led right and left. I turned right along its longer arm, stepping carefully and ready to retreat. The wall on my left was new, made up of laths and hardboard panelling. I guessed the classrooms had been stripped out to make one big saleroom and the corridor partitioned off. Half-way along a door stood partly open. I flattened against the panelling and got my ear to the opening. Still nothing. Where the hell were they?

I got down on all fours and put my head through the gap. Furniture stood around the edges of the room; in some places one piece was piled on another. Cabinets held clocks, china, glassware and bric-à-brac. Down at the front a raised dais held an auctioneer's desk and chair, and in the centre of the room chairs had been arranged in neat rows. Opposite, a door identical to the one I'd come through was closed tight, as was a fourth that must obviously lead to the office. I guess they needed that many to cover fire regulations.

Maybe the big front doors stood open right the way through the sales. Such reflections were interesting but didn't get me anywhere. I opted for the rear door and eased it open. Office on the left, back entrance ahead, open door and basement stairs to the right. I heard Francine's voice. Even without distinguishing words I could tell she was scared. With Jeannie, Donna and Kath on her mind it was easy to see why.

It looked gloomy through the open door, pale yellow light drifting up. I eyed the office. The telephone was in plain sight. I could tell Nicholls where I was.

And if there was an extension in the basement it'd damn well tinkle when I did it. Life is full of booby-traps.

I sent up a little prayer that the basement steps wouldn't creak, forgetting that in a place like this they'd be stone. I really hate to use up favours unnecessarily.

The ceiling was low. Anyone down there looking in the right direction would see my feet coming before I was in any position to know it. Such knowledge offers no comfort. I got my head down level with the top step and still couldn't see a thing. Maybe they weren't looking this way. I trod carefully. Strip lighting on the ceiling would have illuminated the whole place, but they weren't turned on. Sam and friends were being thrifty, making do with bulbs high on the wall and what little dusty daylight filtered through the half-lights.

The basement was stuffed with furniture, paintings, crates oozing straw. Everything, I guessed, destined for the saleroom above. I turned left towards the voices, and when the tall furniture ran out, dropped down to doggy height again. It wasn't a comfortable way to move along but it got me where I wanted to be, close enough to hear what Sam, Francine and Mr Porsche were saying. I eased off my knees and hunkered behind a curvy love-seat, squinting at an angle between that and a bow-front chest of drawers. Francine's eyes were wide, her face nearly as unhealthy looking as the face mask had been. She seemed to be repeating herself, telling Mr Porsche she hadn't made mistakes, she'd done what he asked and all she wanted was to go to Marbella and he wouldn't see her again. Please, she wanted to go to Marbella, she hadn't made mistakes . . . The men ignored her. Sam said, 'Vincent won't see the connection. Relax, Marco, it's over and you owe me.'

'What about the girl?'

'If a problem comes up I'll deal with it.'

Bet he would, I thought, as instinct said the girl was me.

Francine prattled, 'I've got the ticket, look it's here, I can make the plane . . .'

Marco said, 'Shut up.'

'But I . . .'

He slapped her face. She put her hand up and started whimpering. He said, 'Stop the noise.' She whimpered harder and he slapped her again, snapping her head sideways so she cannoned into Sam. Sam pushed her back roughly and gave her a shake. Judas, but I didn't fancy her chances with those two. I turned around, the telephone suddenly seeming like a good idea. Dust came up and a sneeze started. I held it back, half-way between a crouch and a hunker, and went off balance. A vase on the bow-front chest rattled. Marco swore, Francine started screaming and Sam came towards me. Just for a second his eyes locked on mine and there was nothing in them but cold anger. I started back to the stairs, up on the balls of my feet and running, knowing he was behind me. When I glanced back Francine was running too, still screaming.

Adrenaline flooded me, racing my heart, setting it pounding so hard it felt my whole head was pulsing too. A table corner hit my thigh and I hardly felt it, the only thought in my head was getting to the stairs. I heard a flat phutt from behind and risked another look. Francine's arms were outflung as she fell forward, momentum keeping her going and Sam was looking back with Marco's gun levelling on him. He turned, put his hands out and screamed, 'Marco! Don't be a . . .' The second bullet took him backwards, toppling a table as he fell.

I was still moving, feet leaden like in one of those dreams when you're trying to run in inch-long giant steps. I heard feet on the stairs and kept on running, then a bumble bee stung my head with a sledgehammer and I fell down a long, deep hole.

31

When I woke up I was upstairs in the saleroom, lying on a chaise-longue with a mountain sized headache. I put a hand to the sorest bit and it came away sticky fingered. Memory came back. Sidney said, 'It feels worse than it is, love, you were lucky.' I was glad he'd said that. From the worry creasing his face I could have thought I was dying.

I said, 'Marco?'

'He's not feeling too good right now, he didn't want to give up his toy.'

I eased up to sitting and the room spun circles. Nausea crawled in my stomach and threatened to spill over. I took the flask Sidney offered and sniffed it. I really hate brandy but swallowed some down anyway, a couple of seconds later the nausea climbed back down to manageable. I said, 'How the hell did you get here?'

'You had a tail, love, been there since I got the bad news about Jeannie. Sorry I wasn't here sooner.' He felt in his pocket. 'Marco takes a good photo, do you want it back?'

My brain couldn't cope with more than one idea at a time. I said, 'A black Jag?'

'Wasn't supposed to let you see him.'

I said, 'Francine?'

'The girl downstairs?'

I nodded and pain danced in flames. Sidney put the flask in my hand again. Maybe if I drank the lot the pain would go away. I took a long swallow and handed it back. He said, 'Marco's a good shot.'

'Sam too?'

'Yes.'

'Where's Marco?'

'I already told you, he's not up to conversation.'

'Where is he?'

'Downstairs, being looked after. It's your call, Leah, what do you want me to do with him?'

'You got here before Nicholls,' I said. The worry lines flattened out.

'Is he the one I want?'

I sighed, explanations were painful in all kinds of ways. 'Marco gave the orders. Counting the two downstairs the people who carried them out are all dead.'

'What about the photo?'

I took it from him and rubbed both sides on my pants-leg. Now the only prints on it were mine. I remembered Marco's feral smile of enjoyment as Francine fell and didn't regret what I was about to do.

'Another couple of minutes, Sidney, and I'll feel strong enough to ring Nicholls,' I said. 'I guess Marco thought I was dead and drove off. Must have. I haven't seen him around since I woke up. Come to that I haven't seen *anyone* around since I woke up.' My eyes closed in weariness and I prised them open again. 'It was a way to hustle you out of business,' I said. 'Nothing to do with NCIS at all. This part of it has.' I waved a hand around. 'The laundering business. But not Jeannie.' I closed my eyes again. 'Go home, Sidney, before I forget I never saw you.'

There seemed to be a lot of footsteps, but I didn't open my eyes to look. By and by I heard a car start up with a throaty roar.

It took me a while to make it to the office, and when I got there Sidney had thoughtfully opened the door. I punched in Nicholls' number and listened to it ring. You'd think he'd at least be worried enough to sit by the phone. I gave up, and tried his office. He barked, 'Leah, where the *shit* have you been?'

I said tiredly, 'It's nice to talk to you too, Nicholls. Now come and get me before I bleed to death.' I told him where I was, and that he'd need to move two bodies, and then I made my way carefully back to the chaise-longue, laid my head down, and went to sleep.

When the police searched Sam's home they found a new message tape. *Get ready to die, bitch.* It would be nice if all loose ends tied themselves up so neatly, but some things I'll never know, like how big a part Sam played in Jeannie's death. I wish it had been none.

The coroner released her body two days after Sam and Francine were killed and she was cremated three days later. Sidney sat quietly by himself in the chapel until I slipped out of my seat and showed a little solidarity. The fact was I owed him my life, but except for Sidney, Charlie and me, nobody would ever know that.

Lomas went home to face a disciplinary hearing. He couldn't deny his involvement with Francine, there was too much evidence tying them together – like his razor, toothbrush and brand of toiletries at her home, and her perfume and toiletries at his – and he knew better than to try to get out of it. What he did deny was giving her information about the NCIS investigation and unfortunately Francine wasn't around to contradict him.

I wish she had been, my own guess was that pillow-talk had to have been his only attraction.

A couple of weeks after Sidney spirited Marco away he sent his limo around with an invitation to dinner. I got changed into the little black dress that's a permanent stand-by for such unplanned occasions, did my hair nicely, and expected to be driven off stylishly to one of Sidney's clubs.

Instead I got taken to his home.

I guess being allowed to know where he lives makes me one of the chosen few, and I don't plan to share the information. Suffice it to say it's an elegant des. res., not a million miles from Bramfield, but not on its doorstep either. We dined alone and talked of Jeannie and drank our coffee in a room full of chintz and mahogany with enough books and magazines around to make it look like a home and not a showcase. By and by when we'd done reminiscing I got around to something that had been worrying me. Like what had happened to Marco.

'Last time I saw him he was alive and worse for wear,' Sidney said. He got out a pair of brandy glasses and warmed them carefully. 'Didn't want to talk to him did you?' I took the glass he offered and sniffed the amber liquid; it took me right back to Sidney's flask and the saleroom.

'Talking to Marco wouldn't be a pleasure,' I said. 'But I've been wondering what happened to him.'

'What you mean is, did I drop him in the concrete down the roadworks? That what you expected?'

'I don't know, Sidney.'

'I might have if I hadn't known you'd be trusting me not to.' He rolled the glass in his hands without drinking and eyed me steadily. 'Found out every last ugly thing that happened to my girl and Marco got the same. Blow for blow, bruise for bruise.'

An eye for an eye and a tooth for a tooth. I swallowed down some brandy. 'Drugs too?'

'When I say everything I mean everything,' Sidney said flatly.

I stared down at my glass. There were other things besides drugs I wasn't planning to ask about.

'Couldn't find any volunteers for what you're thinking about,' he said. 'Bottles can come in handy though, sometimes.'

I took another drink, longer this time. 'I guess by now he's in the canal.'

'No, he got tied up like a turkey dinner and sent back to his friends. I expect they understood the message.'

Going on past experience the chances of him getting nursed back to health were zero. I passed that detail on to my conscience and let it struggle alone.

Sidney lifted his glass. 'To Jeannie.'

'To Jeannie,' I said, and finished off the rest in one gulp.

A couple of days after Sidney wined and dined me, Nicholls got a fat envelope that shredded the syndicate's web beyond mending, all the way through to the fat spider at the top. He doesn't know where it came from and I don't plan to tell him.

As for me, I'm keeping my mind fixed on other things – like a blissful fortnight in Acapulco and the pink bikini that's going to knock his eyes out.